THE CHARLTON MEN

THE CHARLTON MEN

PAUL BREEN

THAMES RIVER PRESS

The Charlton Men

THAMES RIVER PRESS
An imprint of Wimbledon Publishing Company Limited (WPC)
Another imprint of WPC is Anthem Press (www.anthempress.com)
First published in the United Kingdom in 2014 by
THAMES RIVER PRESS
75–76 Blackfriars Road
London SE1 8HA

www.thamesriverpress.com

© Paul Breen 2014

All rights reserved. No part of this publication may be reproduced
in any form or by any means without written permission of the publisher.

The moral rights of the author have been asserted in accordance
with the Copyright, Designs and Patents Act 1988.

All the characters and events described in this novel are imaginary
and any similarity with real people or events is purely coincidental.

A CIP record for this book is available from the British Library.

ISBN 978-1-78308-166-0

This title is also available as an eBook

This work of fiction has been written in and inspired by South East London. It is dedicated to my wife Sarah, our cat Gobbolino - who can now lay claim to being a writer's cat - my friends and family.

At a broader level, it is dedicated to the community and family of Charlton Athletic Football Club, our supporters and our players, including those I haven't had the pleasure of knowing, or seeing in action, but whose spirit lives on in The Valley, Floyd Road, SE7 now and forevermore.

A special word goes to Chris Powell and the team of 2011/12 whose actions and achievements fully captured a sense of the spirit which defines Charlton as a place and a football club.

Lastly, thanks to all at Thames River Press - editors and publishers - for helping to bring this story to print.

1
The Bare Bones of History

London faced the greatest fight of her life, as dark waves of danger enclosed the Thames River's tremulous coil. The face of night was black and blue, reflected in the water, as if bruised and battered after a domestic row. On the gates of Greenwich, words blazed in the tranquil moonlight, softening sores with caresses of wisdom, knowledge, and evocation. Beneath these cliffs of history, rested two refugees from the day's rage.

'*Tam Minerva quam Marte,*' they read together.

'Motto of England's sailors,' Lance's voice cut through the silence, short and sharp as the sword on London's coat of arms. 'As much by Minerva as by Mars: as much by wisdom as by war, as much by genius as by courage. But tonight it's like nobody's listening.'

Fergus looked up, again, at the names of the two Gods set against maritime images in the moonlight. 'Maybe it's no wonder there's so much fighting in the world. Chocolate's always going to come before common sense.'

'Like women and the beautiful game,' Lance added.

'No wonder people say all's fair in love and football.'

Behind, beyond and all around, Greenwich's haunting greenery, armoured in moonlight, stood pristine as a watercolour from the 1800s. Tonight, as the Thames raced leathery-black and jewelled as a title belt, this wasn't the city of the 1800s, 1900s, any hundreds. Those had been swallowed up by the monstrous appetite of a 2011AD dragon feeding off 3D TVs.

2

Again the refugees struggled for words, feeling foreign in tonight's country. The one on the right, an Englishman, said this wasn't typical.

'Not the heat, nor the madness that's come with it.'

To his left, the flame-headed Irishman sat in shock.

'Wasn't what I expected from my first nights in London.'

The newcomer's name was Fergus Sharkey. Looking out on the river with wondrous, wandering eyes of green marble, he drifted into snapshots of his journey towards a fresh start across the water.

Like thousands of forgotten faces in photo albums, he had caught a boat from Dun Laoghaire to Wales, and followed the ghost trail of immigrants on a train across a less-disputed British border, down to the great city of London.

There he would be anonymous; scattering ashes of the past. Since childhood he had dreamt of a life where seas and windows became one. If he couldn't have that, then the Thames would be a fine substitute.

Deep in thought, and in the whispers of an unsettled tide, Fergus was miles away as his new friend spoke once more.

'It's been a freak show of a night, even for this place.'

The Englishman, with golden locks, and good looks tempered by a heavy sadness in his eyes, made an odd companion for somebody from a place where there's no love lost for soldiers.

But people get drawn together, forging friendships in unlikely places.

'When you're far away from home, serving in a foreign country, every night feels like the end of the world.'

'Like tonight?' Fergus asked.

'You're sitting in silence, waiting for the next attack.'

He could still hear the crackle of shrapnel, he claimed, from the evening's explosions, a couple of hours ago, a few miles down the road.

Whirlwinds of testosterone had swept through the surrounding suburbs, as Greenwich stayed pure, untouched, unmolested.

'As calm as the Armagh mountains,' Fergus whispered.

Everything was much the same as when he had arrived, the day before. This green bay, home of time, receptacle of ghosts, line of demarcation between latitudes, had stayed as white and shiny as in the hour of its first discovery.

To his left stood the glass-fronted apartments where he had rented a room. *Glass, glass everywhere*, he thought, *and no mountains anywhere within sight*. Canary Wharf's sparkling heights dominated the horizon, hard as composite armour and lit up like slot machines at the seaside. Rising high above trees and water, they punctured the bog-black sky; torching clouds, bleeding flame and blue dye into the Thames. Maybe in their own way, they were mountains. *Glass mountains*.

Further uphill, on the slopes of Greenwich Park, in the moonlight, he could decipher the silhouette of the Old Royal Observatory.

Here in Greenwich, he had learned that everything's *old*. Like the Old Royal Naval College, stationed on the riverside, directly behind them; a white stone fortress which seemed a fragment broken off a street in Rome or Athens and transported, like a ship inside a bottle, to the edge of the Thames.

'It's cool living here but it's not *home*.'

This confused the Irishman. 'Where's home?'

He gestured eastwards. 'Over there.'

His grey eyes changed to a pair of blue dolphins swimming, as he swept a hand through the blonde mane he had been growing since coming back from Afghanistan; trying to erase any traces of his soldier's past. At least when sitting down, all you noticed was the top half, as it wasn't so easy to disguise the prosthetic souvenir below his kneecap.

'I grew up in Charlton,' he said, going back to before any battles started, 'in a brown-brick council house, with a whisky-bottle-shaped garden, and a big attic room.'

Again, as several times today, a faraway gaze masked his features in an expression which transformed his face to a pint of Guinness. Golden blonde upwards from the brow. Bitter black beneath.

'After my parents died, the Council took it back, coz you can't hand your home down to your kids in this fucking country,' he gargled bitterness. 'So I went off to fight an idiot's guide to war, while a pack o' pen-pushers gave *our* house to somebody else.'

'Must have been hard for you guys,' Fergus tried to offer sympathy. 'Did you ever find out who's there now?'

'Don't know who, and don't want to, coz I'd probably go out and burn down the city as well.' He was angry, as blood pumped fiercely through his forehead. 'The way things are, I wouldn't be surprised if Afghan kids are sleeping in my old room.'

Strange, Fergus thought, though decided not to say it. England's always fighting everybody else's wars, instead of fixing its own problems.

'I miss that old house, but this is okay.'

The Irishman cast his eyes east. 'Sure it's not far away.'

'Might as well be a hundred miles,' Lance corrected him. 'Greenwich is different to Charlton, same as they're both different to Lewisham, Deptford or anywhere else in this part o' the world.'

When he spoke about these places, stitched together by the Thames' creeks and inlets, you would swear they were scattered out as freely as villages in Ireland's border country. But, aside from the park's sweeping greenery, Fergus could see nothing except for an endless tide of stone and glass. Already he was feeling homesick, as out of place amidst tonight's riots as Lance must have felt on the first evening hunkered up inside a bunker, far from home, holding a machine gun. Perhaps in time they would talk of those days, nights and war wounds, as they had been doing in the afternoon, before the riot started.

'Everything's the same all over London,' Lance insisted, 'even the parts we can't see from here in the south east. Battersea's different from Brixton, and Croydon's a world apart from Chelsea.'

'Never been to Chelsea, but watched them in a few cup finals.'

'Sometimes,' Lance expounded, 'football's the only bridge between bits o' this city.'

'I've read the story of Arsenal crossing to the other side o' London.'

'You know your football then,' lion-like eyes sparkled approvingly. 'Arsenal was born just down the road in Woolwich's army factories. If they'd stayed, the story of Charlton could have been very different.'

'You might have been an Arsenal man.'

'Never in a month o' Saturdays. I'd stay faithful if my boys were bottom of the non-league, and Arsenal next door playing Barcelona. There's no fun in only following the big guns.'

'Isn't sport all about being top dog?' Fergus probed.

'Life's not. Why should football be different?'

'So people can escape from real life?'

'Then it's fantasy, a sporting X-Factor, all show, no substance.'

'Fantasy's okay,' Fergus argued. 'Didn't you ever dream of scoring a free kick in the last minute to win an FA cup final, or captaining England in the World Cup?'

'Of course, but always as a red man,' Lance insisted.

Fergus laughed. 'That's what they used to call me in Ireland.'

'Because of your hair?'

'Aye, because of this, and also *my* football team.'

This made Lance curious. 'Who's *your* football team?'

'I've followed Liverpool since I was a boy.'

The riposte came fast. 'Typical Irishman.'

Suddenly the red man was fired up by this incendiary comment about his home turf. 'What's that supposed to mean?'

'Sorry, no harm intended. Just memories of the Irish boys serving out in Afghanistan.' His tone lowered, then deepened. 'You've no idea what it's like being in a place where it's so endlessly boring. Mostly, you're sitting around tossing away days of your life.'

'Can sympathise, but don't understand what you were doing there.'

Lance chose to ignore the remark, because he had never understood either. 'Banter was the only thing keeping us sane.'

'And most of that was football?'

'Ripped the piss out o' each other,' he recalled, before pausing to reflect on the implosion of irony. Then when the blinding flash and echoes of the blast had passed, he returned to the base of his story. 'Most of the English and Welsh boys supported our home teams, and some of the Scottish too, if it wasn't Celtic and Rangers, but *you* guys follow big-name teams from places you've never been to.'

'Aye, it's a long way from Armagh to Anfield.'

'Long way from London too,' added Lance, returning to thoughts of the riots which had shaped these past few days. 'You'd never have expected any of this on the first weekend of the football season.'

Instead of Arsenal, Liverpool or Chelsea making the headlines, the papers spoke of Hackney, Enfield and Croydon. Then again, all this trouble had started on the turf of North London's Spurs.

'What were you doing when the spark was lit,' Fergus wondered, 'when the police shot the boy in Tottenham?'

He mumbled a quick, angry response, but Fergus didn't catch it fully. Something about growing up, and giving up on games of gangsters. He had no time, he said, for men ten years older than most squaddies, wearing jeans half-way down their asses, and thinking they're hip.

'Know what that means in American prison culture?'

Fergus shook his head, shivering at the mention of prison.

He had come here to get away from the past, and suddenly this conversation was flowing towards somewhere uncomfortable.

'It's a code meaning their asses are somebody's property.'

'There's a lot of myths out there about prisons,' the Irishman insisted. 'People think it's an easy ride, but it's not. Did they teach you anything else interesting?'

'No, but a Crystal Palace fan told us stories of gangs.'

With the change of subject, Fergus breathed relief. For a short while, his heart had been pounding like those days in his childhood, fearing that Liverpool might lose to their deadly rivals Manchester United.

'Just like football teams, London's gangs have their own colours,' he explained. 'And you know where they show them off?'

'Between their bum cracks?'

'Shoelaces,' Lance clarified.

'That why yours are red?'

'I don't wear my colours so lightly,' he responded immediately. 'They're not something I'll grow out of, a year or two from now.'

Suddenly, as Lance lifted up his left hand to unbutton the sleeve of his denim shirt, Fergus noticed, for the first time, that he had a missing fingertip. Another souvenir of Afghanistan, perhaps?

He didn't say, for he was showing off something else.

'This is our club badge,' he said, as the sphere of a tattoo came gradually into view. 'I'd this done before Afghanistan.' Then he laughed. 'You can take the boy out of Charlton, but you can't…'

He stopped mid-sentence, stroking the globes of muscle in his own arm, swivelling colours in and out of the light along the riverside. Across the way, hundreds of thousands more lights lay scattered in fragments of flaming shrapnel, lacing together London's villages.

'Kept me going,' he whispered. 'Like a torch in darkness.'

Yes, Fergus recalled, he had spoken of this earlier today, when he told the story of the landmines. This badge was the sailor's knot which held together his broken body through months of hospitalisation.

'But you struggled through in the end.'

'For a while, thought I was going to die there.'

He was speaking through a bricked-in bubble of pain, as his eyes moved across the Thames' darkening treacle, seeking out the freedom of water. Losing his restlessness, he held his arm steady enough to see the tattoo.

Since the riverside was dark, he could decipher no more than a silhouette at first; the shadows of a story. Gradually, the symbol morphed into focus. Soft black shading surrounded a circle with a white sword rising up like a syringe, clenched in a fist covered in a gauntlet, at the angle of five o'clock, the hour of Saturday's full-time scores. Beneath this, you could see *Charlton Athletic* scripted into his flesh on one rim of the circle and on the underside, in bold, the words **Addicted Forever**.

'A football junkie hooked on your team?'

'A play on words. We're *The Addicks*.'

'Shouldn't it be *A-d-d-i-c-k-t-e-d*, if that's the case?'

'Probably, but I wasn't the ink-gun artist.'

'Looks fantastic all the same. He did a fine job.'

'It's more than just a tattoo though,' the addicted man insisted. 'This goes through the flesh, right down to the bone.'

He knew nothing about tattoos. 'Don't they all?'

Again, Lance's face shone dark and golden as Guinness, watching the moon rise to its highest point in the sky above Greenwich's domes. 'Your kids' names are okay, as everybody does round here, but Japanese lettering that people can't read?'

'I've no tattoos, so wouldn't know, and couldn't even decide what image I'd want if I was ever to get one, which isn't very likely.'

'I carried this to Afghanistan, like a piece of home turf, dug up from the valley, reminding me of who I was and where I'd been.'

'A kind of good luck charm?' Fergus supposed.

Lance gargled fresh black anger. 'Some fucking luck.'

'You survived to watch Charlton again.'

His expression softened. His eyes changed from grey to blue. Holding his arm closer to the light, you would have sworn the red dye had infected his blood, spreading out through the rest of his skin; up towards his bloodshot eyes and stubble shining golden as rioters' petrol bombs.

'If somebody finds my skeleton a thousand years from now,' he joked, 'they'll see this mark and christen me Charlton Man.'

'A thousand years,' Fergus echoed. 'If there's any more trouble in London's villages, we'll be lucky to make it through the week.'

'London's going to survive. Always has and always will,' Lance replied, through the clenched teeth of Charlton Man.

'No matter what this country's taken off me, it's still worth fighting for.'

'And *you* call *us* the fighting Irish?'

Today's battle scenes weren't the first he had witnessed. Back on the island he had left behind, west of Wales, he'd seen as many fights outside the ring, as inside. Growing up, he'd watched rage build and then swell out of control at parades, rallies, and protests. Republicans, waving flags of green, demanding freedom from British rule. Orangemen, draped in Union Jacks, ready to lay down their lives to stay British. Each side righteous, resolute, determined their colours would rise highest at the end. But there was something different about England's troubles.

Looking up at the sailors' words in the moonlight, he spoke again. 'Unlike Ireland, there seems to be no cause here. Only empty rage.'

The same empty rage he had come here to forget, to lose.

2
Scars of Empire

The day had started as many another in Greenwich, during the heat and rush of the holiday season. The crowds came in by rail or through the arteries of the park; the beating green heart of this suburb with a seaside feel, on the edge of the Thames. Then they drifted between there and Blackheath, taking in markets, cafés, Observatory, and the ghostly white buildings of the Naval College.

Fergus had been amongst the swarm, rising early in his new city. Years ago when he pulled back the curtains, the world was green. Here, framed in the glass of his apartment window, he found a river. It was the Thames which he had travelled down on one whole afternoon in his prison cell, a few years ago, reading *Heart of Darkness* by Joseph Conrad.

Conrad's canvas was the colour of duck eggs in the morning sunshine, as smells of the sea drifted up through the peninsula's reed beds. Across the way, skyscrapers stood dressed in turquoise suits of armour. Like a human body, the city was wakening slowly. River traffic was starting to build, painting patterns of boats and barges before his eyes, as the first planes of the morning rose up from London City Airport shielded behind the last remains of an industrial foreshore.

Pretty as the scene might be, he was hungry. Needed breakfast, so headed out into the back roads beyond the Royal Naval College.

Last night when he arrived, this was the first thing he noticed.

'It's a bit spooky,' he had said to the caretaker.

'Yes,' answered the man named Lance. 'If you're looking for a ghost story, then Greenwich is the place to be.'

'I'm not,' he thought. 'I'm here to escape them.'

But there was indeed something haunting about those ghost-white buildings arranged in a set of neoclassical quadrants by the riverside. This architecture formed the face of Greenwich in its postcards and guide books; a set of stone temples embedded with images of gods and demons from English history. Scenes of war screamed out from every corner, sanitised in pediments of coade stone and old gas lanterns.

Close by, he heard tourists crowing. 'So magnificent.'

They were right, he supposed, on one level. Designing the Royal Naval College as a hospital for sailors, Christopher Wren had composed a fine symphony to England's past dominance at sea. Three hundred years later, busloads of visitors, barking foreign languages, snapped and snatched for images scrubbed clean and bloodless in chalk-white mythology.

This is the England I don't understand, he thought. *Is fighting wars all this country's past, present and future's about? Is that what makes its kids so angry?*

There had been trouble in Tottenham and Hackney these past few nights, places where he supposed there was a high concentration of young people and ethnic minorities. He had seen pictures on the news, which seemed a million miles from the peace of Greenwich, as he made his way onwards, past the matching domes at the heart of the College.

'Like Saint Paul's Cathedral,' said the guide book, but they more resembled one large breast, and one small, or two islands, floating in the same sea, with a vast blue gap between them.

The cupola above a chapel had been gutted by fire, centuries ago. The other, rising up from the Painted Hall, remained unmolested by time. Inside, he found a historical pastiche upon the ceiling; again celebrating a shiny, bloodless vision of England's history.

Sanguine waves and golden colours swirled through his field of vision. Clouds, trumpets, drums and muskets surrounded soldiers, sailors, signs of the zodiac and muscle-bound mermen.

Then, in the far left corner, he spied three golden lions, the very same as those worn in battle on the breasts of England's less-conquering national football team.

'Why can't they celebrate sport, not war?'

Imagine a pastiche devoted to the men of 1966, or all the great players who had graced the game on either side of that date. Bobby Moore as the centrepiece, on the shoulders of his teammates, holding aloft the World Cup, the Jules Rimet trophy, of 1966. Then scenes from the comic books, scrapbooks, and magazines of his childhood, from Liam Brady, Kevin Keegan, and Kenny Dalglish, to Roy of the Rovers.

Preston North End's double winners of 1889, Huddersfield Town in the 1930s, Manchester United's Busby Babes of the 1950s, Glasgow Celtic's Lisbon Lions of 1967, Liverpool's teams under Bill Shankly's management, and Arsenal's Invincibles of 2004. FA Cup finals of the 1990s, and a series of greatest goals too.

'*Match of the Day*,' he added in, before his attention shifted to a feature he hadn't noticed.

If you stand close, and look deep, it's there. A series of semi-naked bodies on the fringes of the scene; marble bums, stone nipples, blonde nymphs, mermaids with mesmeric eyes, and a sense of everyday subversion pushing through the royal façade.

'Makes sense now,' he chuckled.

This was 17th-century pornography for bored sailors. Back in those days, people were much the same. Sick of war, but hopelessly entangled in its world-wide web, unable to do anything about it.

Thinking of this, he found a café where he ate a hurried breakfast, and made his way back towards the apartment to finish unpacking. He had grand plans of exploration for the day ahead, but on the way he happened to bump into the Caretaker, who was scrunching a mop through the corridors, whistling a made-up melancholy song as he worked.

'Gorgeous day,' the Englishman said.

'Aye,' he agreed. 'I've been out exploring.'

'They say it's going to hit the high 20s by afternoon.'

'Perfect weather for a pint.'

'Plenty of good pubs along the river,' said the man with a mane of blonde hair, a few days' stubble and eyes as melancholic as his whistle.

'You'll have to show me sometime.'

'I'm shopping this afternoon,' Lance answered, as if desperate for company after a long spell of loneliness, like somebody who's released fresh from prison and needs a friend. 'If you fancy a trip to Lewisham, to help with the bags, you're more than welcome.'

'Sure, we can meet around lunchtime,' Fergus agreed.

Back in his room, thinking of home, Fergus noticed how patterns of colour upon the Thames changed in the shifting morning light.

Up close, pushing against the embankments, he could see shades of anaemic coffee; lots of water, very little milk. But out in the distance there was something else – pigments of soft green like the seaside.

Still, there were no mountains, and he felt trapped by the glass and steel of Canary Wharf's sparkling towers. After a while, looking out, they became prison bars separating him from open sky.

As if taken back to gaol, he felt nauseous. Lying down, to rest and remember home, he was doing fine for a few minutes. Then, in the silence, a face from the past re-emerged inside his skull, as if auditioning for a cameo in the story of Greenwich's ghosts, alongside the likes of Anne Boleyn.

Her distinctive Irish features, aflame with freckles, stormed his mind. That night of the crash, and the last sighting of her face, before they went off the road, was an anthem he couldn't shake out of his skull. She was trapped there, forever a teenager, haunting him with her glassy brown eyes in night's blue-black darkness, and morning's absences.

'Would she enjoy this?' he wondered. 'Seeing me suffer?'

But he hadn't time to figure out the answer as he heard a knock on the door. He had lost whole hours in the flight zones of the past.

'Are you ready?' the Caretaker asked and he nodded.

The Englishman had washed his hair and changed out of overalls, as if he was someone who hadn't socialised properly for a long time.

'Lucky it's not far, in this heat,' he said, trying to defy or conceal the handicap of a limp as they turtled downstairs.

Fergus wasn't sure if he should ask about it, or stay quiet as they moved outside to where the sun had risen high in a Chelsea-blue sky.

'Are we walking or bussing it?'

'Bussing,' Lance answered, fighting crowds.

All the more, in afternoon sun, Greenwich felt like a seaside town. Standing by the bus stop they caught a whiff of fish and chips, and watched the sails of the Cutty Sark flutter in a gentle breeze.

Less than half an hour away, Lewisham danced to a different beat. Inside and outside the bus, Fergus caught shadows of calypso. Like Wren's designs, this too was a legacy of expeditions to faraway places. Caribbean bakeries, Asian takeaways, African food stores and pretty girls brushing and braiding in hairdressers' glass cages.

A few seats across, he noticed a Sikh man, Muslim ladies and a black woman carrying markings of her tribe in deep, peachy carvings on her cheek. A Northern Irishman's marks were far less obvious, he supposed.

'Almost there,' Lance spoke into his thoughts.

Sure enough, the bus came to a sweaty, grunting halt. They would do the shopping first and then go off to quench their thirst.

Lewisham, around them, dazzled seashell-coved in sunshine.

Fergus surveyed a nondescript high street, with a market taking place in a square outside the main shopping centre where fruit baskets, rugs and arrangements of flowers added a sudden touch of colour.

Standing above the market stalls, a clock tower signalled the coming of two o'clock in the afternoon, when the day would be close to its hottest. Women, in bright African clothes, browsed for bargains as Lance told the story of The Battle of

Lewisham back in the '70s, when the police tried to force a National Front march from New Cross up through this area, and hundreds of protestors gathered to oppose it.

'Was madness,' he said. 'Fist fights in the streets, people battering the hell out of each other, and cops charging around on horses. My father said that for a few hours there was an Independent Republic of Lewisham Clock Tower.' He paused then, searching the Irishman's face for reaction. 'I'd friends and family on both sides, because that's how it was in them days in south London.'

'First time I've heard of this,' said Fergus, though the very mention of the National Front, like the English Defence League, sent thorny shivers down his spine. 'We'd enough troubles of our own in Ireland back then.'

'The right wanted to show whose country it was,' Lance carried on, 'because they were losing the bigger battle, and knew it.'

'So what happened in the end?' Fergus asked.

'Town got wrecked by all sides, but cops wouldn't ever again force marches through places where they weren't wanted.'

Moving through market stalls, amidst fragrances of fruit and dusty carpets, Fergus shivered under echoes of his home country.

When change is coming, opposition's most fierce.

But usually, like here in Lewisham three-and-a-half decades ago, you can't stop the tides of change. Come the '80s, they would see black footballers in the national team, wearing the three lions with pride.

'When the first black players came along,' Lance explained, 'there was opposition; bullets in the post and banana skins. But then the likes of John Barnes just became regular guys in their country's jerseys. We'd have been happy to cheer on green men from outer space if they won the World Cup for England.'

'Darth Vader as manager, Luke Skywalker up front?'

Lance laughed, as they sought out a pound shop in the distance. Since he cleaned everything in the apartments, except for the glass frontage, he had a long list of necessities.

'You must know everybody,' Fergus supposed, as they moved along shelves filling baskets and ticking things off the list.

'Just to see,' he admitted. 'Like the girl across from you.'

'I've only been there a day. Haven't noticed.'

Lance's eyes turned dreamy blue as he spoke. 'There's something about her, not so obvious at first, but she grows on you over time.'

'Maybe they're the best ones.'

'Then there's a tall guy down the corridor, dark as Deptford Creek. Bald as a two pence on top, with a goatee beard below. Spends nights upstairs like he's mixing potions and spells, so his nickname's Merlin.'

'And this girl, have you given her a nickname?'

'Yeah, she's easy coz of who she looks like.'

'Who's that?'

Lance paused, tossing a couple more bottles of cleaning fluid into the baskets as he worked his way through essentials.

'Marilyn Monroe,' he said after an interlude.

'I'll have to look out for her.'

Though curious to know more, he didn't want to press the issue. Football and midweek games in the Carling Cup were easier topics. They talked of these on the slow trawl through shopping, and when they had loaded their catch into bags, it was time for a beer.

'There's an Irish pub across the road.'

'And that's probably stayed a republic long after the clock tower's fallen,' Fergus suggested as they carted bags towards it.

The outside was bright and blue as the sky, shifting to cavernous darkness as they stepped through a doorway. Above the optics, a clock spoke of it being three in the afternoon. Already, the place was filling up with refugees from lands of sunlight and sobriety.

'Two pints o' lager,' Fergus requested from the portly barman, as Lance found a seat beneath pictures of Connemara upon the wall.

'Always wanted to visit Ireland,' he said as the cold drinks landed, 'on holiday, as a tourist, I mean, not as a soldier.'

Fergus dipped his head to the table. 'You should go.'

It was a good country, with the best tribes of people in the world.

'So why'd you leave?' Lance asked suddenly.

'Like the rest,' he replied. 'Looking for work.'

'So what's your trade?'

He sipped his pint, for courage. 'I've done so many things at this stage, my mother and father should have christened me Jack.'

Lance didn't get the joke at first, and then looked down, with some suspicion, at the hands which held the golden pint in front of him.

'You're not someone who's done a lot of outside work.'

'Bit o' carpentry here and there,' Fergus corrected him.

'You've fists the size o' sledgehammers though.'

'Used to be a boxer, a long time ago,' he confessed.

'Why'd you give it up? Broken noses and bruises, I suppose.'

'Maybe knowing I'd never be world champion.'

'Something we all have to face sooner or later.'

'What about you?' he switched attention from himself.

'Gardener before I joined the Territorial Army.'

This was the first time he had actually confirmed it, though Fergus had suspected as much from the moment he noticed the limp. And now he was drinking in an Irish bar, in 28 degree heat in London, with somebody who had fought in Afghanistan for the same army that once occupied the watchtowers along the roads and mountains of south Armagh. The same army whose soldiers he couldn't shed a tear for, when he heard of them dying in Iraq or Afghanistan because they shouldn't be there.

You should have stayed in the fucking garden, he thought.

Then he would have never lost half his leg in Afghanistan's poppy fields, from being part of a patrol stumbling onto a series of landmines.

'Yes, it's a series,' he said. 'Off they go, one by fucking one.'

He was out with his colleagues, on one of those patrols labelled *routine* even though the scenery, the heat and the stench made it nothing of the sort; thousands of miles away from training camp. Three months they spent, preparing for battle, in the Norfolk Broads.

'You're standing there,' he said, as if talking about someone else. 'And you're daydreaming about your team getting promotion, about being back at the stadium where you used to go as a kid.'

Fergus held tight to his beer, fearing another man's honesty.

'You're thinking how much you'd love to be back *home*.'

He could hear the roar of the crowd in helicopters overhead.

'And you hold tight to your gun, looking straight ahead.'

Charlton, losing ground in the third division table, were scrapping to reach the consolation of play-offs at the end of spring. He was daydreaming about Leeds and Norwich, top dogs in the battle for promotion.

'You've wandered outa your comfort zone. Brain's switched off, because the minesweepers are up front doing the hard work.'

Listening to the cadence of pain in Lance's voice, he suddenly felt flushes of guilt over his indifference to the fate of soldiers.

'You're crossing countryside, and everything's okay.'

And then it's not, never going to be again. Fast as an aneurysm, the impact comes in a sudden, searing eruption. You feel a click, as if it's the severance of a nerve ripping the earth, hypothalamic agony, as a sudden blinding flash goes through your skull at light-sabre speed.

'Except the pain's spreading everywhere else.'

In fact, your head's the only place not hurting. Suddenly, as all the molecules of time slow down, you're blown out of your skin, up into the turquoise skies of Afghanistan, and you never realised before how lustrously green the countryside looks.

Home's somewhere on the other side of mountains on the horizon. You're hallucinating. The skies are fragmenting. It's as if your body's ripped out of the earth like a rosebush and turned into a flower burning up in 100 degrees of sunlight. There's a gnawing sickness in your stomach because you know that once the flames die down, your stem's going to have evaporated.

Worst of all, as it stretches towards eternity, there's a recurring bass-click of a needle jarred in the groove of your skull.

'This isn't music you'd ever want to hear though.'

It's the vinyl-black echo of the millisecond it takes for someone to step on the trigger of the most feared acronym in the dictionary of any soldier, English or Afghan. *IED*, improvised explosive device.

As time starts going faster and you realise what's happened to you, you're reaching out for an imaginary clock you want to turn backwards, and find the hands of a mother, a lover, someone to hold you.

But your Scottish mate's on the ground chewing on a radio with half an arm and broken gun, and there are no hands coming because they can't get to you until they're sure there's no more mines and then they're going to treat the worst first, if there's anything left of those who caught the full blast.

When they do come, put you on a stretcher and ferry you to the hospital in a helicopter, as if you're no more than a goat's carcass in one of those polo-like games of buzkashi that the Afghans play, you're thinking that you're far too young to end up like Admiral Nelson with half an arm. Besides, you're as unknown as the boys in the unmarked graves of the Somme. Nobody's ever going to create Lance's column in the city's main square, or name the streets of Greenwich in your honour. So you babble, and ask stupid questions like *'my Charlton tattoo's okay, isn't it?'*

And they say *yeah, it's fine* even though they haven't looked because the only football teams they know have names like 49ers and Cowboys. *Thank God for that* you think as you throw your head back and close your eyes, wondering why your brain's gone fuzzy as a static TV screen. But everything's not okay, and your team doesn't make the play-offs.

Nothing would ever be the same again.

3
Empty Rage

Fergus was ready to talk football again, to learn more about Charlton's assault on the playoffs, and help Lance forget about Afghanistan, when a breathless voice pin-pricked this awkward moment.

'Gangs of blacks are gathering at the shopping centre.'

The man who spoke was middle-aged, shaped like a stick of rhubarb. His nose was rhubarb too, pushing through skin of custard.

'They're facing off the police,' he announced, with breathless haste. 'There's going to be trouble.'

Immediately, the portly landlord resigned himself to early closure. 'Finish your beers and go home, gentlemen.'

Lance grumbled. 'No need to be scared of a few kids.'

Regardless of ages, the landlord was insistent. They had five minutes to empty their glasses before the shutters came down.

'Better not forget the shopping,' Fergus said, as they gathered their bags and forged a slow path out of the emptying lounge.

Outside, in the late afternoon air, hooded figures moved through the shadows down side alleys and against the skeleton of market stalls.

Traders had packed up for the day. Boxes stood like gravestones where once there had been colourful arrangements of flowers, food and clothes. Drifting by, you could detect a faint hint of geraniums rising through the scent of fear, and buses parked on the edge of tension.

'You'd swear they were on safari,' Lance said.

'On TV, I saw buses getting hijacked in Hackney.'

'Lewisham's a jungle,' he carried on, as they edged towards the centre. 'They should've sent us here to train, and not the Broads.'

Like soldiers, boys in side alleys started blackening their faces. One, french-kissing a girl through his balaclava, produced a knife that flashed like the infatuated dazzle of her eyes.

Others swarmed behind, like bees from high-rise honeycombs. Stings formed from lumps of wood, clumps of brick, assorted bricolage. You would have sworn they had robbed a junk stall as they made their way downtown.

'All kinds of animals loose,' Lance mumbled, as his eyes tracked movements with the intensity of a sniper's.

Suddenly, there was an air of menace in the streets. Something physical, but not quite tangible, like wind brushing the tips of trees.

Surreal too, as if this was their movie. Everybody else was an extra. They didn't seem interested in shoppers, pedestrians or passengers on buses, like kids zoned out on computer games, zapping aliens.

'What are they going to do?' Fergus wondered.

'Your guess is as good as mine,' Lance replied.

Across the way, a disco-wagon with blackened windows pulled up. Several guys got out, decorated in so much gold you would have sworn they had robbed the Bank of England's vaults.

Since they looked like stereotypical gangsters, Fergus thought, *they probably weren't gangsters*. Back in Ireland, in the '80s and '90s, anybody resembling a TV-show IRA man wasn't really one at all.

The boy in the balaclava, carrying a knife, was taking orders from a gold-toothed smile framed beneath a set of designer sunglasses and a frazzled mane of dreadlocks.

'Like Bob Marley reborn in the gangster rap era,' Lance commented. 'The whole thing's orchestrated by opportunists, amateur criminals.'

Perhaps the police had assumed the same, as they began to arrive on the scene, spilling out of vans, padded up thick as American footballers. They appeared to be trying to encircle the emptying shopping centre, as if closing down on insurgents. Seeing them, the make-believe gangsters strolled back to their vehicle, calm-as-you-like, got in and sped off. Then, for a couple of minutes, deathly silence marked the scene.

'We should probably get out of here,' Fergus suggested.

He knew what happens when the blood's up, when standoffs develop.

'There's no rush,' Lance replied, watching the build-up.

A drove of riot police had started to push inwards on the nucleus of the shopping centre. Batons raised, they had come to do business.

'Lewisham's got the biggest police station in Europe.'

'Thought that record would be Northern Ireland's.'

Already, dozens had arrived. There would be no messing tonight. Surely they had learned lessons from Tottenham on the weekend.

Go in hard and close down trouble before it ripples and spreads, like slicing a tumour out of the body while it's still benign.

'These kids know fuck all about warfare.'

He spoke as a soldier, glancing down at his knee, recalling counter-insurgency operations; the taste and fragrance of fear. Again, he could hear echoes of a click crossing time's ill-defined boundaries.

'If only *our* insurgents had been so casual.'

Wars don't last a decade if you're fighting an enemy who doesn't know what he's doing, who thinks he's resisting a modern form of crusade that has gone on for centuries.

These kids knew shit all about warfare. That's why the police would go inside the shopping centre and disperse them quickly. They would face no landmines or long bearded-banshees.

You could see in Lance's bloodshot eyes some form of psychosis shaping itself around a fantasy of beating the hell out of these boys. Doing so, he could take a truncheon to his own trauma.

Then…licking his lips with anticipation…something else caught his and everyone else's attention. Somewhere over their shoulders, on the far side of the square, an alarm was going off.

'They're smashing shop windows.'

Lance spoke suddenly, surprised by this game plan.

'Now it's the police closed in,' Fergus noted.

Trapped, with backs to the insurgency. Beyond them, teenagers whooped and crowed, coming out the side exits of the shopping centre. There weren't enough officers to keep them inside.

'Little bastards, they're smarter than I thought.'

'Coz they think they've nothing to lose,' Fergus supposed.

A swarm of hooded figures had started to play the shop windows like xylophones. This was like the worst excesses of football hooliganism in the 1980s; gangs of thugs smashing up towns and suburbs as a show of hatred for other teams, other colours. Here, there were no colours on display; the attackers hidden, burqua–like, behind the uniforms of an angry anonymous generation. Unlike football's secret gangs, they probably didn't even know what they were fighting for.

From a distance, entangled in the moment, an open-air orchestra of destruction is striking its first notes. Though the disco wagon's long gone, there's fresh music on the streets of Lewisham; a symphony of smashing glass and burglar alarms.

Some make noise in circles. Others form a high-pitched scream. Amidst all of this, there's a lyric of greed and celebration. Ecstasy, anger, desire and a sense of power. They're able to smash the glass frontage, walk through the gaps, take whatever they want from the shelves, as people watch, acting like helpless voyeurs of riot pornography.

Inside, there's the cry of a masked orgy. Hooded figures hump the shelves, snatching, grabbing, looting and smashing what they can't take. They strip a jewellery store, as if robbing from a rich man's mistress as she sleeps; steal clothes from the flesh of mannequins, beheading them, to make fresh weapons lobbed towards the police.

But they're too late, for as soon as they get to one side of the street, the looters have crossed to the other, cackling and whooping. The girl who kissed the boy in the balaclava is among them, pregnant with delight as she trails designer gear across the street behind her.

'We can't let them get away with daylight robbery.'

Lance, forgetting his wounds and half a dozen shopping bags, attempted to surge forward before Fergus got hold of him.

'There's too many of them,' he insisted.

'But they're only boys,' the soldier protested.

By the look in his eyes, if somebody had given him a gun, he would have opened fire, shooting first, asking questions later. But, for all his knowledge of war games, he was getting one detail badly wrong.

It wasn't just boys playing games of feds and gangsters. Amongst the chaos, behind the masks, Fergus could see girls smashing doors and barricades with high heels, sticks and bricks, before stripping the insides bare in a matter of seconds.

'Like Vikings,' Lance insisted. 'Pillaging their own high street, and there's nothing we can do but stand here and watch.'

By the time police retreated and reassembled, it was too late. The streets glistened with glass and the residue of stolen merchandise.

Still, there was one thing missing from the battle so far; but not for long. Within seconds, an old friend, a veteran of riots entered the fray. Through all the rebellions London had known, from Blackheath to Brixton, one weapon was a constant, as dangerous then as now.

'Fire,' Lance whispered as soon as it appeared.

You could almost imagine its grand entrance, like that of a theatrical superstar from ages past in cameo at the latest West End show. But there was nothing grandiose about this evening's performance.

These kids didn't have time for glitz, glamour or high culture.

'They're going to torch a car.'

Down a street close by, gloved fingers caressed a cigarette lighter. Someone else snapped a door open and turned on a radio. Sounds of the ghetto drowned out jack boots, burglar alarms and riot shields.

'This could turn nasty,' Fergus predicted.

Maybe this was when they should have made their escape, but all the buses had started going in the same direction, towards *Not In Service*.

If you grew up during the Irish Troubles, you knew how to make a petrol bomb, even if you had never actually been responsible for one yourself. These kids had the same knowledge, probably picked up from TV.

'Jesus Christ,' cried a couple of voices in the crowd.

They had filled a long-necked bottle with fuel and then corked it with someone's ripped bandana. Next, they twiddled with a button on a lighter and added a leaf of flame to the equation. At first they didn't seem to know the basic rules of engineering a petrol bomb. You let go as soon as the rag catches light, but they looked as if they might just hold onto it so long that it would explode right in their faces. But they knew what they were doing. Just as it was about to pop, when the flame touched the fuel, they gave way, tossing it through the car window and ran, as the explosion rang out from behind them.

'Burn, you bastard, burn,' they cried in orgasm.

Some rich bastard's car was ablaze, blackening the skies. They had proven who was boss and now they were going to dance; mounting the burning fuselage's white-hot Everest, showing off the colours of their shoelaces for the world.

High above, cameras in TV helicopters beamed their faces into the homes of thousands, the viewing figures for their footage rivalling those for *X Factor*.

Tonight they had staked their claim over one of London's villages. It was their music coming out of the speakers, their show on screen.

'This city's a terrapin on its back,' growled Lance, 'and we're standing by, while kids are attacking it with a sledgehammer.'

'Fuck you!' they cried out. 'Stop us if you can.'

They could have been talking to the TV cameras, or they could have been talking to Lance, who would have gladly picked each one of them out, through a lens, with a bullet in the kneecap as they danced.

'Through the back of the leg,' he added. 'That does more damage.'

Fergus hoped he was only half-serious, in his preaching vigilantism.

'Somebody has to protect us,' he argued. 'They won't.'

Dozens of police officers stood impotent as a couple of girls emerged from the flock of hooded figures. Moving in front of the burning vehicle, they began to dance as the music crackled to a slow death. Shaking their bodies, they slipped in and out of a fever.

Fergus, too, looked on as if in a dream.

'I've seen cars explode like this before,' Lance echoed his thoughts. 'Bombs in market squares, and the stink of burning flesh.'

Fergus shivered, for he had seen, smelt the very same.

'You've no idea what it's like.'

The Irishman stared straight ahead, saying nothing. Dense curls of smoke had begun to emerge from every orifice of the white-hot skeleton. One of the girls moved away, as the heat became unbearable. The second, snaked in coils of dreadlocks, stayed. Arms held to the sky, absorbed in herself, eyes closed on the world, steadfast in a moment. Possessed by X-Factor fever, she was rimming the boundaries of life and death.

But she didn't care for anything beyond the duration of this song, a song of herself, and the freedom to break the rules for once in her life. Above her, Lewisham's clock tower looked down like a Cyclops as fresh battles erupted in the surrounding streets, where flocks of teenagers played matador with the police ranks using bricks, bottles, traffic cones and burning wheelie bins to goad them into a charge. Everybody but Fergus had forgotten the dancing girl and the burning car.

'For God's sake,' he cried out through the thickening smoke, 'somebody stop her, instead of just standing around taking pictures.'

But this was a game, an act of voodoo against the porcelain dolls inhabiting the world of celebrities, TV and magazines. This was her five minutes of fame, her chance to make headlines, appear on billboards.

She was black, she was sexy and she was showing it off, sharing the sights of herself across social media. This was a dance somewhere between reggae and samba, and she was glowing caramel in the light.

'You'd swear she's going to step right into the flames.'

But just as the voice behind them spoke, the reverse happened. Suddenly the engine spluttered and the flames teemed towards her as the windscreen smashed, sending shards of memory through Lance's skull, sniping at the backs of his eyeballs and blackening his vision.

Immediately, and fortunately too, the force of the blast threw the girl forward, onto her hands and knees. She was woken up from her fever.

She had twisted her ankle though and couldn't move, as the flames rose higher. If another blast came, she was well and truly endangered because none of the BlackBerry paparazzi seemed to have the balls to reach out and help her, lift her off the ground and drag her towards safety.

'Do something,' Fergus cried, but nobody did anything.

Then, with a rush of blood to his ginger head, he surged through the crowd to help the girl clamber up off the ground in a daze.

'What the hell's he doing, playing the fucking hero?'

Wanting to stop his friend being dragged into someone else's battles, Lance attempted to push forwards. But there were too many blockages in his way, too great a weight of surrounding chaos. Across the road, barricades from another shop came crashing down. The police, always several streets behind, surged forwards with shields and batons raised. As they did so, the crowd of spectators pushed forwards too.

'Shit!' he yelled as his knees gave way.

He was down, his chest held against a pillow of shopping bags. Like a drowning man, he struggled for breath, fighting to keep his head above water and see what was happening on the shores in the distance.

There was no sign of Fergus. Only feet, chaos and choking smoke. Perhaps he had ridden off into the sunset to appear on next week's breakfast TV shows, telling the world of love unleashed by riots.

Finally somebody stretched out a hand to help him. 'Here.'

A boy, darker than the caramel girl, wearing a ski mask.

'Thanks,' he mumbled, but the recipient was gone.

And there was no sign of the Irishman for a few more minutes, until suddenly his red head came into view, stepping through clouds of mist.

'Had to make sure the girl was okay,' he answered, when Lance demanded to know what the hell had taken him so long.

'London's on fire and you're trying to be a hero. If I'd helped the other side like that in Afghanistan, I'd have been sent to prison.'

'These are teenagers, not the Taliban.'

Blue eyes stared back at him through a prism of humourless rage, and they might have stayed angry all evening if it hadn't been for London transport, and those buses headed towards *Not In Service*.

They had no choice but to walk home, back towards Greenwich, where they would rest on the shore like sailors returning from a foreign war. The villages of London had become a keg of gunpowder, fused and ready to light.

4
Red Men's Rising

Tonight, after twenty-nine years of living across the water from the teams he followed, Fergus was going to experience the first English football match of his lifetime, in the flesh. In some ways it felt like a date with somebody he had known through cyberspace for years. He had grown up with her, allowing her to shape his moods, emotions and desires. Perhaps he had even seen her naked on the screen, what they called cybersex, but it wasn't as good as being face to face, occupying the same physical space, with sounds, smells and touch.

Still, that wasn't the reason he woke up with a hard-on. He had been dreaming of two girls, one who he kissed just once, when he rescued her, and the other who he kissed half a dozen times, but couldn't resuscitate.

Maybe, after a few drinks at tonight's game, he would share his story. Both stories featured girls and cars. Neither would impress Lance. Several times last night he returned to the same argument.

'They're worse than the Taliban, in some ways.'

Well, Fergus thought, *I'm sure a pretty girl dancing samba tastes and smells a whole lot better than a sweaty man with a beard.*

By the end, at least, they agreed on a couple of things. Firstly, when riots happen in other places, there's usually some cause. Second, they would forget London's troubles for one night and concentrate on football.

They would meet at six, catch the train to Charlton, have a couple of drinks and make their way through the turnstiles to the stadium.

'We'll sit in the East Stand's middle block,' Lance had promised, 'where my family's always gone.'

Back in the forties, his grandfather was there on the day German spitfires came in over Woolwich, for the Luftwaffe's first bombing raids on the Arsenal factories. Closing minutes of a derby game with Millwall, locked at four goals each on an overcast afternoon, when the sides of the Thames shook and the sky darkened, and London's long season of suffering began.

As last night progressed, the Charlton Man shared the truths, myths, and legends of his team. He had considered going down the path of honesty too, but resisted.

'I was in prison,' he wanted to say. 'That's why going to a football match means so much, after all those years of lazy Saturday afternoons wasted listening to the commentaries on the radio.'

But you don't go telling people your life story on the first evening you go drinking, despite the drama of the evening. And it had been a dramatic evening, he thought as he pulled back the curtains to look out on the daylight world of ghostly Greenwich. Same as always, Canary Wharf's towers mirrored the sky. Great looms of cloud rolled above its skyscrapers towards the steppes of Greenwich Park, olive-coloured from relentless, rainless weeks.

There was no such sense of calm when he switched on the TV news. Things had worsened in the night. Stories of wreckage clattered headlong off the screen, one after the other. Gangs hijacking buses in Peckham and burning down a bakery, as if it was 1666 all over again.

Every shop in Croydon looted, and flats above them fire-bombed. Running battles on the streets of Woolwich.

Thankfully, reporters said, the piracy subsided in the early hours. Greenwich was largely untouched, free of war wounds, when he left the television behind and went to hunt out a place for breakfast.

Outside, the sky turned red-ash as the sun rose above the Thames. Cinders of the same rebellious heat, as in the days before, rose off the water's surface as he explored new streets, syringing every droplet of experience with all five senses, especially the scents of the park.

Inside a small café, customers spoke of 'madness everywhere', as he ordered a full Irish breakfast, which they had colonised as English here.

Taking a seat by the window, looking out at the traffic, he was back in a world of glass, waiting for his food to be served. Across the way, stale images of last night's battles flickered on a TV screen.

He had come here to escape the fires of the past, but found himself looking up at high-street battlefields, charred bookshelves and birds searching the rubble for scraps. Then a couple of girls on mobile phone footage, freely uploaded to social media, talking as if there was no tomorrow, no comeback from feeding these appetites for destruction.

'World's our oyster, innit. We'll do wot we fuckin' want.'

Seeing the ruins on the streets of Woolwich, and people in pyjamas coming out to survey the damage of last night's racket, he felt his own appetite fading, before the tempting scent of eggs resurrected it.

'Thanks,' he said to the waitress, who was young, hard-working and polite, about the same age as those kids in Lewisham last night.

Then he began to eat his western Atlantic islands' breakfast, listening to the voices of those around him, on the streets and in TV studios.

'Where's this going to end?' asked the commentators.

'The Tottenham shooting was a match in a gas factory.'

'No,' others argued. 'The whole thing's only an excuse.'

This was the underclass rising up, Britain's *Arabesque Spring*. Once they had stripped the high streets bare, they would come hunting in people's homes.

'Bullshit,' argued an old lady with leathery hands, who was having tea and scones.

These were bored teenagers struggling through a hot summer without the cash for a train ticket down to Brighton, where they could release their testosterone into dirty weekends and afternoon swims.

But maybe they don't want that, said another old lady. They want the world without having to work for it. Finishing his breakfast, Fergus recalled what Lance had said about 29-year-olds and games of gangsters.

Then he went to see his friend, to talk about tonight's game.

'How's the head this morning?' he asked.

'Same as the streets o' Woolwich,' Lance replied.

'That's fairly rough then.'

'But there's worse news than my hangover.'

'More rioting?'

'Worse than that,' Lance answered in a sombre tone. 'Tonight's match has been called off, for fear there'd be trouble.'

Fergus felt expectations deflate in his stomach.

'But the news said things had gone quiet.'

'For now, maybe, but they'll be back.'

This time, though, the cops would bring substitutes into the fray. According to the news, London's Metropolitan Force was calling for reinforcements the length and breadth of the country, almost the very opposite incarnation of the miners' strikes in Maggie Thatcher's day.

David Cameron, today's prime minister, was franchising northerners the chance to come down and crack a few southern skulls. And if that didn't stop the feral underclass, they would use water cannons. Plastic bullets got a mention too, but they had never been used on the British mainland, and that was a last resort, like sending in the troops.

'Soldiers on the streets,' mused Fergus, recalling echoes of those wasted years when there was war in his own mountain country.

Those years had been a terrible waste, and he wanted to waste no more. It was time to walk these streets of glass and find some work, despite the gaping baton wound in the spine of his résumé.

He would do anything, if somebody was prepared to give him a start. Security work, bar work, labouring; anything for the price of a pint.

'Sure, if all else fails,' he suggested to his friend with the hangover, as he moved towards the door, 'there's going to be plenty of work in sweeping the streets once this city's come out of its fever.'

When the red man had gone off in search of work, Lance started out on his own; changing a bulb in the corridor close to Marilyn's room. These past few days he hadn't seen her and he missed her presence, though she was no more than a fantasy, a phantom in his world. But when he thought about her, a whole tumult went through his head.

If he could only spend one evening with her, getting to know her, she would soothe his rage, assure him the sacrifice was worthwhile. It was kind of hard to describe why or how. She had become a symbol of England, a white rose lighting up a window balcony in his dreams. Back when he was a gardener, those had always been his favourites.

White English roses. Tenacious roots, strong stems, floury petals, sharp thorns. If he had his chance, he would cultivate love with Marilyn. They would get married, have kids, move to the countryside, keep a farm and horses, and grow old watching their first-born son wear the No. 9 jersey for his country.

Back in Afghanistan, the boys used to talk about girls. The Scots and the Irish thought they had a monopoly on attractive women.

'Can't hold a penny candle to English girls,' he would argue.

'English girls are easy,' insisted the Glaswegian through a haze of smoke, unaware he'd lose his tangerine fingers by the end of the war. 'Great fer a month, but you'd nae want to marry one.'

'Bollocks.' Lance fought the good fight for his country's women. 'There's a reason why we've got the rose and you've got the thistle.'

'And what about us?' the Irish asked.

'Either yah swing both ways with yer shamrocks,' the big Scot replied, 'or else yer always getting caught up in love triangles.'

Suddenly, the light fizzled, snapped on, felt hot in his fingertips. Christ. Again he had dozed into dreams of the past so easily. So real, the voices of ghosts, given flesh, were beside him in the corridors, and in his bedroom in the dead of night.

Perhaps before the explosion, he had done this too; he had this habit of drifting off into daydreams and losing consciousness of what was happening in the real world. Unfortunately, he couldn't remember. He couldn't recall how his brain used to operate in the days before Afghanistan scarred his cerebrum. Back then, did he ever slip into dreams of girls when he watched them through a window, as he did with Marilyn, seeing her kneading dough as she baked, and wishing she made those loaves for him? Or try to reconstruct the past so they'd have met in the months before he left, and she'd have been the girl whose photograph he kept, for sanity, in his wallet?

Perhaps if they had met before he left, he would never have gone there. They would have run away together, somewhere else. She would have found a home in him, and vice versa. Where they lived wouldn't matter, for they would have been in each other, every minute of every day, for two lifetimes.

But he only had one lifetime, one football club and one country. There was no sense in dreaming of this woman across the way, of whom he knew nothing other than the icing on the surface. He'd keep things practical, finish the job, get through the day and forget her.

Probably don't even live in the same world, he reckoned with himself. *If she's a football fan, probably follows Chelsea, just because she liked the jerseys, found their foreign players sexy or something just as shallow. Maybe when she was younger, she'd a crush on Jose Mourinho, their charismatic, sharp-suited manager. She'd be banging him in her head while you're banging her. How the hell's a cripple going to compete with his ivory smile and perfect tan?*

Thinking of suntans, Fergus must have been getting one by now. Several hours had passed since he left to tramp the streets of London, as many of his countrymen had done in the past hundred years. These days you didn't get signs that said 'No blacks, no dogs, no Irish', but it couldn't be easy coming to a new country, whatever his reason, starting afresh. He didn't say much, though there were times he wanted to; moments he seemed like a tortoise, hiding some almighty secret in his shell.

Well, we all have our secrets, he thought as he finished his work for the day some hours later, *and mine's being crazy for a Chelsea girl.*

Getting back inside his room, he cooked a microwave dinner and cracked open a beer. While eating, he watched TV. Sure enough, they'd sent police from every village in England onto the capital's streets.

But still, here and there, every so often, troublemakers scurried through the shadows like cockroaches between gaps in the spotlights. By the time he had his third beer, a newsflash ticker-taped across the screen, drowning out drunken fantasies of how he would make love to his Chelsea girl even if she had her eyes closed and was thinking of someone else.

'Electrical store robbery in New Charlton.'

That was the part closest to the river, on the side opposite to the football stadium and the village. They had come in a couple of cars, smashed windows, robbed a few shops and made a swift exit.

Little bastards. They're not getting away with it.

This was the same as some tanned gentleman coming here to these flats, knocking on Marilyn's door, going inside, keeping the curtains open and having sex with her on the mezzanine, in front of his eyes. Him, on his own turf, having to listen to every laugh, thrust and sigh.

No way, there was going to be no more of this after tonight.

5
Operation Red Man

Through the night, Lance prepared for battle. He made his plans amongst comrades, a cadre of fellow reds, mapping them out on social media, creating codes indecipherable to outsiders. On a second front, he followed TV news, watching London's volcano erupt afresh. Broadcasters used the word *breaking* to describe what was happening: *breaking* news, society *breaking* down, the rise of *broken Britain*.

He spoke at the screen. 'You're wrong.'

This city wasn't falling apart. No, the tide was turning. Across London's villages, diverse groups of people had started to fight back. Turkish shopkeepers in Shoreditch. Bangladeshis in Whitechapel. Sikhs in Southall. They were out there, defending the streets of their country against a common enemy, and re-enacting a wartime spirit of resistance, as in the stories of the blitz his grandfather had told him. He had the gift of the gab you see, through having Irish blood in his veins, from a generation before, when his people crossed the water in the late 1800s. And when he shared his tales, Lance claimed, the lilt of ancestry haunted his voice.

Several times the Nazis bombed Charlton; collateral damage on the Luftwaffe's journey towards the munitions factories at Woolwich. One of his best stories was about Charlton House. That's the red brick mansion rising off a hill, at the end of the village, looking down at Greenwich's riches in a valley. Over 400 years old, built in the Jacobean era, it had its ghosts too. Amongst them, there's a mother and baby killed by a wayward shell in the mansion's gardens.

Once, coming home from a game in the 50s, his grandfather claimed to have seen her, wailing over the burnt-out shell of a pram.

But those were just stories told in childhood to scare you from hanging out on the streets late at night. This, on the other hand, was real. And for the likes of that young mother and the poor dead baby bundled in her arms, the men of his grandfather's generation had resisted.

'These days,' he wrote, 'they'd be called vigilantes.'

He created his own page, and spread the link through various sources. Twitter, Facebook and fans' forums. Very soon, he found a chorus of voices sharing his conversation. Voices crossing boundaries. Charlton, Millwall and Crystal Palace supporters. More besides.

Within an hour of posting his call to arms, more than two dozen people had replied, some of them noting that Muslims were already out on the streets of places such as Birmingham, and that they needed to do the same, here in London, so they could sleep safe in their beds at night.

'There's a danger,' some said, 'of us being seen as thugs.'

'Not if we're open to everyone,' Lance argued.

This wasn't a white fight, or a black one.

'There's only one colour driving this,' he insisted.

The colour synonymous with London, double decker buses, phone boxes, station roundels, poppies on wreathes, roses in gardens, and Charlton Athletic jerseys. This was Operation Red Man.

'Let's not be hasty,' one girl protested. 'It's quiet tonight.'

'Calm before the storm,' cyber-growled a young man who was getting married in Blackheath that weekend and who feared destruction of the reception venue. 'If the police don't sort this, there'll be chaos.'

The mood was unanimous. 'We've got to do something.'

Even if you go on Twitter, others said, you'll find tweets from footballers - black, white, foreign or British - saying enough's enough. After four days of madness, everybody was craving ordinariness.

'This isn't England anymore,' declared a woman with Saint George's cross as her avatar. 'We're losing our country.'

Probably, thought Lance, she had never held the deeds to any part of England, but he understood, and feared, where she was coming from.

'Let's meet in the village at five,' he suggested.

They would play the troublemakers at their own game, separating into cells, keeping in touch via social media throughout the day.

'Be careful,' warned Saint George's girl. 'Way things are these days, we could be the ones who get banged up in the end.'

If they arrested him, well and good. He would be a martyr for his cause. Tomorrow he would make a stand for his community and his country. Once he turned off the computer he had one thing to do before going to bed. This was an act, a habit or perhaps a ritual, maybe even an addiction, a shot of methadone rather than heroin, one last time before giving up for good and concentrating solely on the higher causes of tomorrow.

Going up to Marilyn's window, he saw she wasn't there. But this was for the likes of her, even though she would offer no more than a second glance, or disdain, when she read of it in the papers.

He thought of this as he went to bed and had dreams of her through the night; dreams where he went to her door, knocked, and asked if she could please stop coming inside his head as he was trying to sleep. What would she do, in the real world, if he asked her this question?

He might never know and had no time to find out, as he woke.

'There's work to be done,' he said, switching on the computer.

New voices greeted him as he entered the site he created.

'We're signing up,' said a couple of teenagers.

'Roll on *Red Man*,' added another.

But after days of heat and rage, London's villages had fallen silent. *They* had taken the trouble northwards and outwitted the authorities again. As scores of riot police flooded the streets of the capital, the focus of the insurgency shifted direction in the night, becoming nationwide. *They* would be back, though, and London's villagers would be waiting for them.

As always, the morning passed slowly. After a couple of hours on the computer, he mopped the stairs, observing the passage of daily life. Around ten, Merlin the magician left his room, going downstairs with a bike and a rucksack loaded with books, perhaps a collection of potions and spells. Shortly after, smiley, sharp-faced Somali kids came out to play.

A blonde girl, no more than seventeen, stepped fresh out of a shower and through the door of a city banker's apartment. He was young, suave, and he disappeared at dawn, towards tunnels and sparkly towers.

There was no sign of Marilyn though, and for once he didn't care. He had found a higher cause. Going back to social media, he was creating a poultice to absorb the dull ache of this prosthetic life. It was like being back in Afghanistan, boys off duty, sharing banter. Supporting different football teams, but all fighting on the same side.

You could follow any team and be a part of this. West Ham, Welling, Crystal Palace, even Chelsea and Millwall. Team colours didn't matter. You could be black, white, green, red, navy, claret and blue.

'If the police won't stop this, we will,' they agreed.

Operation Red Man was going to begin in the streets of Charlton. That was where he was born, where he grew up, watched his first football match and had fallen in love with his local team. The colours of his tattoo ran bloody deep. Defending those colours was worth the fight.

He was thinking of this when he heard a knock on his door.

'Police?' he wondered, first of all.

Then he realised this was paranoid. There was as much chance of finding Marilyn standing at his door, fresh out of the shower, in damp London-red lingerie.

When he finally answered, his visitor was the ginger Irishman.

'You look happy. Did you find work?'

'Possibly,' Fergus replied, stepping inside.

'I'll make us a drink to go with the story.'

Strong caffeine would rouse them for the evening's battles.

'Yesterday, I must have tramped every street in south London,' the Irishman said as his large boxer's hand grabbed the handle of a cracked and chipped Charlton Athletic FC coffee mug.

Generations of Irish had done this, he supposed. Years ago, he had an aunt who had walked the soles out of her shoes, through Knightsbridge, until she found a sign, in one of the big houses, for a job as a maid.

'Tried bars and building sites,' he said, 'with no success.'

'Everything's done by agencies nowadays, I reckon.'

Fergus sipped the coffee slowly as he spoke. 'Aye, and I was about to give up on my way back home through Deptford.'

'What happened there?'

'I came across advertisements for a community project,' he replied. 'Looked good, so I went inside and talked to people.'

He could see flames of excitement in Fergus's emerald eyes, hope at the end of all his hopeless tramping. 'What kind of work?'

'It's a project that gives young people training and education through sport,' he explained. 'Teenagers from sixteen to nineteen.'

'Don't you need particular qualifications?'

'They're looking for assistants more than teachers,' he clarified, 'and they're looking for people who can identify with these kids. Some of them are what you'd call troubled and need a second chance, even a first chance if they've never had one in their whole lives.'

'I don't get it,' said Lance. 'Why you'd go for that?'

'I've trained kids before. Taught them sports.'

Finishing the coffee, he shifted awkwardly in his seat. Once a week, those last years in prison, he had worked with kids from a young offender's centre, teaching them boxing, football and carpentry. Sometimes, honesty was easier with strangers.

'You do know these kids are going to be black, right?'

The Irishman shrugged. 'So's the guy who promised me an interview. He didn't make a big deal of my colour.'

'Jesus, I'd have expected a few ginger jokes thrown in.'

'That'd be racism nowadays,' Fergus hit back with a sharp riposte and a playful punch, across the table, to his friend's shoulder.

'Any plans for this evening?'

'Maybe a pint to celebrate or a run in the park.'

'You could come across to Charlton.'

'I didn't know there was a game tonight.'

'There's not,' he replied firmly, searching his friend's face for reaction as he made his proposal. 'We're going out to defend our streets from the rioters. Come and join us if you like.'

'Dunno,' Fergus was unsure at first; he was calculating in his head all the reasons why he shouldn't get involved in someone else's fight.

'Don't worry. There's going to be no trouble. We're not attacking anybody, just defending ourselves. If they won't arrest troublemakers, they'll not arrest us.'

Fergus shifted his eyes across the room. 'Okay.'

'I'll make another coffee and tell you about it.'

The second coffee, though not as strong, gave fresh impetus to his battle plans. If someone such as Fergus, new to the city, could rise up and fight back, there was hope for London's resurrection.

'We're going to wait and beat them at their own game.'

'What's their game?' Fergus wondered, trying hard not to think of the friendly guy who had promised him an interview.

Gambian, with a smile wide as a dream-catcher.

Lance spoke furiously. 'Move and attack, attack and move.'

They hit one place and then, before the police could react, they shifted to the next, destructive as foxes going through rabbit hutches.

'Yeah,' thought Fergus, 'that's what his smile was like.'

White rabbits set against the dark peace of summer nights.

Lance barked on. 'Tonight we'll be ready for them.'

'For whom?' his friend wondered, but didn't voice his fears.

Instead he headed back to his room to rest for a few hours before they would set off around five. On his way, he caught sight of the girl called Marilyn for the first time.

Momentarily, he paused to introduce himself. But then hesitated, unsure of what to say. She was gone by the time he had formulated the most simple of possibilities – "*Hi, I'm Fergus. I'm Irish. I'm your neighbour.*" She had faded inside behind a bike and bags of shopping.

She seemed as untouched by the riots, as her skin by the sunshine. There was nothing *so* special about her, though she was fashionable. Visually arresting too, wearing a loose blue dress and shoes to match; closer to Chelsea's sharp navy than Manchester City's soft azure. He couldn't say more than that, for she was gone in a matter of seconds with the speed of a hunted rabbit.

A few hours later he was the hunter, going to Lance's room, knocking on the door, having to wait a few minutes for a response.

He had been getting ready, he said. Putting on his battle dress.

Fergus was shocked, but tried to make light of his fears with a joke. 'You're taking this as seriously as Churchill.'

Lance, as his costume suggested, was in no mood for joking. Combat fatigues, khaki jacket and a pair of boots high enough for the legs of a hooker. He had his hair slicked back, darkened by gel, and the bristles of his unshaven face glistened black as boot polish.

'Let's go,' said the leader of Operation Red Man.

They stepped out into the evening air: it was spitting rain, as if Nature was sending them a message. Things needed to cool down before somebody got killed, or whole streets got torched to the ground. But passing through the white blaze of Greenwich, they saw that everything was quiet. Shops closed, barricades up. Park and College gates locked.

Battle lines were drawn against an invisible enemy as they started to make their way towards Charlton, on one of the few buses that were still running. Then, somewhere along the half-deserted Woolwich Road, came news which seemed to douse Lance's excitement in a sense of dejection.

'Word's out they're going to attack Eltham.'

That was up near Charlton's training ground, he said. Headquarters of the club academy, which developed young players for the future.

'Maybe it's not our turf, but they need our help.'

Getting off the bus, then catching another one in a different direction, Fergus was starting to wonder what the hell he had let himself in for. Caught up in someone else's turf war, without even being able to point out any of these places on the map. He shouldn't be doing this. The last thing he needed was to go back inside, especially to an English prison, now that he had a good chance of getting a job and rewriting his life.

By the time they reached Eltham, blood was already boiling. They could see shops and doorways shuttered and ready for an onslaught. Hundreds of bodies lined the streets; men, women and children.

Fuelled by rumours on social media, they had come to stop the bushfire sweeping towards them, through London's villages. Like the woman with the Saint George's avatar, they were going to defend a country, and a way of life, which didn't really belong to them anyway.

'That's not how they see it though,' Lance explained after they had decided to have a pint in one of the few pubs on the high street. 'They're seeing their community taken away by strangers.'

'Strangers like me?'

Lance shook his head as they stepped into the darkness and made their way towards the counter. That was different.

'The Irish came here to work, not live on welfare.'

'But they didn't want us at the start either,' Fergus remarked as his friend forged a path through to the counter, to order drinks.

Inside this bar, he could see a lot of football jerseys, tattooed bodies, gold chains and Saint George's crosses. Sometimes you got all of these together, in the form of big swaggering men in England shirts.

It was a far cry from the three lions on the roof of Greenwich's Painted Hall or on the jerseys of the country's multi-ethnic team. Things had changed since the seventies, battles in Lewisham and banana skins thrown onto football pitches. But you got the impression that these people inhabited a 1950s time zone. Then again, others had reached the 1960s; stepping into a tardis in the gents' toilets, they came out the other side with glazed eyes and powdered noses.

'Some people have weapons,' Fergus noticed.

'They're not weapons. They're just for defence,' Lance assured him, pausing to sip his pint. 'Those little bastards carry guns, you know.'

Fergus surveyed the assortment of cudgels, baseball bats, lumps of wood and tools from garden sheds. Seeing this makeshift army beside its arsenal, they were like the cast of the '80s TV comedy *Dad's Army* caught up in a reality gardening show. The guys in the corner were sporting West Ham's colours; talking of how they might get into Europe next season.

'All shades of London are here,' Lance remarked. 'Chelsea, Millwall, maybe even Manchester United!'

Though Chelsea and Millwall shared shades of deep blue, the badges were different. Millwall's was a lion on the breast, perhaps a distant, more ferocious cousin of the national team's three lions.

'Down through the years we've had our differences,' he remarked, 'but we're all one tonight, in this fight together.'

As he spoke, Fergus looked around the bar. There was nobody fighting here, and of all the places in London worth looting, Eltham possessed few of the city's crown jewels.

This was a plain shore of everyday existence; a suburban combination of council estates, half-emptied for the evening, and terraced houses, further out, where distant shadows watered gardens in the receding heat.

'We've a Paddy with us,' someone spoke into Fergus's seclusion, having caught his accent as he ordered a second pint.

'You're one of us now,' insisted a tattooed man at the counter, making him wonder if this was a sign of integration, or testament to how far he had fallen in a single evening.

Outside, the sun was starting to dissolve as he headed back towards their table. TV cameras had arrived in Eltham.

'God, it must be a quiet night elsewhere.'

'No,' Lance insisted, 'this is big news.'

He had grand visions of Big Ben sounding out stories of football fans fighting to defend their streets, in the spirit of Sikhs in Southall and the men of his grandfather's generation in the Second World War. But the English Defence League had come along as self-appointed guardians of the nation, stealing the thunder of Operation Red Man.

Suddenly, the news monster had its feed of stories for the night.

'Let's go and see what's going on.'

'Okay,' Fergus agreed, 'when I'm finished.'

He stretched the closing mouthfuls of his pint like accordion bellows, to delay going out into the glare of TV cameras. But Lance was having none of it, impatiently drumming his fingers on the table. At least, outside, the night was cloaked in darkness.

In the back of his mind, Fergus feared that somebody back home - or, even worse, the man from Gambia who had offered him an interview - might see him on the 10 o'clock news.

He imagined the words coming at him and sweat rising. 'So what were you doing out on the streets with those Nazis last week?'

'I wasn't,' he would protest. 'I was only looking.'

'Soliciting,' his interviewer could tease.

Yes, that's what he was doing. Getting a taste of life as a football supporter on a night of chaos. Seeing Lance's aspirations crushed beneath the wheels of somebody else's agenda. These guys, who had turned up as darkness fell, seemed part of something more sinister than the families who had blocked streets in the hours before.

Grannies, more at home in holiday camp wrestling bouts, were suddenly pushed aside by men who had more in common with a world of bare knuckle fighters than Big Daddy and Giant Haystacks. Some of these guys were probably ex-army, Lance admitted. In fact, it was most likely. You could see traces of it in their build, their tattoos and cropped hairstyles. Generally, people don't tattoo "England" across the side of their faces forever unless they feel they've got undying personal investment in the place.

'Different England,' Fergus suggested, 'to the football team.'

'There is only one England, the one that's here now.'

But those guys, parading in front of the cameras, preaching a narrative that was embarrassing, had a different view of the nation.

'Their tattoos are for a country that's dead and gone,' added Lance, gesticulating towards the half of the leg he had lost in Afghanistan, 'and has no more chance of coming back than this ....'

'Like tattooing an ex-girlfriend's name on your neck,' Fergus supposed, 'and facing those memories in the mirror every mornin' for the rest o' your life when she's off shagging somebody else.'

'Worse for them,' Lance said, 'because the way these guys see it, she's probably out there shagging their worst enemies.'

Perhaps it was this knowledge and the kettle tactics used by the police on the main street that boiled their blood more than ever.

'Blacks are back on the streets of Woolwich.'

They tried to inflame the crowd, but the police told a different story, and TV people who mingled amongst them did too.

'Everything's quiet in Woolwich tonight.'

The insistence fell on deaf ears. 'Lewisham also.'

'There's an army of looters on the march.'

'We should go meet them in the middle.'

A huge cheer rose up from the underbelly of the crowd. Then, as an almost empty bus passed down the street, some amongst the mob caught sight of half a dozen black kids on the upper deck. The crowd surged forwards, then sideways, snaking towards the vehicle in a giant conga as it stopped at traffic lights. The police, with dogs, tried to come between them as one of the boys in the upper deck turned his head and smiled, sparking off further rage on the ground.

They were the posse, shouted a man with a megaphone, sent in to check what was happening before the rest of the cavalry arrived. This was Conrad's *Heart of Darkness* in reverse, a native mob surging towards unwelcome guests to cannibalise them. But before they could do anything, the lights had changed and the bus was gone.

Those kids were most likely nothing more sinister than students making their way home to the halls of residence at the nearby university campus. But in the drunken, dehydrated minds of the crowd, this was a hostile provocation.

'See how they're laughing at us.'

In the background, somebody started singing songs about being English and foreigners going home. Fergus felt like a fifth columnist, glad to see the taillights fade into the far side of town.

By now though, blood had boiled to the same temperature as the scorched cars in Lewisham a few days before. But instead of smashing and looting shops, they were going to take the fight to the enemy.

'You're not going anywhere,' the police said.

'It's a free country. We'll go where we like.'

But the cops were right. Besides, deep down, they had no intention of marching several miles to Lewisham.

What would they find when they got there? Fergus mulled over the possibilities in his own mind. *Tower blocks in darkness and people asleep in their beds.*

'It's just for show,' his friend agreed.

He too was tired of standing around and posturing, sick of people losing sight of the real issues and reducing everything to race. There was no fucking point, he said in the taxi they caught home, targeting everybody with black skin. Chris Powell, his team's manager, was as Caribbean black as his blood was Charlton red. So too was Bradley Wright-Phillips, their star striker, who grew up in Brockley, on the edges of Lewisham. Like most people, they had nothing to do with the riots.

'A few kids and everybody's screaming apocalypse.'

'It's over now,' Fergus assured him.

The explosion of rage had happened on all sides and the episode was closed. Rain started to fall in silver freckles on the taxi windows. One side had voiced their discontent, showing how they could smash up the artefacts of a society in which they had no stake. Another side expressed their right to fight back, to be refused, and then feel a sense of grievance which convinced them further they're losing their country. Tomorrow the clean-up of London's villages could begin.

'Goodnight,' Lance said, as they reached Marilyn's light.

Tonight's boxing match had passed her unawares, probably. Making a nightcap, Fergus wished she would pull back the curtains so they might at least get to make eye contact through the window.

But she didn't, and the world behind her window stayed a mystery. One thing he had learned these past few days, through all the madness, was that London is a tale of different cities, alongside its many villages. Looking at glass sparkling in the night, again he longed for mountains, the way they had been before he ever went joy-riding through them.

6
Ghosts

After the stand-off in Eltham, several days of rain swept in across the Thames, dousing the last flames of empty rebellion. The maelstrom was gone as quickly as it had arisen the week before in Tottenham. Normal service resumed for life and for the football season. All that remained was for somebody to create *London Riots – The Musical* – and the summer's events could be sanitised, scripted, storyboarded and set up in the sparkly lights of West End showrooms.

'England does riots, not rebellions,' Lance said when they met for the first time in days on the Saturday after Charlton's latest league game, a 2-2 draw with Scunthorpe United.

Usually they ended in bloody, heroic failure. Victories for the king, and gallows for the vanquished. Several times, in centuries past, Blackheath had seen such rebellions. This time, the heath's crisp gorse remained untouched as places such as Lewisham suffered. Greenwich too had got off lightly, and Deptford, where Fergus had his interview.

'How'd it go?' Lance wondered.

'Great,' he answered. 'I'm going in for training next week.'

'I thought you were going to be the trainer.'

'Training for the trainer,' he clarified.

He had done a good interview in front of a panel which included the Gambian man, with the bright smile, a middle-aged white guy who looked ex-military, and a woman who was a PC, equal ops dragon. Something about her posture brought to mind a rhinoceros as she asked a dozen or so difficult questions, all theory, no practice.

'I'd swear she hadn't been in a classroom for years.'

She had probably never talked to the boys as he did on his way out the door, not expecting to get the job or even hear from them again. Then the Gambian guy, the good cop on the panel, called him up.

'They liked what I said.'

'What did you say?'

'You know the Irish. We've the gift o' the gab.'

He wasn't ready to share the same story he'd told the panel. Coming into the building, sitting in the waiting room, watching angry boys with loose trousers and attitude, he saw aspects of his own past.

He recalled being with his friends on the edge of town, seeing a car, deciding to steal it, breaking the lock, getting in, starting the engine, and speeding off into the darkness, destined for a twisting noose of back roads in the countryside, described to the panel.

'Why are you telling us this?' asked the ex-military man.

'Even though some of these boys are from very different places, we've an awful lot in common. I'm Irish, and I'm an immigrant.'

'Well, you'll find that everybody likes the Irish,' said the Gambian, 'and in Africa, we've claimed Guinness as the black man's drink.'

Instantly, rhinoceros eyes rolled disapproval.

'We're not talking colour though. We're talking life.'

The ex-military man leaned forward, shuffling papers.

'I've been to the same place as some of them might be headed.'

He took a sip of water, going stale in a clean glass tumbler.

'When I was nineteen, I was a boxer, going to be Olympic champion. That was all I dreamed of. Representing my country. Winning gold. Standing on the podium with *The Soldier's Song* playing.'

'I thought you're from Northern Ireland,' the ex-military man spoke.

He admitted he was, but saw himself as Irish first.

'Life can be boring when you grow up in a small town on the Irish border, and you've a limited choice of friends. Not everybody dreams of being Olympic champion, and maybe they try to drag big dreams down.'

All three interviewers nodded in agreement.

'One September evening, a few of us decided to steal a car a couple of weeks before my friend was going to teacher training College.'

Three sets of pupils, across the way, tightened to a headlock.

He heard a voice in the back of his mind. 'Slow down.'

It was hard though to stop. He was young, free, and at the wheel of a car, feeling a whirlwind of emotion. They'd kissed as he was driving, turning his head, luring her mouth towards his, and almost going off the road in the process. But they'd survived. Then kept going through a lunar landscape of bare thorns and moonlight on pine forests bearding the Irish borderlands.

Mountains lined the distance, crossing boundaries between north and south, nippled in the last traces of British army watchtowers that made you want to sing Bob Dylan and Jimi Hendrix songs just to be resistant.

There was a whole concert playing in his head at this stage. The light was blue through the windscreen. Lucy's pale, freckled face turned the colour of melancholy. She was huffing, bunching up her freckles around her eyes, wanting an end to this, but the air was cool, the feeling good, and his sole fastened on the accelerator.

Behind, there was light and in front of them darkness, like the town they'd escaped from contrasted with the open road. He was young, a champion boxer, and invincible. Life, then, seemed like a joyride, with a glorious highway ahead.

He'd paused, to have another sip of stale water. 'The sea was hours away, miles away, down back roads, past hundreds of fields, through a dozen small villages in the shadow of mountains.'

They'd reached speeds of maybe seventy, though anything over forty was dangerous on those narrow, winding roads. Always he thought of it as *they*, for the boys in the back were as much to blame as him, egging him on to keep going, almost to the edge of the speedometer. Lucy was the only one who was innocent, protesting that this was too fast, getting crazy, achieving nothing. The guys in the back were laughing.

'It's okay Loose,' he assured her, 'I'll take care of you.'

Her name was short for Lucille, taken from her mother's favourite song, which she'd hated ever since her childhood as a freckle-faced tomboy, playing ball with the best of the boys, and always fighting for the underdog.

Happy to have her back, he drove deeper into memory, to the depths of the brain's inner lobes, returning to the past, feeling free and loose.

'The car was light as a cloud, heading towards the Mournes, the famous mountains from the song you might have heard,' he hoped for connection but was met with a shoal of blank, shaking heads.

He was sweating, under the black suit he'd hired from a store in Deptford High Street, full of people in bright African clothes looking for formal funeral gear. Inside his skull, the car was going faster, journeying deeper into cerebral hemispheres towards sunset, as if surfing the pages of a dictionary. There he'd find the first syllable of what he was experiencing. /dʒɔɪ/ - vivid emotions of pleasure, gladness, and extreme passion, from the old French word *joie*, rooted in the Latin *gaudium*, meaning to rejoice.

Then, thumbing forwards, you reach the less cultured part. /rʌɪd/ - of Germanic origin with many connotations, one of which is common amongst teenage boys. In Ireland, it's slang for sexual intercourse, or a girl you'd like to have sex with. Boys desired Lucy because she was beautiful, strong-willed, and independent. That's why, when together, he called her Loose. They'd slept together once, though the panel didn't need to know those details.

She'd been with another boy, so knew what she was doing. In fact, she was the one doing the riding, above him, outside in the open air, on the green grass of a Gaelic football field, during a disco, in a clubhouse across the way, and soldiers up in watchtowers, in the mountains in the distance, maybe watching them through a rifle lens.

When you're 18, you just don't care. It's your hard-on which matters absolutely in that moment, and nobody else's.

'So we're about ten miles from the sea, young, free, high on life, and it's like we're on a road that's never going to end, and then we struck an almighty speed hump.'

Coming out of nowhere, it changed everything, like one day you're in the shower, safe in a cocoon of suds and water, when you feel a lump, out of place, protruding through the lather, intruding on dreams of the future.

'We heard sirens behind us, police and soldiers too.'

The rhinoceros lady suddenly changed her posture to that of a giraffe, as if preferring the sound of this, a moral edge to the parable.

'Loose said the game was over, that we needed to stop.'

'Boys should listen more to the advice of girls,' the woman preached.

'Yes, but we thought we'd escape.'

She rolled her eyes and tutted, as the military man stared frostily ahead, while the Gambian sat up straight, drinking in the tale.

'So I did as the boys asked and put my foot to the accelerator, driving on even though I knew they could open fire on us, as they'd done to kids in Belfast. They'd shoot us and wouldn't even get prosecuted. At least if we gave up now, Lucy protested, we'd just get done for theft, and dangerous driving. But the boys said that we could shake them off.'

His heart was racing at this stage, his temples knotted in a fever. Then, light appeared from the bend in front of them. Suddenly, they were trapped helpless as rabbits in a set of headlamps.

Going too fast to stop, the scene froze. Coming towards them, they caught a flash of grilled windows and green shell; a speeding tortoise in composite armour.

'The British army,' said one of the boys in the back.

Deep in the lobes of memory, his thoughts wheeled towards Lucy's sudden sigh, a voiceless scream, and freckles on a fear-hardened face in the mirror.

The two drivers hadn't seen each other's lights in time, and hadn't slowed down till it was too late, so one had to swerve.

'No,' Lucy screeched, as the wheel turned.

Then her gasps became wordless, as front tyres pierced the ditch at sixty miles an hour, and the malignant fingernails of thorns scraped glass and metal. Briars that seemed so hard through the windscreen in the moonlight suddenly eviscerated under the weight and speed of the vehicle. Then, on the other side of the ditch, there was a drop, twenty or thirty feet; he couldn't be sure.

His sense of time and distance dissolved in the very moment they went off the road, and then started falling, tossed sideways in their belts.

'Minutes before, they'd been so tough in the back. Suddenly, they were scared. I was scared too, though there was hardly time to feel fear, going down the edge of a steep, tree-stubbled slope, head first.'

Lucy threw her arms against the windscreen's last layer of protection, as the car struck the ground like a bare fist punching a stone wall. Then it spun for what seemed an eternity, turning full circle from his side to hers, driver's to passenger's, before crashing to a halt against jagged rocks.

'Jesus,' he heard a voice from the back, as another moaned.

First he took a deep breath, relieved to be alive, and feeling dirty great crystals of glass from broken mirrors laced through his hair.

Then as the darkness gave way to moonlight coming through the silhouette of trees, the full horror of the crash came into view. He could see Lucy's freckles splashed in blood, her eyes glazed, and mouth hanging open. They'd rolled down an embankment right to the edge of the sea, crashing blue and stiff against a seaweed-reeking beach in the foreground.

Fergus could make out shadows above, emerging from their tortoise shell, scrambling down the hillside. Thirty seconds later, they were pulling bodies out of the wreckage, the twisted fuselage that could turn to a fireball at the slightest ignition.

At that moment he didn't know whether to hate or love their accents from different parts of England; the working class voices he knew from *Match of the Day* interviews, and the soap operas his mother watched. Perhaps these were the last two things he'd think of, if he died here on the edge of the Irish Sea, and both of them as British as fish and chips. Coronation Street started the Troubles, his mother always said, as much as the TV news of civil rights in America. Elsie Tanner and Hilda Ogden showed the Catholics how people lived across the sea, and gave them hunger for the same freedom. The freedom of football games on a Saturday, which he'd never see again if this car was to blow, taking them over the mountains to Heaven. At least they'd know then what history was all about, and if it had been worth fighting for.

Then suddenly he noticed that one of the soldiers coming towards them looked like John Barnes, slim with broad thighs, and bushy eyebrows framing his coffee-coloured Caribbean features.

He could have been stepping from the dressing room the night before scoring for England in the Maracanã stadium against Brazil back in 1984; one of the finest goals of all time, and England's best since the 1966 World Cup.

Fergus had tried to think of football, and great goals, to block out the horror of what was happening around him. They were cutting him out of the car, to separate him from Lucy, but he didn't want to go.

He couldn't resist them though, hoisted upwards and then outwards, onto the damp ground, watching them cut the seatbelt off Lucy's bosom, as if severing a chord, a layer across her heart between life and death.

'She's mine,' he tried to call out.

But he was stuck fast to the ground, feeling shards of glass, like shrapnel, burning his skull; cutting through the skin, and sinking into the sponge of his brain, where memories began to flare, then explode in fireworks. Speaking in a Caribbean accent, carrying traces of Scotch or Irish ancestry, Lucy's soldier was shaking his coffee-coloured head.

'Any sign o' life?' asked a Geordie, who smashed the remaining glass with a gloved fist, and reached inside to turn off the engine.

Fergus didn't know much of what was happening, or what they were saying in their mix of strange accents and codes, but he could tell that something was wrong.

The Caribbean soldier raised Lucy's lifeless body towards the moonlight. Momentarily, her freckles, grainy brown as sand on the shore, reflected the night's white fire. A loose tendril of hair fell against the lineaments of her face, as sudden spumes of jealousy spread through Fergus's mind. The brown man had his hands all over her body, as if she was a ghost-white cigarette he was drawing breath from.

'She's mine,' he wanted to shout again.

'He's giving her the kiss of life,' the Geordie said, as if seeing his distress, sensing the metaphysical pain he was suffering.

'No.' He wanted to be the last one whose lips touched hers.

For a second he thought back to TV pictures of that classic goal, to block all of this out. Like reading a line of poetry, the act's over in a matter of seconds but the echo, the memory stays with you for a lifetime. Casting off the rucksack, he's out on the left wing once more, ghosting into view. The ball's on his toe, triggering this way and that, through the mass of bodies running backwards, until he steadies himself and shoots.

Then he could hear sirens, gradually changing to birdsong and heavy traffic, and whispers from the soldiers arrayed upon the shore. She was gone, gone for good, and he'd never see her face or hear her voice again.

'Joyriders?' cried out one of the soldiers, as they carried Lucy's body away from the wreckage that was starting to burn, and would be a fireball in a matter of minutes. 'Death-surfers would be a better name.'

Fergus paused to take a sip of water, to relieve his burning guilt. 'The story was in all the papers, and I was arrested, then charged, and sentenced.'

'So you've spent time in prison then?'

'Yes. To crack down on joyriding, the judge gave me the maximum sentence for death by dangerous driving; almost ten years.'

After sharing his story, he couldn't read the panel's reactions, not even when the military man asked if he was sorry, and he said of course, that he'd have to live with a girl's death for the rest of his life. He'd made one mistake, but learned from the experience.

If given a chance, he could teach others to avoid the same mistakes. Then, by doing something good, he might lose his guilt and shame, and she might stop coming into his dreams, all these years later.

Both their hopes had screeched to a halt, in that flaming wreckage by the sea. At least he had a chance to be the teacher she'd wanted to be.

'We'll have to call you Mister Chips.'

Suddenly Lance's words brought him back to the present. 'Wait until we see what I'm like in the classroom,' he replied. 'At this stage, I'm surprised they even wanted me in their team.'

Everyone makes mistakes, they said when offering him the job.

'These boys just need someone to believe in them,' Fergus echoed the Gambian man's words, 'and they've put their faith in me.'

'Like Chris Powell, Charlton's man of faith,' Lance suggested.

Back at the start of the year, Charlton's board invested their hopes for the future in this novice manager who'd been a star player of the past. He had taken over a team drifting on the borders of the play-off zone, and set about rebuilding the club in his image. He was inexperienced, and some said too nice to be a football manager. You had to be tough, dirty and nasty to survive in this game. But he had ploughed on regardless.

'And we're still unbeaten in the new season.'

'So how was today's game?' Fergus asked.

'Mixed emotions,' answered the man in a short-sleeved Charlton jersey as he rose to the fridge and returned with a couple of beers. 'We'd been leading two-nil, and the party was in full swing, like back in the Premier League days. You're sitting there, singing songs, dreaming of promotion, thinking this is the best team we've had in ages.' He paused for a sip of lager, shaking his head as he spoke. 'And then it's typical Charlton.'

'What's typical Charlton?'

'To be two goals to the good and flying,' Lance replied, 'and then to let them come back, draw level and cost us two points.'

'So this is a habit of theirs?'

'Habit? It's a part of our religion.'

To test the supporters' faith, down through the years, the team would bleed hope out of them in a series of short, sharp sword wounds.

'When things are going best, we're champion at screwing them up,' he explained. 'When we've a great start to the season, you know we'll crash after Christmas, or if we're lucky enough to find a kid who could become England's Maradona, we'd sell him for half a million, use the money for bog rolls and get relegated six months later.'

'Lots o' bog roll in half a million quid.'

'We've spent ten times that much on shit before.'

'Things seem to be going okay for you now.'

'Hopefully we're through the bad times,' he said, touching wood. 'You probably know our crash was spectacular.'

'Yes,' Fergus mused. 'Like a joyride.'

'We thought the Premier League years were going to last forever,' Lance said sadly. 'Then we spent a lot o' money on shit, got relegated, couldn't get back up again out of the second division, went bust, got even worse and ended up relegated into the third division.'

'Unbeaten in three games,' his friend said, 'that's recovery.'

'I suppose.' He nodded hesitantly, as if superstitious against false expectations of hope. 'Let's see where we are at Christmas.'

'It'd be good to see a Premier game at Charlton.'

'Good to see any game,' Lance corrected him. 'When you follow your team it's like being in a marriage, for better or for worse, for rich with Russian owners, or about to be kicked out for bankruptcy.'

'Wouldn't know,' Fergus said. 'Never been married.'

'Me neither,' his friend replied, 'but in the months before I left for Afghanistan, I'd an affair with a married woman.'

Again, he sipped his beer to douse the flames of memory.

'Maybe that was the reason for going in the first place, to get away, because it had been an addiction, like heroin, and when she stopped seeing me and went back to her husband, I was in cold turkey.'

'Feels like grief, I suppose'

'Somebody's dead to you, but they're still alive,' he replied. 'It's like wakening up in the night and there's a part of you amputated.'

'Unlucky in love, unlucky in life,' Fergus thought to himself.

'So now I'm looking for somebody to replace the two parts that are missing. One below the knee, and one inside the heart. Thank God there's football, though I don't really believe in God, because if there is one, Charlton would be champions, not Manchester United.'

'Thought there's more to football than Chelsea or United?'

'Yeah, you're right. I'm just feeling sorry for myself again,' he said. 'Wouldn't change following my local team for anything.' Then he laughed. 'Still, must be nice to be born in Barcelona.'

Then he would have known nothing of the suffering of supporting a small team and of being caught up in the passion of an affair with Charlton. Probably if he had been Catalan or Spanish or whatever, he would have never been out in Afghanistan either, playing so far away from home.

'There's a story I remember from school.' The former soldier changed direction suddenly. 'It's about a guy called Martial Bourdin, who made me think of Charlton the very first time I heard it.'

'Was he a player from the past?' Fergus wondered.

'If he was, he definitely played on the far left.'

He was a Frenchman, so probably preferred rugby to football, though he was little more than five feet tall, which might have been a problem. That was if he liked sports at all, for he was an anarchist and a ladies' tailor, Lance explained as he limped off to grab a couple more beers.

Around the 1890s, he moved to London and got himself caught up in plans to bomb the Royal Observatory in Greenwich. Maybe, like Lance, he'd been unlucky in love and needed methadone for his empty rage.

Whatever the reason, which nobody would ever know, this angry foreigner decided he was going to blast a hole in the walls of time.

'So what happened to him?'

'One February evening, just after Valentine's Day, he turned up in Greenwich, on a tram from Westminster, in a hurry and a fluster. Like he was on a team that's losing in the last minutes of a Cup match.'

Fergus imagined him as Lance described a small man nervously stroking a moustache, starting his ascent of Observatory Hill. 150 feet above stood the meridian line and the home of time. Cradling a package under his arm, it's as if he's playing a game at Twickenham.

'He's getting right near the top as it's starting to go pitch dark,' Lance tried to impersonate a Victorian sports' commentator. 'He's cradling the ball to his chest, approaching the goalposts, shimmying, swerving, ducking tackles from big ugly fuckers on all sides of him, about to score the winning try for France over England.'

Then Lance stopped talking for a second. His eyes darkened. Much as he hated Bourdin for what came next, he understood the suffering. It was as if, in this moment, he stepped into the minute Frenchman's shoes.

'He's right on the edge of the line, by the walls of the Observatory, and all he's got to do is to gently put the package down, calmly walk away and the show's over, but the left winger stumbles right at the very last second, and then it's boom… goodnight Irene.'

'So he ends up as an accidental suicide bomber?'

'Suppose so.'

'But what's this got to do with Charlton?'

'Well,' said the man with the sword tattoo, 'we always seem to screw up at the last minute, especially when things seem like they're going perfectly to plan, and all we've got to do is cross the finishing line.'

Ten years after the lights went out on Bourdin's mysterious mission, Charlton Athletic Football Club formed in a back street by the Thames. Sometimes over the years, it seemed that black acid from Bourdin's bomb had seeped through the soil of Greenwich, dyeing the river dark. Then, come spring, the anarchist's failed spirit resurfaces in South East London, taking revenge on those inside a red steel fortress.

'It's just a story,' Fergus said. 'There's no such thing as ghosts.'

'Don't say that too loud. You'll wreck tourism in Greenwich.'

'I take it Bourdin's not part of the official story, then.'

'Written out of history.'

As Lance spoke, he caressed the circle of his own tattoo.

'There's something else about this, what it means in my life,' he spoke again suddenly. Fergus sensed traces of emotion buried deep in the reflections of red and black ink in his friend's damp blue eyes.

'I told you I got this before Afghanistan. She was the one who did it.'

'The woman you'd an affair with?'

'She was a tattoo artist,' Lance whispered. 'An Asian girl born in England, married to somebody she'd never loved but couldn't leave.'

'Would you tell this to the guys who hijacked the other night?'

He hadn't meant to be so direct, but Lance didn't seem to mind.

'To hell with them,' he growled. 'We loved each other and couldn't be together, but I've got this tattoo that's as much hers as Charlton's.'

'So your whole life story's told in that club badge?'

'Not all of it,' his friend corrected him. 'But once you're caught up in an affair, and you've been through a war, there's not much left of what you used to be, and if there is, it's buried under a mountain o' rubble.'

'Well, hopefully it's a fresh start for both of us.'

'You don't give much away about your story.'

'How could anyone compete with a tale like yours? It'd be like going head to head with Stephen King in a short story contest.'

Lance laughed, crossing to the fridge for fresh drinks. Again, Fergus had diverted attention from his joyride and the lonely years of his twenties.

'I'd like to see a game sometime,' he said as an August sunset laboured on the river before sinking into darkness. 'If this is a fresh start for me, maybe my football team should be fresh too.'

Lance's eyes shone as blue as robin red breast's eggs with pride and amusement. 'Well, if you're going to start following a team in division three, at least nobody's going to accuse you of jumping on the bandwagon.'

These past weeks he had found a new place to live, a new football team, a new job and a new friend. Deep down, he wanted to share his story. But there'd been enough ghost stories for one day, so they sipped beer and spoke of football, sometimes glancing out on Greenwich's waterfront, where they caught snapshots of Marilyn's window and sailors' cannons from bygone wars, standing guard over the present.

7
Temple Grounds

On Saturdays in England, towns and teams steered a path through the uncertain waters of league competition, bringing together north and south, east and west. They became ships navigating a voyage through four seasons rolled into one, across the geography of each division. Charlton's division, the third in a series of four (or seven, if you counted the semi-professional lower ranks) covered most of England.

Up in the North West you found Carlisle, resting on the borders of Scotland, after a journey through the rolling countryside of the Lake District. On the opposite shore, you could sail into Hartlepool, where they had hung a monkey, mistaking him for a Frenchman. To this day they kept a monkey as their mascot, Lance informed Fergus.

Moving away from the North East, going back towards the centre, and then westwards again, you crossed through the bygone mill towns and Gothic architecture of Lancashire. Preston, home of former cotton factories and England cricket captains. Rochdale, trapped like a spinning wheel in the foothills of the Pennines; famous for fourth-division football and Pablo Fanque's Circus Royal of 1863.

Then there's Yorkshire, with its dales, cloth caps and curry houses. High in the hills, there's the sprawling town of Huddersfield, one of the promotion favourites. Slightly southwards, you'll discover Sheffield's deadly rivals, United and Wednesday, who like the Steel City's industries had known more glorious days in the past. Beneath them, on the edge of Derbyshire, you'll see Chesterfield's Parish Church with its crooked spire, and former winners of the Anglo-Scottish Cup.

Getting to the Midlands, you're greeted by Notts County's Magpies from Nottinghamshire, the oldest professional football club in the world, and the town of Walsall, once attacked by Martial Bourdin's fellow anarchists. Across the way there's Colchester, England's oldest Roman town, and Milton Keynes Dons as you move further south, careful not to tread on the sensitivities of football history. Like one of those wasps that use other insects as a surrogate for their babies, MK Dons birthed from the dying body of Wimbledon Football Club.

Soon you're in London, wandering through Wycombe and having stopovers in Stevenage before reaching Brentford's Griffin Park with a pub on every corner. Moving on, you'll come to Leyton, where you'll find a small team called Orient, hidden away in the back streets of the East, beneath the encroaching shadows of the 2012 Olympic stadium.

Taking the road out of London, you come to the blue seas and high cliffs of Bournemouth; everybody's favourite away game unless you prefer drunken weekends in Bury, Scunthorpe, and Tranmere.

Following the island's sole through Dorset, you pass the burnished sandstone cliffs of the Devonshire coast that jut out into the English Channel, and turn inland for Exeter's cathedral and canals. Then, heading west through picturesque villages, you end your travels in the Somerset town of Yeovil as you quench your thirst with cider.

Today, though, in the September sunshine, it was a home game.

'Exeter City, the first live match of my lifetime.'

It had been a long time coming.

'We'll go across early,' Lance suggested. 'That way, I'll be able to show you round before the place gets too crowded.'

They departed in morning's upper reaches from Greenwich Station, with the array of historical buildings shining virgin-white, except for the Observatory's red-brick cruciform above the park's rusting greenery.

Beside them, a couple of pretty girls drank lemonade and gossiped, travelling three stops without exchanging a glance. Reaching their destination, they climbed the stairs from the platform, passing a swarm of yellow-coated transport police, which made them glad they had paid the fare instead of, as they sometimes did, bunking a free ride.

'So this is Charlton,' said Fergus as they stepped out into a rough and ready place with none of Greenwich's airs and graces.

Though newcomers, from Romans to Royals, had settled here since the days of the Iron Age, there were no cliffs of Portland stone greeting visitors.

'You're not so impressed.'

The Irishman shrugged his shoulders as they passed a couple of deserted takeaways, side streets full of bins and bedsits, betting shops, groceries, off-licences and a shabby coalition of social clubs.

One was Liberal and the other Conservative, though they both displayed the same frontage of Saint George's crosses, torn and tattered as a burglar's trousers after a scrap with a Staffordshire. Already, not five minutes out of the station, he had seen half a dozen bull terriers.

Lance grumbled. 'Leftovers of last summer's World Cup.'

Flags, Fergus presumed, and not those badly-trained dogs dragged around Charlton's streets as weapons by macho owners who drunkenly watched them decorate the pavements in adverts against tourism, and not give a shit.

'Probably not the prettiest place in the division,' Fergus admitted, 'from what you've told me about some of the others.'

'This is just one stretch of road,' Lance defended his home town.

But the guest wasn't impressed as he took his first steps through Charlton. This wasn't glass or mountain. It was everyday stone; bricked terraces. A cluster of tower blocks, dipping in and out of heights, offered a stark contrast to Canary Wharf's sparkling towers in the background.

'Floyd Road,' a sign read as they rounded a bend.

'Valley, Floyd Road,' Lance spoke softly, tracing out the lineaments of every syllable, 'is the name of our club anthem.'

Going around the corner, Fergus saw the stadium for the first time. Soft-red, rectangular, clamped in spikes and turnstiles, nested between terraced houses, a railway bridge and a tree-bearded slope to the east. They passed the club superstore on one corner, and a six-foot mural on the opposite side, showing the club badge, the same as Lance's tattoo except for the wording.

'So what do you think now?'

'It's got character,' Fergus answered.

Set against curls of clouds and patches of blue in the late-morning sky, the Valley moulded itself to a red-hot fireball, an open-top volcano.

You could almost smell the fumes of the past as the old stadium creaked towards the onset of another match day. Here you realised there was far more to football than you would ever see in a TV game.

'Like drinking flat beer from a plastic glass,' Lance said.

'Cybersex,' Fergus thought but didn't share it.

'Bartram's will be opening soon. We'll have a pint.'

'Bartram. He's the man on your wall.'

'That's right,' Lance answered. 'Our greatest goalie ever.'

Then he paused to add that the great man was married in the very same church as his own parents – Our Lady of Grace down the road.

'Told you the colours of this club run deep in my blood,' he carried on, but his friend was thinking of something else at this stage.

Every match day's like someone's wedding, Fergus thought as they made their way towards the western side of the stadium. There's hundreds of things to be done before the ceremony starts.

Coming here this early, you could see the plans taking shape. Caterers, inside and outside, unpacking for the day's action. Stewards, beefy and brusque, arriving early. Souvenir stalls setting up.

'Chris Powell T-shirts, only a tenner,' declared a sign buried in a bundle of scarves. 'Fridge magnets free for a fiver.' They chuckled at this as they drifted towards the promise of beer, drinking in the smell of fresh cut grass.

There was something else, strong as horse manure, used to treat the surface before games, so that at three o'clock it's ready to take as much abuse as a racecourse.

Standing guard over the stadium's west side, they saw a statue of the goalie who had volunteered his name to the lounge beyond.

'Sam Bartram,' read the plaque.

'He loved this club, loved this place. Even though he was born somewhere near Newcastle, he was a Charlton man.'

At first glance you would have sworn the statue had been sculpted out of anthracite, shipped out of South Shields, down the waterways and through the divisions of a country for which he had never been capped.

'Because o' another bloody war,' Lance grumbled.

Touching the body of the ex-serviceman goalkeeper, Fergus expected to come away with dark stains on his fingers. But the metal was soft, smooth and clean as the wings of a plane rising into a silky sky.

'He's got an air of legend.'

'Always smiling, watching over the streets of Charlton,' Lance replied, 'even when there's not much to smile about.'

Through successive relegations, he had kept his head high.

'Every detail's so perfect,' Fergus remarked.

Like a piece of wood cut, smoothed and sanded to perfection, you could tell that this was the work of a master craftsman. Every aspect carried the intricacy found in a line of good poetry.

The Irishman's eyes tracked the artwork from head to toe, starting with swept-back hair coming off a broad forehead in a lather of silvery waves softly falling into the long strand of his face.

Then his clothes, the playing costume of creased shorts, folded socks, laced boots and round-necked jersey. Next, the tools of his trade, an old-fashioned stitched football rose up in his right hand, and in his left, a cloth cap, like those worn by old men from his childhood.

Lance must have been thinking the same thing.

'Whenever I see this statue,' he said, 'it reminds me of coming here with my grandfather, as a boy.' His eyes dampened again. 'He died the very year this statue was unveiled, back in 2005. I've a picture of us standing together, alongside Sam; him bent over on a stick, but still enjoying the tradition of going to a Saturday game.' Suddenly, his mood changed, followed by the eruption of a bitter laugh. 'I'm glad he never got to see me being the one who was unable to stand up straight.'

'Come on,' his friend replied, 'it's time for a pint.'

Going inside Bartram's just a couple of minutes after it opened, they found a seat beneath an olden-day picture of an FA Cup winning team.

'They're the men of '47,' said Lance.

Sam Bartram was amongst them, wearing the dark clothes of a goalie, as a cadre of outfield players, in white shirts and baggy shorts, shouldered a happy captain across the Wembley turf, holding the silverware high and proud as Bobby Moore was to do a couple of decades later. 1947, to Charlton, was what 1966 represented for the whole of England; a moment of being on top of the world.

'Like an old friend,' Fergus said of the trophy.

'So you watched Cup finals in Ireland too?'

'Watched them? Football's always been Ireland's third religion.'

'So you didn't hate everything about England?'

'Loved comic books, crisps, comedies and Cup finals.'

Lance rose to get the drinks, since beer was part of Saturday's football ritual, up and down the country, from Hartlepool to Torquay. Looking around the gallery of snapshots from Charlton's history, Fergus could see football's version of Greenwich's Painted Hall.

'I'll tell you the story,' Lance said, returning to the team of '47. 'The potted history of the Valley in a single pint.'

After sitting down and taking the first sip, he started talking about when this place was a gravel pit and about the team newly formed a few streets away.

'Hundreds of men,' he said, 'got together to make a pitch out of the pit, mostly river workers on their days off, doing the digging. We're so close to the water, you see, it's like this team's a part of the Thames.' Taking another sip, he glanced up at the shiny trophy with its big lugs. 'Haunted too, you know, as full of ghosts as Greenwich.'

'How so?' asked Fergus, intrigued to learn more.

'According to my grandfather, when they filled the pits, they used earth from an ancient graveyard in the grounds of a local hospital.'

'So maybe there's more than Bourdin haunting the place?'

They must have been kinder ghosts in the early days, for the '30s and '40s brought great success to the club and its stadium, which had one of the biggest capacities in London but not the supporters to fill it.

'We'd a great manager,' Lance explained. 'Another northerner, by the name of Jimmy Seed. But, as happens, Bourdin's ghost got inside the boardroom, we got rid of him and caught a fast train downhill.'

The '50s to the '80s were dark years for Charlton, potholed with strange episodes such as the story of Allan Simonsen, European Footballer of the Year, turning up at the Valley for a cameo in 1982.

'Then health and safety became an issue,' he sighed, his glass half full, half empty. 'We had to renovate.'

He talked as if the club was as much his flesh as the tattoo was.

'So we moved to Selhurst to share with Crystal Palace.'

You could feel the disdain in the way his teeth lingered on *share*.

'Was supposed to be temporary, but we spent a whole seven years on the road, becoming the gypsies of British football.' As he spoke, his eyes brightened and the years rolled back like clouds over tents of blue. 'Maybe at the start it was fun, an adventure, being a boy, being able to get inside the empty ground, running on the terraces, kicking a ball on the pitch and smashing things that were going to be fixed anyway.'

But the years dragged on. Smashed things remained unfixed. The pitch, with its missing squares of turf, slowly turned to a ragged, untended garden. Long grass and brambles grew over the first beer cans and empty cigarette packets of a London boy's rite of passage.

'Seemed like we'd never get back home,' he said. 'But we did, we bloody did, and the knowledge of this was what kept me going in a hospital bed in Afghanistan when I feared I'd never walk again.'

Sick of waiting, fed up with broken promises, the supporters took the matter in their own hands, in a fine Charlton tradition of resistance to bad decisions, from changes in bus routes to closures of parks.

Volunteers got together and started tidying up, clearing terraces and turnstiles of long grasses and brambles, before feeding residue to bonfires; letting red sails of pride rise again through dark smog.

'If we could do this, then I could walk again, see straight and think straight without hearing explosions all the time,' Lance growled through clenched teeth. 'But there's always obstacles, speed humps that come along and slow your journey down.'

Even though they had resurrected their home, a few miles from the peninsula that featured in T.S. Eliot's *Wasteland*, the speed hump of bureaucracy came along and blasted them below the belt.

'Greenwich Council wouldn't let us go back,' he said bitterly. 'But you don't give up, even though the first days and nights are dark.'

Physically he was here, alongside the FA Cup team of '47, but mentally he was somewhere else, in a hospital bed under a foreign sky.

'You have to hoist yourself up, concentrate and learn to fight.'

Charlton's supporters chose the ballot box over rage and riots.

'We formed a political party,' he declared with such passion that Fergus could feel the suffering of his people in those days of fear and doubt. 'We fought elections and took seats in the town hall.'

Suddenly London's political establishment shivered in the flames of change rising high as the nine-foot, sun-blazed statue across the way.

'They had to listen to us at last, and after seven years of being gypsies, we re-opened the turnstiles to our one true home.' Again, his eyes hazed and his voice deepened. '5th of December 1992, the most important day of our lives.'

Christ, Fergus sensed, the colours of his tattoo surely ran deep. Bizarrely, that date had shaped his life as much as the explosion had.

'Were you there?' he asked to soften the mood.

'We didn't get tickets to go inside the ground that day,' his voice burned jersey-red with nostalgia, 'but I watched from a tree on the heights above the old East Stand and it was fucking freezing, but with seven minutes gone I was glad.'

'What happened?' Fergus asked.

'Colin Walsh scored the first goal of our return and no matter how cold I was and how far off the ground I was, I wouldn't have swapped positions with anybody in the world.'

Suddenly, his eyes shifted to the slopes above a tower block.

'Sometimes when I was lying in hospital, far from home, half-awake, half in dreams, inside my head I'd go back there to that tree house,' he said softly, returning to Afghanistan for a moment as he finished his pint.

Then it was time to go and get ready for the game.

'We'll have some haddock and chips,' he suggested as they stepped outside. 'It's a tradition going back to when the club first started, when we got our nickname 'the Addicks' on account of our sponsors.'

Going back towards the station, where the streets were suddenly full of people and a few police officers mounted on horses, they felt the mood of a match day smother all memories of torn flags and bull terriers.

The place was buzzing as they ordered the best fish and chips he had eaten since the evening of a death ride to the seaside long ago.

Strange how she followed him here and then went out of his mind quickly as she had been in the habit of doing lately, except in his dreams, ever since he had started working with his team of angry young men. Lucy wasn't part of his new life, his new religion, his new teams, and he wasn't going to let anything spoil the loss of his football virginity. As he finished his chips, she became no more than an anonymous face in the red-breasted crowd of thousands drifting back towards the stadium.

'Sometimes there's more police,' Lance said, stepping into synch with the rhythm and flow of his people as his limp miraculously disappeared, 'especially against Palace and Millwall.'

'Different atmosphere then,' the visitor supposed.

'If it's a small team like Exeter there's never going to be trouble,' said the former soldier as he quickened his step. 'At least not outside the ground. Just carnage on the pitch sometimes, like last season when they came here and hammered us three goals to one.'

That was 'football for a fiver', he added. A feast cooked up by the club's marketing people as a kind of honeytrap to lure fresh support through the Valley's turnstiles. Over 20,000 people turned up, as if catching cheap flights to the Mediterranean. But on this day the plane crashed in flames, in spectacular fashion, and little Exeter, brought as lambs to the slaughter, put the home side to the sword.

'Embarrassing,' Lance said, 'but we'll make up for it today.'

On the pitch his team would erase the ghosts of the past as he carried on a family tradition going back decades. They would watch from the East Stand, as he had done since he was a little boy learning the folklore of his team. Every game, every day, was a reservoir of a thousand memories.

'We're early,' he said as they entered the stadium at half past two, 'but that's good because you can soak up the atmosphere.'

'It's different to Gaelic football back home,' said Fergus, leaving behind fragrances of burgers and fried onions on the streets outside, passing through turnstiles and red steel tunnels. 'So much security you'd swear they were expecting a riot.'

'Been like this since the eighties,' his friend replied.

Something about the scene reminded him of being in a cage, of prison walkways and the watchful eyes of screws. Then the sight of the pitch soothed his nerves. At this stage of a match day, the stadium was peaceful as a cathedral. Slowly the congregation gathered. Up in the North Stand, amongst bugle horns and drums, a choir practiced.

On the pitch, players from both teams warmed up. Fergus flicked through the pages of a match programme to attach names to faces.

Lance did the same. 'Most of them are new.'

'That must be Chris Powell,' Fergus assumed, pointing to the well-dressed man on the sidelines whose proud, pearly smile blazed like foam on a summer's pint of Guinness.

'Yeah,' Lance said with pride. 'Best left back to ever play for us, before he became a coach, and he played for England too, though that was late in his career.'

'I was often left back in the dressing room.'

Lance wasn't listening; he was too absorbed in Chrissie Powell's story. 'When he was called up for England, the papers asked '*Chris Who?*' But on the night of his debut against Spain, he was better than Beckham. He's a great guy and he's trying to build a great team too.'

Then he went through the players, for Fergus's benefit, so that by knowing them better Fergus might take them to heart.

'Ben Hamer's the goalie, blonde guy, tall and slim,' he explained. 'That little guy leaning to the left, kicking to the right, is Chris Solly. He's a full back, a local boy, came up through our academy.'

'Up in Eltham?' Fergus asked, and Lance nodded as his eyes swept towards someone taller and darker who might well have been foreign.

'That's Rhoys Wiggins,' he said. 'Our left back, a Welshman.'

He had moved from the blue seas of Bournemouth in the summer. The two centre halves, Michael Morrison and Matt Taylor, also crossed the country. Morrison, moving from Sheffield, added steel to the defence. Taylor, his new partner, was previously captain of Exeter City.

'Yes,' Lance admitted. 'Part of *football for a fiver's* disaster.'

They had added a trio of new midfielders as well, though only two of them appeared on today's team-sheet. Dale Stephens, a playmaker from Lancashire, wearing the number eight jersey. Then Danny Hollands, already nicknamed 'the Dutchman'. Like Wiggins he'd been snatched from Bournemouth, though started out at Chelsea.

'One of the best players in the lower divisions,' Lance insisted. 'And we've also signed Mikel Alonso who's injured at the minute. Brother of Real Madrid's Xabi who used to play for Liverpool.'

'Very continental out here in SE7,' Fergus supposed. 'Having a Spaniard and a Dutchman at the heart of your team.'

But today, a couple of Englishmen, team captain Johnnie Jackson, and Scott Wagstaff, were the final members of the midfield quartet.

'Jackson, wearing number four,' said Lance, 'takes free kicks like a Camden Ronaldo and gives 220% every time.'

Wagstaff, academy graduate and local boy, plays on the wing, setting up chances for the forward partnership; one older, one newer.

'Number ten is Bradley Wright-Phillips, the Brockley Pelé,' he explained. 'Chris Powell's first signing back in January, and the bigger guy alongside him is Paul Hayes, another summer signing.'

By now, the players had almost finished their warm-up. When it was complete, they applauded the fans and disappeared down the white canopy of a tunnel which led towards two sets of dressing rooms.

'There's a sign inside the tunnel,' Lance explained. 'It says "THIS IS THE VALLEY QUALITY IS EXPECTED EFFORT IS DEMANDED."'

Seconds later, a sudden explosion of joy drowned out Lance's voice. The day's teams had emerged from the west side of the ground.

'Let's hear some noise,' demanded the match day announcer. 'Ladies and gentlemen, it's your home team, Chaaaaalllllton Athletic.'

Immediately, the congregation of about 15,000 rose to their feet. Hymns erupted in the North Stand. Finally, in the flesh, Fergus had experienced the sound of a match day. It's a noise that's both solid and liquid at the same time, coming upon you at thunderstorm speed. When thousands of voices congeal into one mighty roar, nobody's alone anymore. They're a part of Charlton in a way they can never be if they just pass through its train station or walk its scruffy streets. Clapping to the same rhythm as the folks around you, you feel the same blood's eddying through your veins, deep red as the players' shirts.

'Makes me feel like singing,' Fergus admitted, though he wasn't sure if his accent would be out of place amongst these Londoners.

Then all of a sudden, just as it seemed the mercury was going to shoot its load out of the thermometer and spill onto the streets of SE7, the thunderstorm silenced. Everybody sat down and they once again became strangers watching players shake hands and go into battle stations.

The scene was set, like when you are sitting in a plane, waiting for take-off. The atmosphere was building up. It was a clear day fragranced with fish, chips and beer. This time around, there was no turbulence expected.

Across the way, Exeter fans had mustered a rousing chorus despite being vastly outnumbered on enemy territory. The Jimmy Seed Stand had perfect acoustics for a small group of supporters making lots of noise. Today it was a chessboard of red and white, matching the shirts of the team from the west country, as striped as a stick of rock.

'Take off,' Fergus thought as the game kicked off.

'Come on, you reds!' the men around them chanted.

One fellow, a couple of rows down, stole a sip of whisky from a hip flask he had managed to sneak past the wardens at the turnstiles.

Beside them, a boy in puberty croaked, 'Get the bloody fink.'

Exeter City weren't going to be a walkover. These past few years, they had climbed through the lower divisions with successive promotions. Back in 2006, Lance said, when Charlton was in the Premiership playing Chelsea, Exeter had been facing the likes of Canvey Island. You don't come so far so fast without being organised and tough to beat.

'Come on, Charlton!' willed the men on the east side.

Gradually the reds began to get into their rhythm, as if they too had the taste of whisky warming their blood. Chris Powell's new team was starting to chip away at the sticks of rock surrounding them. Dale Stephens and the Chelsea Dutchman, found on Bournemouth beach, drove forwards from the centre at every opportunity, matched by the full backs pushing up from defence in a red blaze that reminded Fergus of Phil Neal and Alan Kennedy playing for Liverpool in his childhood.

'Haven't seen a team like this in years,' said Lance.

Since Premiership relegation, they had been a side with a soft centre, a great soggy doughnut. Something had changed. These guys had been together only a few months and they were already playing as a unit, working in harmony, helping each other out, pausing for contemplation before passing the ball, anticipating where their team mates might be.

You could feel the breeze of hope blowing through the Valley, and every so often it turned to drum rolls in the North Stand. When players did something special, the supporters chanted their names in chorus.

'Bradley Wright-Phillips, he's better than Shaun.'

That was his brother, Lance explained, who used to play for Chelsea. Then he fell silent as Exeter forced their way back into the match. Seconds later, one of their shots seemed to sail across the line before Ben Hamer managed to crab-claw it back out of the goal.

'Phew,' agreed the home support, 'bloody lucky.'

The referee hadn't seen it. One of the Exeter forwards was furious. He crossed the pitch to remonstrate with the linesman and found himself sent off for an early shower. Reduced to ten men, Exeter found that its sudden improvement had been thwarted. The reds were in the ascendancy once again, let loose like kids at the seaside. Danny Hollands went Dutch through the centre, sending a shot high and wide. Chris Solly surged forwards with two efforts soon after, prompting songs from the choir.

'Only five foot three, but better than John Terr-ee!'

'He's actually a few inches taller,' Lance pointed out, 'but I guess they couldn't find a defender whose name rhymes with seven.'

Then, just before half-time, the song on the jukebox changed as somebody turned up the volume once more. Wright-Phillips had managed to flick the switch, with a swish of the ball off his chest and an interchange with Paul Hayes, as he breezed towards goal. Taking a return pass from his strike partner, he shot low into the corner.

Fumaroles of sound erupted from every direction, aside from the stiff-lipped Jimmy Seed Stand. 'One-nil to the reds.'

Lance threw his arms around Fergus as everyone in the East Stand rose up simultaneously to celebrate and applaud the scorer. There was whisky flowing through all of them now, heating up their insides, speeding up the heartbeat, sending them into mass delirium. Chrissie Powell's management team and all the substitutes were up and dancing too; the gaffer's smart black suit and tie unruffled.

'Christ,' Fergus thought. 'It's nothing like this on television.'

This was love in the flesh – compared to cybersex. You had every sight, sound, taste and smell magnified a hundredfold. Images of a blonde girl in her boyfriend's arms, hip-flask man stealing another sip, the silver flash of sunlight dancing on bugles. Shouts, sweat and spittle, streams of whisky, and cold burgers infused with fresh life.

Huddles of bodies and tremors of excitement, the sense of anticipation, of wanting more, like the goal had sparked off an addiction, reminding junkies of how good the needle feels.

Echoes of drums and domination continued through the half after everyone had calmed down and continued watching.

'We need more of the same in the second half,' Lance said as they headed for another beer to keep alive the ecstasy of that goal going in, and the dream of promotion when the season's wheels turned full cycle. 'It's time to exorcise the ghosts of football for a fiver.'

But Charlton tend not to do exorcisms or early victories. In recent seasons, they had been here many times before. They dominate, take the lead, fail to build on it, and then concede a soft goal in the dying minutes. This season, things might be different. There was hope in the air as fans stuttered back to the stands for the second half.

Another mighty roar greeted the players as they emerged onto the pitch. The game resumed and the big screen showed 45.00 minutes ticking downwards as clouds silvered a four o'clock sky.

Once again the red men had the ball, stroking it gently across the green baize as if afraid of cracking the bones of the dead.

'Come on, Charlton,' cried hip-flask man. 'Get stuck in!'

'Whack the bloody fink!' yelled the boy in puberty.

Fergus imagined this bloody fink as a mythical sea beast that crawled out of the Thames; jellyfish-shark that for several seasons had enwrapped Charlton's terrace-swimmers in tentacles of misery.

Perhaps the bloody fink was the game itself, which the men in red were trying to kill off, inflicting a series of small cuts on the Exeter defences when all that was needed was to go for the jugular.

This was where armchair supporters get themselves a cup of tea or another beer, but there's no such luxury when watching football live. Again his mind began to drift, reacting to the rhythm of the game. He listened to the catcalls of tattooed men and watched their greying heads swish from side to side as they followed the action.

Sometimes, their voices set against drumbeats, the fans on the north side would sing a few lines of a song and then suddenly stop and sigh as the men in red surged forwards once again, before reaching another dead end. And all the while, as they worshipped in their Saturday temple, stewards watched every move from the sidelines, taking him back to games, not so long ago, on a radio inside an Irish prison cell.

Then, as the game was drifting to closure, Dale Stephens stepped forwards from midfield to impale the bloody fink. Slowing down for a second, he swivelled his hips and then straightened up, like he was a young Kate Moss pausing, and posing for the cameras on a Parisian catwalk. Okay, she's better looking, but just like her, for a few seconds, Charlton's playmaker holds the attention of a thousand-dozen men.

Shooting low and strong – you would swear this was more *Roy of the Rovers* than a 3rd division football match. Almost in slow motion, the mythical sea beast becomes tangled up in the back of the net.

The sigh of relief and the upward surge of bodies were immense. It was a case of job done and three more points collected on the road to promotion, as Chris Powell would say in post-match interviews.

Going in, the walk was slow and measured. Going out, everybody was hurrying home. There was no place for a crippled man in the rush.

'What'd you make of your first game?' Lance asked as they lingered in the emptying coliseum, applauding the gladiators.

Fergus drank in the closing scenes before answering. 'Great.'

At the start, he had been interested in the spectacle and the novelty. By the end, he felt a part of something. He wasn't sure he would ever tattoo the badge on his arm like Lance and let this club become part of his blood and his body in the same way, but he would come back again. That was for sure, he thought as they hobbled home together out of the empty stadium.

8
Boys Being Boys

Come Monday, as life returned to normal, Fergus could still feel the hot red blood of the weekend flowing through his veins. He was back again amongst his boys, hearing stories of court cases, scraps and girls. They would talk of *life in the ghetto* and release their aggression on football pitches and in boxing rings, then chill out over games of pool in the common room; kids against adults, playing doubles alongside Omar, his Gambian colleague.

Sometimes they would chat for hours. They said he understood them better than most teachers, even Omar. Hearing this, he felt a candle of pride warm the back of his throat. Though he was an assistant rather than a teacher, his life had taken on some purpose.

Amongst these boys he felt young again. Though he couldn't get back the years he had lost, he could steer others in a better direction.

He would feel contented walking home from Deptford to Greenwich as the College's misshapen breasts came into view. The same ghosts resided there as before, while the trees changed colour. Coming through the courtyard, in the evenings, he would stop off by the Painted Hall, where he could see England's history in sanguine glory.

Sometimes his mind would drift back to the riots and to how those fevered nights seemed so long ago. London's villages had found a sense of peace again as the fires of empty rage died down.

Then one evening things changed.

'You can't come this way,' said a sudden voice.

He had been daydreaming when a police officer appeared like a great black cloud blocking out the last spark of sunlight on the river. Up ahead there was motion outside the apartments, and the cop was a part of that; he was directing people away from what gradually became a commotion the closer you came. But most of the scene was blocked off, with crowds directed towards the riverside. All races of the world had gathered on the banks of the Thames as if Noah's Ark was setting sail. He recognised some of the faces and could see others looking out the windows of apartments. Merlin was amongst them, drawing apart the curtains so that his sharp eyes gleamed in the half-light. Lately, he had a visitor staying – a boy no more than fifteen or sixteen.

'Arsenal fan,' Lance noticed from the hoodie he wore.

There was no sign of the boy now, with his bright eyes and cropped hair, as police addressed the crowd. 'Stay back.'

Spectators had phones and cameras ready, but Fergus couldn't work out what was going on. He could see police cars, glassy and buzzing as bluebottles; then specialist cops swinging semi-automatics on their hips. Women screaming, mostly African, all dressed up, sporting an arsenal of Bibles, babies and designer handbags.

'Lord save us!' they hollered up to the darkening heavens and down the street where kids lurked, feral as foxes, in the shadows.

Perhaps these events had something to do with Merlin. Unmasked as a bomb-maker, he could have felt this was his last stand, a final siege. These days anything was possible and everything happened fast.

Something stretched on the pavement was being cordoned off. He couldn't see what exactly. There were too many bodies in the way.

'No photographs please,' the cops cried out, as helpless to stop the tide as they had been on the night of rioting in Lewisham.

Requesting this from the digital generation was like asking bees to stay away from jam. Whatever chance they got, they pushed through to the front of the line, recording scenes on their electronic devices.

Okay, somebody was dead. He had figured that much out. The rest didn't make sense and heavy rain wasn't helping piece the clues together.

Getting closer, that's when he noticed what the police were doing. They were moving everybody from one side of the road to the other.

Amongst the figures crossing the tarmac which was closed off to traffic, he caught the splendid blaze of a bleached head.

'Lance's Marilyn,' he realised.

She was standing by the edge of the Thames, a bicycle pressed against her body, acting as a shield between her and the crowd. A guardian of the waterfront, like Ben Hamer in Charlton's goal. But a lot more beautiful.

For weeks she had been coming up in his conversations with Lance. He had caught glimpses of her through a window too. This was his chance to go and approach her, to put a voice to the face and the hairstyle.

'What happened here?' he asked, suddenly so close he could see the colour of her eyes – cornflower blue with a faint hint of green.

Surprised he had selected her from amongst half a dozen people, she looked up, for she was a couple of inches smaller. 'I was coming across the road and I heard a shot.'

She spoke with a northern accent, though he couldn't place it.

'Then there were all these screams as I came closer.'

Maybe there had been more than one person killed in the shooting.

'It seemed to be coming from one of the side roads,' she explained, 'and that's when I realised it was from the church.'

'Somebody was shot inside a church?'

'Yes,' she confirmed his assumptions.

'Any idea why it happened?'

'They reckon that a group of boys pulled up in a stolen Mercedes,' she said. 'They'd hoods on when they broke through the doors.' She paused, then pointed across the road. 'It's a gospel church.'

Momentarily, he was going to tell her. 'I know. I live up there.'

But something stopped him – preserving the mystery.

'Whatever his reason, one of the boys shot a singer in the choir, then turned around and ran away while the place was in panic.'

'Sometimes people don't need a reason,' Fergus suggested.

When he said that, she lowered her head, fixing her eyes on the pattern of raindrops dancing on the puddles forming at her feet.

Close up, she wasn't quite so much like the American actress, but there was some similarity in the shape of her face and in her blonde hair.

'Did anybody ever tell you you look like Marilyn Monroe?'

He had spoken suddenly, without intending to voice these thoughts.

Blue eyes danced playfully before she replied. 'Yes, but they've also told me that I look like Myra Hindley.' She uttered a soft laugh. 'I hope it's the bleached hair, not the heart of ice.'

'I can see the resemblance,' he said, then tried to correct himself. 'Between Myra and Marilyn, I mean, not between you and Myra.'

She lifted her head, looked him in the eyes.

'You're talking like you know these women.'

'Does any man ever know any woman?'

'Only as much as she's willing to let him.'

Perhaps this was the cue to get to know her better. 'What's your name?'

'Isn't Marilyn as good as any?' she asked.

'A rose by any other name,' he quipped in response.

By now the police were starting to move non-essential bodies along the street, closing off the church to let the forensics team go inside. Press and TV cameras had arrived on the scene, interviewing anyone who would talk, though those who had witnessed it were mostly silent. The body of the dead boy was still on the street, covered over in tarpaulin.

'If it's a boy,' she said, 'gangs can hurt girls too.'

'I saw plenty of them in action on the night I arrived.'

'Girls or gangs?' she asked, mischievously.

'Gangs,' he replied, 'on the weekend of the riots.'

'Quite an introduction to the capital, then.'

'Yes,' he said and then realised he might only ever get one opportunity such as this. 'Maybe I can describe it over a drink.'

She drew back, retreating inside the castle of herself.

'Not tonight,' she said. 'Perhaps another time.'

'Okay,' he replied, feeling partially rejected.

He had Charlton games and beers with Lance for consolation.

She spoke again. 'I know you live across the way.'

His eyes lit up with the thought of her noticing him.

'I've seen you with the guy who I guess was a soldier.'

'Yes, he fought out in Afghanistan,' Fergus replied before realising he should be promoting himself and not his friend.

'I've gone on several marches against wars,' she said. 'I don't see the need for sending armed gangs to the other side of the world.'

'Nor do I,' he agreed. 'Or even across the water.'

'I've only been to Ireland once,' she said, 'as a child.'

'You're always welcome in my Irish embassy.'

Her blue eyes softened. 'Maybe we could go for a drink some night. I'll stick a note through your door when I'm free.'

Those were the last words she said as police waved her through. A couple of minutes later, when he headed upstairs to see his friend, her Chinese lantern sparked to life. Lance was excited about tomorrow's game against Chesterfield when Fergus stepped inside, though also curious about what had been going on with the commotion outside.

'Saw you talking to *the* girl.'

'Yeah. We just had a quick chat.'

'So what did you talk about?'

'Gangs and guns,' he replied.

'You're a dark horse, a fast mover.'

'Wasn't like that,' he argued. 'I'd no agenda.'

'Everybody's got an agenda.'

Maybe now would have been a good time to tell his story, to explain how you lose all sense of agenda when you wake up every morning inside a prison cell, with only the goal of getting through another day.

It was easier to talk football. 'Going to tomorrow's game?'

'Sure,' he replied. 'It's *football for a fiver* again. Want to come?'

'Okay,' he agreed, and found himself, almost a day later, back in the East Stand, watching the game but thinking of Marilyn.

Like planes in the sky above, she would drift in and out of his thoughts. For today's match there was a new player in the Charlton squad.

'Yann Kermorgant,' Lance said. 'Signed from Leicester.'

Chris Powell called him a calculated gamble. His former manager Nigel Pearson had referred to him as a wild card when he first signed him from the French League two years before. Having survived leukemia as a child, he had a different outlook from that of many footballers. Positive and determined. Conscious of what's important in life.

But he hadn't succeeded at Pearson's Leicester City, missing a penalty in a play-off final that had cost them promotion to the Premiership.

He was coming to Charlton with a point to prove. Paul Hayes knew that and was making all the effort he could to keep himself in the team. Less than twenty minutes gone, he shinned the ball into the net.

Ten minutes later the score was doubled when Dale Stephens rolled a free kick into the box smooth as a manoeuvre in a game of snooker, teeing up Johnnie Jackson, captain, to sink the black.

'Game's as good as over,' said Lance.

But out of nowhere on 72 minutes, Charlton conceded a penalty. Game on, as Chesterfield scored. Eighty minutes in, two goals to one, it was time for a change. Chris Powell sent on Yann Kermorgant for the tiring Paul Hayes who was given a standing ovation.

Some fans grumbled. 'We don't need another striker.'

But a few minutes later the Frenchman made his first contribution to Charlton Athletic Football Club. Moving into the path of a Johnnie Jackson cross from the left, he trapped the ball on his shin before spinning it up towards his chest. Letting it drop, then rest on the cradle of his thigh, he flicked it inch-perfect onto the boot of Scott Wagstaff, whose pass curved towards the diving figure of Wright Phillips. Seconds later the ball was in the back of the net from a header propelled at full stretch. Bradley's sixth goal in as many games had sealed the 3-1 victory. They had exorcised the spectre of previous disasters in 'football for a fiver' and Yann Kermorgant was doing the same with the ghosts of Leicester City. After nine games were gone, they were top of the league with twenty three points.

'I could get used to this,' Fergus admitted afterwards.

'One thing about following a team from the lower divisions,' his friend said on the way out of the stadium, 'is that you can be sure times won't always be as good as this. So when they're good, enjoy them.'

These days were certainly good and full of promise for Charlton fans. Autumn was here. A cool frost glistened like broken glass on the stubbled grass of Greenwich Park each morning, nights grew darker. Meanwhile, back at work, he continued giving everything to his cause, making sure none of his boys turned out like the kid shot in the Church, or his own ghost on a night of empty rage long ago.

All week he waited for news of Marilyn. Finally, on Tuesday, she dropped a note through his door, making plans for Saturday.

'You can meet me at twelve o'clock by Greenwich Station,' she wrote. 'You can decide where we go from there.'

He was glad that when she left the invitation, Lance was travelling to a game up in Milton Keynes. Though he wasn't exactly sure why he was glad, he didn't want his friend to know too much.

He was happy too to hear the game on the radio as he lay in bed, with the light off, having an early night, like he used to do in prison, except here he could open the window and let in the smell of the Thames.

After the summer's heat had passed, it was fresh again. But on the weather forecast, between reports of the night's football matches, they said there was going to be an unseasonal heatwave at the weekend.

'Maybe we'll go to the beach,' he mused.

His mind drifted in and out of daydreams and descriptions of action on the radio as Charlton fell behind. Then with 72 minutes on the clock, SE7's newest import emerged from the dugouts.

Three minutes later, having barely broken sweat, his name flashed through Fergus's mind once again. *A cross comes in from the right towards Kermorgant*, said the commentator. Suddenly, he had risen high and straight as the sword in Charlton's club badge, as if his heart and soul was going into making connection with that cross.

He's touched it with his forehead and the ball's in the net for an equaliser. It's the Frenchman's first goal in a Charlton jersey.

And that was how it finished as Fergus drifted towards sleep, switching thoughts between his seaside date with Marilyn and calculations of the table where Charlton sat on top, two points clear of Preston. Some hours later he was awakened by the dull thud of footsteps in the hall. He thought of his friend coming home, but buried his head deep in the pillow to go back to dreams of a girl.

9
Indian Summer

During his time in prison he had often dreamed of the day when he would be free to get on a bus or a train and go to the seaside. On Saturday 1st October, less than a year after he got out, his waiting was coming to an end with a trip to the Kentish coast on a morning showered in spectacular sunshine. When he pulled back the curtains in his room, light danced on the Thames in such abundance you would have enough electricity to power a whole city if you could harness solar energy.

'*I'm off to Sheffield,*' Lance had texted him. '*Early start.*'

He was going on one of the coaches the club runs for away games.

'*It'll be boiling,*' Fergus texted back, '*on the journey.*'

Then he added '*good luck to Charlton*' in their promotion battle with Sheffield United, one of the third division's biggest teams. Only a couple of years ago these sides had faced one another in the Premiership.

But Fergus was going to forget about football for the rest of the day. He would concentrate on his date with Marilyn, and a trip to the seaside.

Outside his window, the glass mountain turned to a greenhouse as the sun rose higher and clouds retreated. He prepared some breakfast, though he scarcely felt any appetite from the weight of his expectations.

After the struggle to eat and finish, he tidied his flat.

'You have to be prepared,' he figured.

You never know, she might come back with him at the end of the night, even if it's only for a coffee. He had been so long out of the dating game, he wasn't sure of the rules, if there were rules anymore.

When you're eighteen there are rules, but late twenties, early thirties didn't seem much of an age for playing by the rules, at least until you're married, and then it's a whole different ball game, he imagined.

He made a promise to himself as he made the bed. 'Whatever happens today, I'll take it as it comes.'

When you're free your days are unpredictable, meaning anything could happen tonight, from when they caught the train to the seaside till they came home all hot with sunburn and the moods of evening. But that seemed far away, as time became trapped in a tortoise shell. Slowly morning passed by until the clock reached half eleven, his cue for a slow stroll through Saturday's crowds towards the station.

Lance would be somewhere on the motorway, baking inside a coach or stopping off at a service station, joking with his fellow supporters about this weather being more like an 18-30 sun holiday.

Coming towards the station, Marilyn was prepared for the sun. Framed beneath the entrance, looking far more relaxed than he felt, wearing a straw-coloured summer hat, and a black dress which was a paradox, incredibly hot, and cool at the same time.

'Such white skin,' he thought. 'It dazzles.'

Under the arch of the station doorway, she was Greenwich incarnate. Chalk-white, stoned immaculate as the College by the riverside.

'Hello,' he said, as he approached her. 'You're early.'

Close up, her limbs glistened in sunscreen and lips in balm as she spoke. 'Let's see what time the trains are running.'

But getting inside the station, they encountered a problem.

'There's delays on the line to the coast,' said a tomato-faced officious man planted at a desk behind a glass screen. 'Signal failure.'

'When are they going to be running normally?'

'Perhaps an hour. I haven't a crystal ball.'

'We could have a coffee,' she suggested, then seemed to sense the disappointment in his face. 'Or try something more imaginative.'

Was this the part where they skipped the train journey, the seaside, the coffee, and the smalltalk? They'd go back to the apartments, cut through the chase, and sculpt the rules of desire to suit themselves.

'If we can't go to the sea, then it can come to us.'

'How's the sea going to come to us?' he wondered.

'We have the Thames. Maybe it's not the sea, but today we've got Spanish weather, and London's shores have more sand than Brighton.'

'Brighton's got stones.'

'Shingles,' she corrected him, focusing her eyes on his. 'Probably thousands of people too. Half of London, on a day like this.'

'It's decided then. We're having our date by the Thames.'

'I never said this was a date.'

'Of course it can't be a date,' he retaliated as quickly. 'Sure you haven't even told me what your name is yet.'

'A girl has to keep some sense of mystery.'

Half in shade, under a sunhat, the woman by his side kept herself mysterious as they made their way down the high street, passing through the park which was filling up with sun-bathers out of season.

'We'll get some food,' she said, as they furrowed a path towards the crowded indoor market, 'and have a picnic.'

'Sounds good,' he agreed, as they melted together into a cocoon of flower baskets, ceramics from Palestine, and canvas prints of movie stars which he scanned for a sighting of his not-a-date's lookalike.

Finally they reached the far corner, where they witnessed wars fought out between the cuisine of continents. His eyes feasted on Japanese sushi and noodles shrouded in steam behind red-lantern signage, and then Brazilian barbecues, cooked in stone, alongside Turkish sweets for dessert.

'Have you got any preference in cheeses?'

'If they're good enough for a mousetrap, good enough for me.'

'Actually, mice can't digest cheese. How about wine?'

'Any colour's okay, except blue, or mouse-grey.'

'Don't ever audition in the comedy club on Creek Road,' she countered. 'I'm fairly sure they prefer style over cliché.'

Seeing her lift bottles from the rack, holding them to the light, studying the labels, he felt emasculated by his own ignorance of these things, after so many years. Finally she chose one, and switched her focus to assembling a salad basket, before insisting upon paying.

Slowly, they forged a path through the crowds back into the sunshine, as he struggled to make conversation. 'We can get to the river through the College, and don't worry, there'll be no detours in the direction of the comedy club.'

She paused a moment, leaning close. Her face was all in shadow, under the sunhat, and dark as the dress she was wearing. Aware of his hunger, she used language as a layer of desire.

'What would our neighbours say if they saw us?'

'Don't know any. Just the soldier.'

'You like to keep your own company?'

Before he could answer, she said she was the same, enjoying doing her own thing, whether that was reading, baking, or designing. 'I'm not into fads, popular culture, or reality TV.'

'I never got into those either; just football.'

'Hate football with such passion it's a form of suffering.'

They'd hit a dead end before reaching the river. But coming through the College, passing through a series of keyhole-like arches, she softened again, reaching out to touch him gently on the forearm.

'I can be moody,' she admitted, 'but it's a self-defence mechanism. Maybe if we ever get to know each other, you'll understand why.'

'Well, we've this whole baking day to get to know each other.'

When he was in prison, dreams of the seaside sustained him. On getting out, he swore he'd spend as much of his life there as possible. He'd been keen to see English seaside towns, compare them with Irish. Perhaps she'd the same urgency, as she echoed his thoughts.

'It's not the sea, but we have to make the most of it.'

'Close your eyes and you could be there,' he said, as they made their way down to a shore speckled in a swooping cacophony of gulls.

On the river's edge, the tide was out as they sat down on stones, preparing for their picnic. Shingles, seaweed, driftwood, fragments of shells, and small patches of sand accentuated the seaside atmosphere.

If Greenwich was a fragment of Rome, then this stretch of water was a hidden corner in the jigsaw of the world's rivers. You could follow it from here to central London, as tourists on clipper ships were doing; waving as they passed, busily snapping shots of silhouettes in the distance which she could name, one by one, as she fingered their delineations. Of course the opposite direction could be interesting too.

'That's towards the Thames Barrier and Charlton's football ground. Perhaps we could go check those out later.'

'London's got far more to see than anything to do with the madness of being paid millions for kicking a ball around.'

'That's me told, but doubt Charlton's men get millions.'

Canary Wharf, on the far shore, decanted shades of sea and cloud as she poured wine into paper cups, then set about unpacking, cutting, buttering, and layering the bread in a causeway of cheese.

Where this pathway might lead, he wasn't exactly sure. Like the geography of the river, this was a new and ever-shifting landscape. Behind them, curls of smoke and smells of locally brewed draught rose from the waterside pubs once graced by Charles Dickens.

'Big crowds for before one in the afternoon. I'm enjoying this. I'd prefer these Indian summers to the ones we have in Ireland.'

'I'm enjoying being down here in the quiet having a picnic,' said his not-a-date as she passed him a cup of wine, and bread with cheese.

In truth though, he was more of a beer man than a wine drinker. Maybe if their lives were stretches of river, they'd be opposite shores. She'd be the Isle of Dogs, and the sparkling towers across the way, while he'd be the industrial foreshore leading to Charlton.

But they weren't rivers. They were people, with first sips of wine flowing through them. On the far shore he could hear seagulls mewing again, and imagined sounds of a funfair in their voices. If he could rewrite history, he'd never have driven to the coast long ago. Instead, he'd take this girl, Marilyn, to an Irish seaside town. There they'd drink beer and drift down to the beach, where they might see a wild salmon leaping in the distance, and race across rocks, breathless, to catch a souvenir snapshot. And in the distance mountains made of rocks, heather, and earth, not cones of steel and glass pushing against the curdled clouds.

He still missed home. This was a river, and not the open sea.

'Does anything actually live in this water?'

'Just because you can't see it, doesn't mean it's not there. This whole area's teeming with life, everything from plants to insects, safe places for frogs, moths, and dragonflies, to nesting habitats for seabirds. We've conservation projects for miles.'

'*We*,' he thought. 'This is her city, her river.'

She'd been involved in so many causes and dozens of projects to help clean up the river, including one at Deptford where they converted a series of abandoned boats into a nature reserve for wildfowl.

'There's no point in living,' she said, as she reached out to fuel her energy with bread and cheese, 'if you don't do something for the world, if you're not a tree which produces some form of fruit.'

As she spoke, a thought nipped his mind. Perhaps he'd misread the character of this girl. Like a dyslexic turning sounds upside down, he'd heard *Chelsea* when she was actually whispering *seashells*.

Words flashed through his mind as if in an email from his emotions to the segment of his brain responsible for actions. 'Lance was right. She's different, like every minute of her life's a journey, but not a joyride. This girl's got something made to last.'

And that was the moment he knew that he wanted to kiss her. His heart instructed him to lean closer, and push towards her mouth and teeth through which words glinted in shoals of leaping salmon. But his head was warning him that he'd probably get a smack in the mouth.

'I suppose that's why I hate football so much,' she said, as the salmon gathered speed. 'There's so many things people could be doing, so much they could be changing, taking action instead of passively following the herd, and treating a silly game as a religion.'

Then she paused, closing her eyes on the taste of cheese; allowing him to steal a glance. Again he wanted to kiss her.

'I don't have any religion. Do you?'

'Born a Catholic. Not sure I still believe.'

However, there were times in prison when he had prayed. He'd asked the God he didn't believe in to speed up the months so that he'd be free.

And here he was, free, picnicking with an English Rose. Enjoying the taste of bread, cheese, chillies, and olives washed down with wine. Already he could feel tremors of intoxication, drifting towards eddies of fantasy, as his not-a-date subsided back into silence, sitting on rocks, peeling fruit, set against the coming-closer tide of afternoon.

Keeping her eyes on the water, she began to speak of religion again. There could be no God, she argued, as her face filled up with flame, because people are every bit as much flesh as bananas, and once they're rotted there's no going back to when they were white and pure.

'Very deep for a lazy Saturday afternoon.'

'More so than football,' she snapped. 'Can't you handle it?'

There followed an interlude of silence, a consciousness of their surroundings, river instead of sea, glass instead of mountains. Then she spoke first, suggesting they move on towards the Thames Barrier.

'Down by Valley, Floyd Road, home of Charlton FC.'

'If that's what truly rocks your boat, then we can go.'

As they began to walk, he admitted not being so bothered.

'If I was a true fan, I suppose I'd be in Sheffield.'

Instead, he was wandering on this not-a-date along the side of the Thames, discovering old stories and new angles. First they passed the last of the great riverside pubs from the days of Dickens along a street of Georgian houses, and then the old Power Station's chimneys blasting up from ivy-lapelled walls to pierce the sky beyond the College domes.

Further down they encountered a gaggle of black-faced geese, pecking through a terrain of old boatyards and wharves reclaimed for the purposes of conservation, which formed the keel of their conversation as they funnelled through narrow alleyways out to where the river widened.

This meandering, shape-shifting stretch of the Thames was fascinating, explained his not-a-date. There was no singular sense of identity. Instead you had historical remnants, several centuries of architecture, and secluded pockets of natural shoreline stitched together in a microcosmic tapestry of London's history.

Losing track of time, and feeling the delayed onset of wine, they stopped in several places, sitting down, drinking in the view, to quench a growing thirst. Fergus could taste salt on his lips, and again thought of the sea, wiping sweat off his brow in the 3 o'clock sun.

Somewhere north of here, in the same 20 something conditions, Lance's red knights would be starting battle with Sheffield's *Blades*.

'Shall we go inside somewhere?' he asked, as the heat became too much to bear as they rounded the Blackwall Tunnel, and the chestnut spikes of the Millennium Dome's crashed-sideways spaceship.

'Sure. There's a Thames Path pub crawl.'

She'd never tried, though if you were brave you could go the whole dozen between London Bridge and the Thames Barrier. You could even keep going to where one river becomes another, and then the sea.

'Let's stop at the first one we come across, because this heat's brutal, and I'm bursting for a piss, and tempted to use the Thames.'

'Classy,' she said, as they moved on in search of relief.

But distances can be deceptive after a couple of wine bottles. They passed what seemed like miles of boats and a yacht club rising out of the river on wooden stilts, as full of glass and verandas as one of those Queenslander houses you find in Australia.

Eventually they reached a pub on the river's edge, close by the silver shells of the Thames Barrier; operatic and iridescent.

Once there, Fergus dived into the urinals where such a mighty wave of relief surged through him, he feared the Barrier's alarm system might go off from sensing a biblical flood.

'The team that you, and the soldier follow, is winning today,' she said, as he returned. 'I caught it on TV.'

'What's the score?'

'Think it was two goals to zero.'

Sure enough, as he went to check the score, ordering a beer for himself and wine for his becoming-more-of-a-date, Lance's red knights rode closer to the holy grail of promotion with a two goal lead. Again, the French fusilier, Yann Kermorgant, had stepped off the bench to score with a header, and then create a second for Wright-Phillips.

'Top of the table,' he told her, as the game finished and they sat listening to the cries of seagulls resting on the Barrier's shells.

But she'd heard enough talk of football for one evening. The night they first met, he'd offered her the chance to visit his Irish Embassy. She wanted to hear about Ireland, and so he told her a dozen or more stories, without ever once touching on the past decade of his life.

'It hasn't been a bad day, even if we didn't get to the seaside,' she said, as the sky began to darken shortly after six, reminding them of something they'd half-forgotten, this being the 1st of October.

Shortly after, they finished their drinks and followed the last stretch of river before the Barrier, where birdsong drowned out the harsher melodies of wasteland, aggregate factories and recycling plants.

'We can't just leave it like this,' he said, surveying the Thames, sensing the loneliness of closure, 'Surely we have to end by going to the Valley?'

'Okay,' she agreed, as they made their way there.

The surrounding streets were in darkness as they reached their destination, and only grainy silhouettes of the stadium visible as they settled down by the boots of Sam Bartram.

'What exactly are you expecting from me Fergus?'

He paused, wishing he could forge words as intense as his feelings. 'Just to be a friend, two small people, smaller than Sam anyway, in a big city, sharing days like this.'

When he said this, her eyes turned bright blue as a peacock's tail in a mating dance. Like the statue of Sam Bartram coming to life, he took flight across the pitch of the moment, edging towards her open mouth with the furtiveness of a goalkeeper.

At first he feared falling flat on his face. But her mouth drifted to meet his, timed perfect as Kermo's header in Sheffield's steely sunshine. Suddenly, he could taste wine flavoured in fruit on her breath, as their two bodies became closed together, letting time pass and die in the cell of one another's presence. He'd waited all day for this, giving up hope along the way, and finally, cheered on by a soundtrack of seagulls, scored his goal. Released from the terrible absence of prison, he held and kneaded her body, going underwater, swallowing salt, determined not to let go until they're almost drowning. Coming up for air, regaining a sense of time, his rage was cooled. But, burning inside, with the numb feeling you get waking up, coming out of a dentist's, there was a sense he'd never kiss anyone so good again.

'I don't even know your bloody name,' he broke the silence.

'It's not Marilyn,' she laughed. Then as she focused her blue eyes on his, a few sparks of the mating dance still flickered. 'My name's Katy Prunty and I'm from a town called Huddersfield.'

'They're one of Charlton's biggest rivals for promotion.'

'Charming,' she said, without a hint of irony. 'Typical guy, talking about football when we've just stumbled into a romantic moment.'

'We've just had our first kiss outside a football ground.'

She sighed, turned around to walk away, hesitated, and then shared their second kiss, standing up against the body of Sam Bartram. This time he was kissing both Katy Prunty and Marilyn Monroe.

It was time to step out of their cocoon and go home, bringing an end to this afternoon of wine, cheese, and an imagined seaside. They walked to the station, kissing for a third time on the way down the steps by a *Charlton* signpost, before rushing for the train. When they got to Greenwich, she said goodnight. She wasn't going to make this easy for him, his first act of chasing a woman after prison.

'I'm going to meet friends,' she claimed, with a final peck on the lips. 'Though I hadn't planned for this, we'll see each other again soon.'

When she was gone, he headed home; passing Merlin's boy on the walk by the Thames, not far from where today's action started. Finishing a smoke, he tossed a stub into the water and squirreled away.

'Strange fish,' Fergus thought, recalling his own days of secret cigarettes and thinking the world's worst thing was getting caught.

Then he ascended the same pathway, smelling the sea in his thoughts, and the mists of night rolling across the Thames in numb kisses. Though still warm, summer's nights seemed far away. The powder keg of London's villages, once mirroring his own empty rage, had cooled.

10
Dark Days after the World's End

Sometimes you dream of a thing you want more than anything else in the world and spend hours anticipating its arrival, only to find that when the package arrives it's empty or it's for the guy across the hall. Didn't Fergus use to be a boxer once upon a time? Well, if this was a fight, he had struck a hell of a punch these past few weeks.

A blow to the heart, as quick and dirty as a knuckle to the nuts.

'Maybe it's like the story of Mikel Alonso.'

He thought this aloud on the morning after he had gone to the game. Like his seduction of Marilyn, plans had been falling into place. Charlton, unbeaten all season, had a home match against Brentford in the Johnstone's Paint ~~Pot~~ Trophy, on a Wednesday night.

It's one of those minor cup competitions that's a whole lot less important than promotion, but you still expect to beat Brentford. They're London rivals, after all, and you don't waste derby games.

Besides, after weeks of missing in action, the mystical Mikel Alonso was making his first appearance in a Charlton jersey. Though things had been almost perfect in the season so far, the missing piece of Chrissie Powell's jigsaw was being put in place.

Soon they would have a Spaniard and a Dutchman in the same team. Danny Hollands, providing industry, alongside this newcomer who would introduce a touch of Basque poetry and continental philosophy to SE7. It would be as good as having Albert Camus as Ben Hamer's understudy. Camus was a goalkeeper, a philosopher and a Frenchman too.

'Get stuck in!' supporters demanded at the outset.

There was a small crowd because the game was being shown on TV. Gloomy evening too, which didn't add to the atmosphere. It was one of those skies that you look up at sometimes and you think to yourself, '*That could be a mirror showing the insides of my head right now.*'

Down on the pitch, he could see reflections from the same mirror. Whatever the reason, weather, atmosphere – too many reserves on the field, or stage fright in front of the cameras – the team never got going. For the first time this season, they seemed as lethargic as in years past. Two minutes into the match, Brentford scored an opening goal.

'Wake up, for blazes sake!' cried the man in front.

But instead of rising up, the red men sank further into nightmares. A quarter of an hour later, Mikel Alonso made his first contribution. When Brentford's long-legged African midfielder charged through Charlton's soft centre, the Basque No.23 made a senseless challenge.

Supporters swore beneath their breath. 'Certain penalty.'

'It's not Christmas yet!' someone else called out.

But he had gifted Brentford the chance of a second goal. Instinctively, without even a word of thanks, they accepted and then scored a third. Three nil defeat, at home. The bubble had burst. Walking back to the station past the house where Italo Svevo once lived, you could almost smell the ghost of Bourdin surfacing through the autumn slush.

When he was waiting for the train, a fan told him the story of Svevo.

'He was Italian, as his name suggests, and a friend of James Joyce,' said the man who was a blogger on fans' forums. 'He wrote a book about somebody who tries to give up smoking so many times that in the end he becomes addicted to the idea of one last cigarette.'

'Like us,' Lance laughed, looking around the carriage of sad faces. 'Telling ourselves every bad game's going to be our last.'

Getting back to Greenwich, he looked up the story of this Svevo guy. He had lived in Charlton for a while, and *Confessions of Zeno* was the name of his book. Sure enough, it was the story of a hopeless addict. The guy gets hooked on the ritual of quitting and planning a new life around this. But the change always starts tomorrow because for the length of today's last slow-burning cigarette, he's still a smoker.

'There's a bit of Svevo's character in us all,' the former soldier thought to himself in the days after the game, and the days after his defeat. 'Tomorrow's always going to be the time we take action.'

If he had taken action weeks ago, gone and knocked on her door, things might have turned out differently, before she had started a romance with Fergus, transforming her from the mysterious Marilyn across the way to an English girl with the very real name of Katy Prunty.

Tuesday, he had seen them together as they walked home from a pub. Since they didn't go inside one another's rooms, as far as he could tell, they probably weren't sleeping together, but the whole thing wasn't fair, even the thought of someone else kissing her. Like some essential fiction helping him to survive, she had been in his head for months.

Now he had to switch off and tell himself some hard truths. 'The whole thing was fiction and there never was a Marilyn and me.'

He had become addicted to a fantasy, and now he had to live with his friend putting flesh to that fantasy, taking her for nights out in pubs and afternoon walks by the riverside, changing the landscape of everything around them, even Sam Bartram's statue. That was where they had kissed for the first time, Fergus claimed, as if that's something you want to hear when the Valley runs in your blood, as if you want your favourite memories polluted.

He had a couple of choices then. One was to give up. There are many soldiers who do the same after coming back from Afghanistan, many more after Iraq (twice), Northern Ireland and the Falklands. He had a river outside his window, to make it easy; he could become another statistic, a casualty of civilian life and source of embarrassment for the military.

But that was the easy way out, giving up without a fight. If he had struggled through the horrors of war and post-traumatic stress, then he would find a way of recovering from this addiction, replacing Marilyn's heroin with some kind of methadone to get him through each day, so he would be able to reclaim Sam's statue and everything else he had lost.

Later in the week he spoke to Fergus, unsure of the day because they had all blurred into one since Alonso night at the Brentford match. All he knew was that it was getting close to Saturday and a home game against Tranmere, not so many seasons after playing Liverpool.

'I've come up with an idea,' he announced, trying hard to swallow the sailor's knot of emotion pushing up from his chest into his throat. 'I'm going to create a community garden.'

'Where?' the Irishman wondered.

'Right here,' he replied. 'The Council and the government give funding for community projects and food growing ventures.'

'Before the war you were a gardener, right?'

'I am a gardener. The war didn't change that.'

'Sorry, I didn't mean anything by it.'

'You don't have to apologise. You can help though,' he explained. 'I'm looking for volunteers to clean up a space in the back garden of our apartment block and then to start work on building the site.'

'But isn't the garden like a bloody jungle?'

'Just a wilderness,' he replied, 'and that's not quite so bad.'

His red-headed friend laughed softly. 'Okay, I'll help.'

'Work starts Saturday morning, and more on Sunday.'

'Can do Sunday,' he said, 'but on Saturday we're going on a date to some winter gardens Katy says she likes, up in a place called Avery Hill, so you're not the only one interested in flowers these days.'

Briefly, the lump in his throat tightened to a cramp in his chest. But he had to be gracious, even in defeat, because maybe it wasn't really a defeat if he had learned some new valuable information about Katy.

'Enjoy yourself,' he said. 'See you Sunday.'

'With gloves and a shovel,' the Irishman assured him.

Then Fergus was gone, smiling like a lucky bastard who had won the lotto. But if this was a battle for Marilyn's – no, Katy Prunty's – heart, then the winner was going to be the one who would impress her most with rose gardens and freshly cut flowers. Maybe this was a new symptom of addiction, pricking his finger on thorns of the past, but they had something in common. He could name every plant in the steaming glass gardens, from towering palms to thorny dwarf cactuses, built around a fountain statue of Galatea, a Roman sea nymph who was a sculpture brought to life by a creator who had fallen in love with her.

'Her name means milk-white beauty,' he recalled from books on London's gardens in his horticultural-college days.

He could recall Avery Hill's gardens more than most for they were beside Charlton's training ground and academy in Sparrow's Lane.

'If she's interested in gardens, I still have a chance.'

Again, he found himself using her as the basis of his motivation. Though it couldn't be healthy, she became his muse, inspiring him to produce leaflets calling for volunteers for the weekend's clear-up, before catching a bus up to Eltham where he bought some tools and was tempted, briefly, to travel on towards those Winter Gardens.

'But no,' he assured himself, 'there's no rush.'

He had lost Marilyn to Fergus's smooth talk over gangs and guns, but he would win Katy with freshly cut flowers. Catching the bus home, going past the Valley, he felt Svevo's last cigarette spark to life in his imagination as he caught traces of autumn mist rising off the Thames. They would clear the wilderness by the weekend, lay fresh soil, plant seeds and have the garden full of white roses by the late springtime. Then he would go to her door with freshly cut flowers. This was going to be a long war.

11
Season of Mist

As Fergus's season of mellow fruitfulness gathered pace, traces of the Indian summer lingered in the mists rolling in from the Thames. Things were going well with Katy Prunty.

There had been more nights of wine and cheese, detachment in the cellars of a jazz club in Greenwich, and walks by the riverside. One afternoon they followed the water all the way to Woolwich, talking loosely as they walked, sharing stories of their lives. He told her of his boys in Deptford, which she didn't seem so interested in, and she spoke of her career as a freelance fashion designer and consultant.

'I'd never work in an office,' she said. 'I get claustrophobic and need space. That's why I live in a place facing the river.'

Strangely, he had not been inside her apartment so far, and she had shown no interest in crossing the corridor and the stairs towards his. As they worked on the community garden, Lance had asked if they were shagging yet, trying to pretend he was cool about everything.

He had made light of the comments, preferring to chat about the Carlisle game where Charlton returned to form after a periodic blip.

Lance described how Kermorgant scored twice, both of them beauties, Hollands once, and Wright-Phillips the same, as kids in the crowd sang *'we've a Dutchman, a Cantona and a Brockley Pelé.'*

4-0 winners, at the end of a textbook performance.

'Third of the season gone and we're top 'o the league.'

There were two further reasons for celebration, he said. Firstly, he had been successful in his application for a grant to develop the project. Second, after all this time, his compensation money came through.

'I'm buying a car,' he said, 'but it's not just any car. It's an old Ford Torino, same as the one from *Starsky & Hutch*. And I'm getting it specially fitted so that even a cripple like me can race on the roads o' London.'

'Sounds like a good investment.'

'Seven grand,' he said. 'But worth every penny. You'll have to come for a spin sometime. Might even let you take the wheel.'

Fergus smiled and nodded, despite a shiver running down his spine. He hadn't driven a car since the night of Lucy's death. Maybe the suggestion was just banter. He would never let another man sit at the wheel of his machine. Even if he offered, there would always be some excuse. Besides, he was trying to seduce an English rose.

'I've bought us a river rover ticket,' he told her a few days later when there was no gardening work, because Lance had taken his new car for the longest test drive possible on the map of England.

'Hartlepool,' Katy laughed, 'that's even a thousand miles from Huddersfield from what I remember. God, if he goes much further he's going to drive over the edge of England into the sea.'

Deep down, he wanted to tell her the truth.

'I once drove over the edge of Ireland into the sea.'

But the words wouldn't come out, so he spoke of roving instead.

'With these tickets you can go anywhere,' he said.

'Maybe not as far as Hartlepool,' she quipped.

The name of the town in the North East of England had become a dirty word. Hearing it, he thought of tyres crunching into shingles, and a stolen car slipping over the cliffs with *Starsky & Hutch* giving chase.

'Come on,' he said. 'Let's see where the day takes us.'

'Okay,' she agreed as they steered a path to the marina.

There they came across Merlin and his boy amongst the crowds.

'Something unnatural about the way he treats that kid.'

'I never notice how the neighbours act,' she answered as they got on board a boat bound for Westminster, 'just that the man's a very sharp dresser, but the kid's always in scruffy jeans and hooded tops, even when the sun's shining.' She paused, lowering her voice to a whisper. 'And there's no physical resemblance either.'

But Fergus wasn't concerned with Merlin's, or the boy's, physique. Landmarks along the Thames soon became the focus of his attention. Katy, up front on the deck, stood at the centre of the afternoon's architecture as the catamaran began its sinuous journey westwards. Against the distant shadows of the city's sights, she was radiant in an emerald dress that matched her strapped sandals and eyeshadow, and a cream scarf around her neck, to resist the creeping autumn breeze.

'This side's more crowded than the paths we've walked,' she said. 'There's few secret places for wine and cheese.'

Moving away from Greenwich Reach, they left behind the stoned blaze of everything that was old: the College, the Observatory and the riverside pubs where Dickens used to drink.

Loud as a brewery, the vessel wrestled a tag-team of wind and tides. The couple retreated to a window seat, then ordered glasses of wine as they passed through landscapes new and shiny as crystal. Deptford's waterside, and Rotherhithe, site of London's first Chinatown, as she had once read somewhere. Then the Isle of Dogs, moving backwards, forwards and to the sides at a moment's notice as the river bends.

'Like scissors in a haircut,' he thought then decided to ask a question of his date. 'How long have you been blonde?'

First she looked at him strangely, over the rim of her wine glass. Sometimes he could see a guard dog in her eyes, warning him against trespassing; readying herself to snap his question mark in half.

She pulled her scarf tight as a bandage then spoke. 'I'm not naturally blonde.' This was hardly news, as her dark eyebrows suggested. 'When I first came to London, moving down from the North at the age of seventeen to study fashion, I had long dark hair.'

'You'll have to show me a photo sometime.'

Again she tightened the scarf and the drawbridge of her mouth, closing doors on the castle of herself. 'I don't keep photographs.'

'Maybe one day you'll go back to being dark?'

'No,' she said, 'I can't go back to being that girl.'

Just for a second, it seemed she was going to say something more about herself, but as they drifted towards Tower Bridge and the hulking figure of the museum ship *HMS Belfast* she changed the subject suddenly. This was the route Nelson's funeral procession had taken from Greenwich to Whitehall, two and a half centuries ago.

'Do you know that he lay in state in the Painted Hall?' she asked. Fergus nodded as Katy loosed her scarf and her castle doors. 'If he was Irish, you'd have had a wake.' She laughed then, showing skin. 'Everybody would get drunk but Nelson would be ahead of them all.'

'How?' Fergus wondered. 'Wasn't he dead?'

'Yes,' she agreed as his eyes followed the trail of scarf across her bosom, 'but they say he was shipped home from France inside a cask of brandy.'

Drinking a second glass of wine as they crossed under London Bridge, Fergus started to feel like they two were in a case of alcohol. This close, touching one another with eyes instead of words, scared to sever the skin of desire with the blunt and awkward instrumentation of language, they could have been inside a ship in a bottle. Slowly, they bobbed past a series of grand buildings including Saint Paul's Cathedral, also designed by Christopher Wren, the architect of the Royal Naval College.

'That's us,' he said as the boat drew to a halt.

Getting off at Westminster Pier, a black bronze statue of Queen Boudicca came into view on the steps above. She was a commandeering figure with a spear raised to the heavens, moving in a flurry of horse hooves and scythed chariot wheels, about to smash headlong into Big Ben and the Houses of Parliament. He had read of her long ago in school, of how the Romans stole her lands, tortured her and played games of *tournante* with her teenage daughters. But like her fellow Celts, the Irish, she had fought back against foreign invaders.

'Didn't she march on the old city of London and burn it to the ground?' asked Fergus, as Katy watched on wide-eyed, silenced.

'I think so,' she said dismissively after a few seconds. 'But let's go. Something about this statue always freaks me out.'

Again she tightened the scarf, skipping up the steps towards the golden stalactites and Roman numerals of Big Ben's clock face. They could sense winter on the horizon, in the breeze, as they crossed Westminster Bridge – the site of a famous poem by Wordsworth, she said. Where Bourdin set off from too, with his Valentine's bouquet, in 1894.

'Never heard of him,' she admitted.

If he was a French poet, she might know him.

'More than likely he's a footballer,' she supposed.

'No,' Fergus said, 'but there is a football connection.'

Then he told her the story as they skirted the Houses of Parliament and a few tents of anti-war protestation camped on the lawns opposite. Bourdin's blast made her shudder as they passed caricatures of Bush, Obama, Blair and bearded bogeymen drilling for blood in the sand.

'Let's go to a pub,' he suggested.

'So we can forget this?' she asked.

'Maybe,' he replied, wondering what Lance would make of these protests,' or just to get drunk and stop feeling so damned useless.'

Whatever the reason, they sought out a riverside pub and half-forgot the protests acted out in the shadow of Churchill's statue.

'It's like we've got a seat on the edge of autumn,' she said.

Watching leaves fall in giant freckles on the embankment, they discussed wars, protest, the taking up of causes, the giving up of causes, and the indifference of many people nowadays.

'I feel sorry for the young soldiers,' she said, 'like your friend.'

'You'll get to meet him at Blackheath Fireworks,' Fergus told her, more confidently than before. 'But go easy on him.'

She laughed. 'Don't worry, I'm not going to hold him personally responsible for all the bad things that happen overseas.'

By now, it was dark and time to go home. Again, as they passed the statue of Queen Boudicca, Katy shivered. She was still shivering as they got on board a boat bound for Greenwich, standing on deck once more, making Fergus burn as Boudicca had burned the old city of London. Maybe he should turn back now before the heat destroyed him.

There was such silence going downstream that he could hear the bells of Saint Paul's Cathedral ringing softly in the background, echoing like a chain of wind chimes on the bascules of Tower Bridge.

Together, deep in a lagoon of private thoughts, they moved away from other passengers, to a hidden corner of the windy deck where it was as if they were alone in a dark cellar, with the city's lights turned to floating candles on the surface of the Thames.

'Is there something you want to talk about?'

There was a serious look in her blue eyes. The bones of her skull tightened into themselves, and her breath came out thick as the steam in the rainforests he had read of in the prison escape of Conrad's stories.

'About what's going on with us.'

'In what sense?'

'I'm sick,' she replied. 'Sick with wanting to fall in love with you, and sick with not wanting to fall in love with you. You make me so sick I just want to run away and hide in a forest where no other man's ever going to be able to find me. And that's not good, because I've a lot of layers, Fergus, and I'm not really sure you're ready to see them.'

'I don't know what to say.'

Her voice became a whisper. 'If we sleep together it's going to be heavy, probably heavier than anything we've ever been through before. It's a weight that could crush the both of us.'

'I don't understand,' he said, and he really didn't.

'There's something I haven't told you about myself,' she admitted, 'and I'm not going to tell you tonight after wine, but I'll tell you eventually because if we're to take this further then I have to.'

Then she sank into silence as the lights of London snapped back into focus, as if the eyes of a million foxes nested in the darkness. When they reached Greenwich, everything was small, antique, and village-like in comparison.

'It was a lovely evening,' she said as she kissed him on the cheek, on the steps of the Pier. 'Let's do it again.'

There had been so many of these goodbyes. Tonight though, they had reached a crossroads. If they went off in separate directions at this stage, they would probably stay apart or end up as nothing more than friends, if Charlton boys and Chelsea girls can ever do so. That's when he decided to make the move and to signal his intentions.

'Can I come inside?' he asked suddenly.

'Inside where?' she said, confused, before realising that he was trying to seduce, or at the very least, deduce her. 'Why tonight?'

'Maybe to see the young girl with dreams and dark hair.'

'You won't find her there,' she insisted. 'You'll just have me.'

'That's enough,' he answered, playing along with her game.

Going up the stairs and making their way inside was like climbing the steps at Wembley to receive the FA Cup for Charlton's men of '47. No, this was going out through the tunnel before kick-off.

'The game still has to be won,' he mused.

When they got inside, Katy made cups of hot chocolate while he surveyed the room. Sure enough, there were no pictures of the dark girl on display. Few pictures at all amidst a life of uncluttered mystery.

On the ceiling, the Chinese lantern he had noted before. A Dream catcher in the window and plants on the sill, herbs or clover perhaps. Spices for cooking, in her kitchen area, and the tools of her trade scattered around the minimal presence of a foldaway desk. He could see naked mannequins, sketch books, a laptop and glass torsos.

She made light of this as she passed him the chocolate. 'I hope you don't have to spend your days in school with so many dummies.'

He wanted to say something clever but was tongue-tied in Katy's territory, caught like moths' shadows in a lantern's layers.

'Does it get lonely working alone?'

'Sometimes,' she admitted, 'but when you're designing something, you're never really alone, because it's coming alive through you.'

When she said that, a spark of passion flared in her eyes, drawing him closer until he was almost on his knees beneath her, smelling the chocolate off her breath as she looked down from above.

'You smell of warmth and safety,' he whispered.

Again she retreated. 'Why do people always want that, a world of safe, pretty things and routines like football on a Saturday?'

'Maybe we need an escape. Seven days a week there's a lot of hardships which make us feel small, helpless. But for just a couple of hours on a Saturday, you've got power, as a part of something.'

'I didn't know football fans thought so deep.'

The thought grew deeper with the fragrance of her breath as she leaned closer, coming down beside him, as if giving way to the sickness. Suddenly, as their bodies melted into the same bubble, she transformed, in his arms, to a chocolate shell with as many layers of foil, to unwrap, as an Easter egg.

Hungrily, drunk on the scent of rich, dark chocolate, he tore at the wrapping until the colours from head to foot, changed to milky white. He thought of Galatea, in the winter gardens, and then Boudicca as she rose up from under him, took his hand, and led him towards the bedroom, upstairs in a mezzanine full of books, CDs, and even more books, surrounding him with dizzying force.

'If this is what you want, if you're certain.'

'I'm not, but I'm listening to my heart.'

Then they lost a sense of time, moving through forests of passion, torching every part of the other's body, using words as a second skin, selecting books from the shelf, and reading passages in between, turning each other on by the feel, scents, and whispers of paper brushing against naked flesh.

Between her legs, he pressed a dictionary and this excited her, as if the language of desire, in all its definitions, synonyms, and collocations came alive. Words broke off in fragments, as the spine of the book aroused her, opening up between her thighs; suffusing her flesh and taking her to a place of pure seclusion, as if naked in the lexis of a damp, green forest.

'More,' she begged, as if seeking water to douse the fire on the mezzanine, closing her eyes to seek out clarity in the darkness. 'I want this to be about words, not bodies.'

Hours later they reached the forest's end, having scrambled through the mossy undergrowth of desire to the shade of a treehouse where they made love amongst books, tossing, and turning; burning, then melting inside the sighs, symbols, and syllables of every image, sentence and page.

'Goodnight,' she whispered, when her fever died down, as if sweated out of her in passion, and then drifted off into a deep, impenetrable sleep in his arms, jet-lagged from first night travels in a country of words.

Everything's changed now, he thought as he watched her shine in sleep; white as the Portland-stone facade of the Old Royal Naval College by a coffee-black river in the moonlight. She was Greenwich, and Greenwich was theirs tonight. After all the rage of summer's riots, as the fires of autumn began to burn, Minerva had triumphed over Mars.

12
Fireworks

A few days later, Fergus returned to his other inchoate love on the afternoon of Guy Fawkes Night, Saturday 5th November. When he got there, the stadium was aflame with noise; a fire of hope stacked and coming to light. It wasn't a case of starting to believe in promotion.

Belief had already been born high up in the North Stand as drums sounded and supporters sang, 'Chrissie Powell's men are we.'

Across the way, Jimmy Seed was a chessboard of black and white. Preston North End were today's opponents. One of England's greatest clubs long ago, they had won the first ever League and FA Cup double. Like Charlton, they had fallen on hard times recently and found themselves caught up in the stone-cold sobriety of the 3rd division.

'There's a nip in the air,' Lance said as the match kicked off.

'Yes,' Fergus agreed, though he didn't really.

These past weeks, the cooling air was like whisky in his blood. Detached from autumn's decay, he found romance in everything.

'Good start,' his friend remarked as the league leaders dominated the early stages, supported by a chorus of 'Valley Floyd Road'.

Sixteen minutes gone, a whole firework factory exploded. Johnnie Jackson, captain of the guard, scrambled home an opener from close range. Six minutes later, after the Preston keeper struggled to get to grips with a corner, Michael Morrison's debut goal doubled the lead.

By now the home choir was in full voice but there was still some way to go before the end. Following Charlton, you've always got to fear the presence of a piss-drenched squib intruding on the pyrotechnics.

Sure enough, feelings of déjà vu came minutes later. But this time, it was echoes of the Carlisle game, and not the ghost of an anarchist. Bourdin's fellow Frenchman Yann Kermorgant latched onto a loose ball from a tame back header. But before he could stir his body into a shooting position, their Greek goalie, who was having a nightmare day in the nets beneath the Jimmy Seed chessboard, pulled him down for a penalty. Again there was déjà vu as Johnnie Jackson stepped up to score the spot kick. Three-nil, and there was less than half an hour gone.

'This isn't just promotion stuff,' Lance said as three sides of the stadium shook. 'This is a championship performance.'

By half-time the Brockley Pelé had added a fourth.

The scene was set for six or seven but they had to be satisfied with one more firework lighting up this bedimmed November day.

Rhoys Wiggins, racing down the left, delivered a high cross that seemed impossible to reach. But to show this was no ordinary team and no ordinary season, Danny Hollands rose towards the ball at full stretch and directed a bullet header into the top right corner.

'Our flying Dutchman!' someone shouted.

As the last leaves of autumn started falling and the bonfires on Blackheath stood stacked and ready to light, they had seen perfect poetry on the football field. The day's fireworks ended in a 5-2 victory.

'Time for another kind o' fireworks,' said Lance.

Every year, on the closest Saturday to the date, thousands of people assemble in Blackheath on the borders of Lewisham and Greenwich. There, like rebels gathered on the heath in centuries past, they watch sticks of flame torching the night sky above church spires and the highwayman's mansions in the ancient forests of Shooter's Hill.

'Biggest fireworks show in London,' Katy said.

Though the whole show lasted no more than fifteen minutes, in these times of cutbacks and recession it was an essential ritual in the lives of south Londoners. For one fragment of one night only, the biggest, brightest circus in town was on this side of the Thames.

'And it's about far more than the fireworks,' she insisted. 'It's the whole fizzle and dazzle that goes with it, the sideshows.'

One of those sideshows was the need for her to dress up and go to a party afterwards with a crowd of fashion designers who would make an exodus from Shoreditch, for one night only, down into New Cross.

'You'll come too,' Fergus had said to Lance.

He might meet a woman there. They would find him someone handsomely exotic, a worthy cause who probably couldn't even speak their meta-language.

'I'll drive,' he said, 'but I'm not dressing up.'

'You have to,' Fergus insisted. 'Katy says so.'

In the end, he agreed. They found him dressed in a black rubber skeleton suit when they met at seven outside the apartments.

'Lance, meet Katy, and Katy, this is Lance.'

'We've seen each other,' she said, 'but never spoken.'

'Yes, you've passed me when I've been working.'

'Coming in with muddy bicycle tyres,' she apologised.

He laughed. 'Yeah, that keeps me in a job alright.'

'So are we going then?' Fergus wondered.

'Sure,' Lance replied as he took out the keys to the Torino. As they walked he spoke to Katy again. 'So what's your costume?'

'Can't you guess? Isn't it obvious?'

'Green dress, green hat, stockings, sexy boots.'

'These boots aren't sexy,' she protested. 'They're second hand.'

'Is the previous owner coming tonight?' he asked.

'How would I know? I got them in the high street.'

'That's a pity,' he said as they reached the car.

'There'll be plenty of girls for him to meet, right?'

'Maybe.' She paused. 'We'll find him the right one.'

'I've got it.' He spoke again suddenly. 'You're Greenwich.'

'Yes, she is,' thought Fergus, picturing the immaculate architecture and the white blaze of her body in bed beside him these mornings.

But that wasn't what he was talking about as they got into the car.

'Green Witch,' he said. 'That's clever. Cheesy, but clever.'

'Glad you said that. I like people to say what they think.'

Dragging his leg into position in the driver's seat as they got into the back, he felt honest in Katy's presence.

'And do you know who I am?' Fergus interjected.

Lance started up the car and moved slowly through the traffic. 'A ginger man with a black moustache, in a brown suit,' he said. 'Maybe one of those guys from the *Tintin* stories. No?'

'Martial Bourdin,' Fergus clarified.

Lance laughed at his visual awkwardness. 'He was a tailor and your date for the night's a fashion designer and that's the best you can do.'

Again he noticed his friend's wandering eyes in the mirror, straying towards Katy's stockings and thigh-length boots. He felt uneasy, aware of fancily-dressed competition and subterranean caves of desire as they headed for Blackheath Hill, where Lance parked the Torino.

'Do you need a coat or anything?' he asked Katy.

'If it's cold, I'll give her my jacket,' Fergus answered, feeling a strong whisky of jealousy distilling in the back of his throat.

'I'll get us some punch,' the skeleton suggested as they mingled with tens of thousands of bodies on a slow crawl through the darkness.

This was London, city of glass, but there was something about the emptiness of the heath that makes you feel like you're in the midst of wide-open terrain, smelling the gorse of mountain country.

Chinese lanterns floated in the cormorant-black sky above as Lance came back with three steaming cups of fruit punch.

Then they stood and sipped in silence, waiting for the day's second spectacle.

Several times he noticed his friend's eyes straying to Katy's costume, undressing her in his thoughts or imagining the taste and smell of punch on her lips. Or maybe he was just standing there, half-afraid of hearing echoes of Afghanistan in the flash and roar of fireworks.

'This is my first time since the war, being at anything like this.'

'Don't worry,' Katy assured him. 'I've never liked crowds, so this used to be hard for me too, but you'll be able to cope with it. You're not fighting a war alone anymore. You're here with your friends.'

Fergus felt a cramping pang of jealousy as his handsome friend turned around, smiled, and their eyes connected for a few seconds. Again he was either being paranoid, or he caught a sudden spark of change; her pale eyes torched bright, wolf-blue in the darkness.

But the countdown had started. 'Ten, nine, eight.'

Within seconds, there would be a rupture in the skull of darkness; landmines in the clouds.

'Three, two, one.'

A hundred thousand voices struck zero. The former soldier's chest tightened, fearing a sudden blast. But there was just a crackle and then a whistle; a tassel of light shooting between Chinese lanterns.

Snaking towards the arc of the sky, the tassel stopped suddenly, suspended like the moment before Johnnie Jackson's penalty kick. Briefly, he was back in Afghanistan. Seeing laser traces light up the darkness on night patrol. Space-age stuff the Americans used.

But instead of guns he heard the excited chatter of children.

'Whoosh!' they cried back in the present.

The first fireworks crackled then imploded. He shivered, focusing straight ahead. Suddenly, the sky was pregnant with colour. A second whistle came, followed by gasps and sighs, and exploding pinwheels.

Close by, Martial Bourdin stood beside a gorgeous green witch. Further back, he caught sight of a tattooed lady's Staffordshire.

'Poor dog's more scared than me,' he thought.

Classy act, bringing a dog to a fireworks display. Seeing the animal shivering, he knew he was home. This place of kids, and parents wearing poppies, as they watched from a safe distance, wasn't Afghanistan.

Still, the sounds were similar as fresh thunder rolled off the heath and turned the sky to a 3D triptych of flame disgorged from the smouldering crater of night.

He could imagine the ferocity of battles fought here in days past, but was trying to forget about war, so thought of colours, spread for miles above the heath. Charlton reds, Chelsea blues, West Ham purples, Watford gold, Plymouth greens, Blackpool tangerines, coming together in a single promenade. Spiralling, leaping, dancing, whistling sharply, shaking tails, creating images of butterflies in flight crystallising to comets crashing down on South East London's orchard.

Strangely, cured of his malady, he was enjoying the show.

Once or twice though, when children lit sparklers unexpectedly, he felt an urge to dive for cover and cower beside the Staffordshire.

But when he turned his head to run, he caught sight of Katy's eyes, softening the scene of the auditorium after the night's show had ended.

A few minutes later he heard her voice. 'It's over.'

The last sparks of the fireworks display had fizzled out, fading and falling to a black dust of shrapnel on the bruised and muddied heath.

'Time for the party,' Fergus said, linking his arm in Katy's, reminding Lance of being the one on the outside of this triangle.

'Our first fireworks,' she whispered in response as they began to trudge their way back towards Blackheath Hill, caught up in crowds as big as you would find at Wembley Stadium on Cup final day.

Strolling along under the soft glow of streetlamps, she looked like Marilyn again; dipping her blonde head towards camera flashes.

Just at that moment, everyone's attention shifted as a sudden, sharp shark's fin of noise pierced the tide of voices and footsteps.

'Police sirens,' those in front presumed.

But Lance recognised it as something different.

'My car alarm!' he cried out and started running.

Knocking bodies aside as if on a rugby field, he pushed his way through the crowd, charging towards the Torino's intensifying shriek. What happened next was as much of a blur as the morning of Marilyn Monroe's death; a mixture of hard fact and speculation. Though there were a couple of hundred metres between them, and several hundred people blocking the path, Fergus could hear Lance hurtling towards the car, moving on his one good leg and dragging the bad one behind, screaming '*fukkkerrzzz*' out of his lungs as he came upon the scene.

Afterwards witnesses would speak of seeing different things, as if dazzled and half-blinded by the spectacle of the fireworks' display. Some said three, others four, when asked about the boys on the far side of the Torino; a set of hooded gangster-rap mechanics snapping open its side windows and then its doors. One thing they agreed on; given another few minutes, they could have hot-wired the engine.

'But the victim got there just in time.'

Soon as he shouted at them, they scarpered, jumped out of the shrieking Torino and disappeared into the darkness, scattering in multiple directions. Obviously Lance couldn't chase them all. He had to make a choice. He would never capture the elfish kid who had sprinted downhill, or fish out the whale-bellied hulk who had gone to the flats.

He had some hope of going after the others though.

'We could hear shouting,' a witness said, 'echoes in open space, and then a sound like a pack of foxes running through bushes.'

'He went after them furious as a terrier,' another added.

'Then there was a struggle,' said the previous, 'and you could tell somebody got hit, because there was an almighty whine and tumble.'

Several people ran to his aid. By this stage, the bushes were empty. He was alone on the ground, on a hill above the lights of Greenwich, trying to use his fist as a barrier against a sweeping tide.

'Shot or stabbed?' they firstly wondered.

The full picture came into view as they got closer to him. There was a slit in the side of his skeleton costume, suddenly dyed in the same ink as the circle around his tattoo. Now he was a Charlton man for sure, bleeding the colours of his favourite football team. He was in a bad way, maybe worse than when he had been injured in Afghanistan.

'He's been stabbed,' screeched a young girl.

Behind them, the Torino was also screeching.

Katy took charge. 'I'm calling an ambulance.'

Lance was on the ground, trying to scramble to his knees, to reach his car and turn off the sound. Finally, after a few seconds of feeling helpless as a mouse in a glue trap, Fergus got down beside him.

'It's okay, mate,' he said. 'Ambulance is coming.'

'The car,' he mumbled, as if to trying to forget the wound in his side and get back to what was important, 'the fucking car.'

'I'll take care of the car.'

He had said the words without thinking. Seconds later, Lance's hand was in the pocket of his costume, fumbling for keys. When he finally found and passed them across, they came stained in sticky blood. Behind, the sound of sirens closed down on the scene.

'Come after them,' he pleaded. 'In the car.'

That was when the pounding in his temples started; the realisation of what he had agreed to. He hadn't driven a car in over a decade. But it was too late for excuses. Even if he had never renewed his licence or wasn't insured, that was small compared to what his mate was suffering.

'Turn off that bleeding alarm,' Lance begged as it sounded out a constant reminder of how he had ended up in this condition.

But it was Lance doing the bleeding as a couple of ambulance men cut through the crowd, lifted him onto a stretcher and ferried him towards the waiting vehicle with lights flashing blue as Katy's eyes.

There was blood, lots of blood on the trail to the ambulance.

'Come on,' she said. 'Let's get in the car.'

'I haven't driven in a long time.'

'You don't forget,' she answered. 'It's like riding a bike.'

When they got there and turned off the alarm, flashes of the crash went through Fergus's mind like fireworks. Suddenly his head was pregnant with images of Lucy's freckled face during the fatal joyride. She had been gone for a while but was back again with a vengeance.

The memories made him nauseous, needing to sit down before his legs buckled. When he took the plunge, getting into the driver's seat, his heart began to hammer, probably hitting a hundred beats a minute.

The keys in his hand heaved with a sense of best-forgotten history. Holding them tightly, he felt sharp edgings cut into his palm and open a stigma of old wounds. For a split second, a psychological sclerosis had consumed his upper body and he couldn't move. But he had to move, for the sake of his friend inside that ambulance.

'What's wrong?' Katy asked.

Suddenly, feeling impotent in her presence, he thrust his arm towards the ignition system. Thinking of the here and now instead of the past, he felt the sclerosis ease. He took a deep breath and fumbled with the keys, in foreplay before the first wet seconds of intercourse.

There was no sudden wave of shock or blast of memory, just a gentle sighing of the engine, which could as easily have been a dying.

'Time to go,' he said as he slipped the gearstick into reverse.

'It's only a couple of miles,' she remarked as they made their way out of the car park and nosed into a slow conga of traffic.

Around them, the colours of the streets blazed more intensely than even the fireworks from an hour before. The lights of Blackheath became neon projectiles searing the surface of the Torino's windscreen and wing mirrors. Looking down on his costume, he wondered if Martial Bourdin had sweated as much on his journey over a century before. The ambulance was long gone, down the road up ahead, where cars shuffled in an endless over-sized deck towards Shooter's Hill.

Looking out on the road ahead, Katy drummed her fingers impatiently on the dashboard. 'Will he be okay?'

'He should be. He's survived worse than this.'

'Knives don't care if someone's strong or weak,' she whispered. 'He shouldn't have gone chasing after those boys.'

He had no answer to that as the Torino shivered and sweated like its driver with every jolt and shudder. Each time they hit a traffic light or saw the headlamps of cars coming in the opposite direction, a cold shell of terror abscessed his insides. Memories of that night came back in every flicker of amber to green, every freckled star in the sky above.

You don't have to be a soldier to suffer post-traumatic stress.

'You're quiet,' Katy said after a few minutes as the traffic became lighter and she reached up to caress his face with gentle fingers. 'My God, I've never seen anybody sweat so much in my whole life.'

As they came out of the conga onto the open road and gathered speed, trickles of hot fluid dripped from his temples and splashed on the dashboard, steaming up the sequence of metres below his eyes. Suddenly he had a desire to share the full horrors of the past with Katy.

'I need to say something,' he closed his eyes and spoke.

'Careful,' she cried as he drifted through an endless sea of words beyond the windows. 'You've just broken a red light.'

'Sorry,' he said as a series of parked ambulances signalled the hospital's entrance. 'For a few seconds there, I was miles away.'

'Where were you?' she wondered, but there wasn't time to explain as they pulled up inside the grounds of this former military hospital.

Since the side windows were broken, they parked in the light close to where groups of people stood outside smoking, some in pyjamas. It felt ironic, entering a hospital through a cloud of nicotine. Going down the wide corridors, they sought out the Accident & Emergency area. When they got there, the nurses were helpful. Yes, they knew about the guy who had been stabbed in the ribs at Blackheath Fireworks.

'The ribs!' Katy exclaimed. 'Is he going to be okay?'

Nurses and doctors don't answers questions like that until they're sure, so they ensconced them in a side room near an operating theatre. They could hear voices, so they guessed that Lance was in there.

After a few minutes of silence Katy spoke first. 'Back in the car, there was something you wanted to tell me.'

She was right. There had been a moment. Maybe it had passed. Sitting here in the soft light, it was as if they were in a dream.

'What is it? What's troubling you?'

'It's not that important,' he started to tell the story, 'but it is too.'

Suddenly flashes from another hospital came back as the same sobering sense of dread filled his subconscious. Waking up after a blackout, feeling that something terrible has happened, memories coming back to him in random fragments rather than full sentences.

'When I was a teenager,' he said suddenly, 'I was part of a gang that stole a car, took it for a joyride, crashed, and somebody died.'

Katy's blue eyes went cold and she didn't react for a moment. Then she spoke in a soft, high-pitched way. 'You were in a gang?'

'Not really a gang,' he tried to explain. 'Not like the gangs they have in London who go around stabbing and shooting each other.'

She was looking at him with a vacant stare and when he tried to touch her, she pulled away. 'I never pictured you as the kind of guy who'd belong to a gang. I thought you were different to other guys.'

'Gang's not the right word,' he protested once more.

Besides, it was strange to be preoccupied with that part of the story. For years he had carried around this burden of guilt, thinking that the main confession would always be connected to Lucy's death. Katy though seemed to think being in a gang was a bigger deal.

'Maybe we don't know each other so well after all.'

He stood up, about to put his arms around her, but fate intervened. One of the doctors came into the room, bringing news about Lance.

'How is he?' Fergus asked. Katy stayed silent, which was strange because up until now she had done most of the questioning.

'He's through the worst of it,' said the doctor.

He had had a lucky escape. There was more blood than lasting damage. The blade had missed his lung by little more than a sideways inch.

Fergus wanted more. 'Can we see him?'

The doctor shook her head. 'No, he needs to rest for now. You should go home, get some sleep and come back tomorrow.'

Going out of the hospital, back towards the car, in their fancy dress costumes, neither seemed in the right mood for a party.

'You've lost your moustache,' Katy pointed out as they got into the Torino, started up and headed out on the road for home.

In all the commotion, he hadn't noticed.

'Are we still going to the party?'

'No,' she said. 'No party tonight.'

'We'll have a drink then, when we get to Greenwich.'

'No,' she said sadly. 'I'm tired. I just want to go home.'

'I can grab some things and stay for the night.'

'No,' she said again. 'I want to be alone tonight.'

'Is it Lance?' he asked. 'Or is it what I said?'

'It doesn't matter,' she answered. 'I'm just tired.'

That was more or less the end of the conversation. They drove back to the flats, where she got out and walked to her room with nothing more than a kiss on the cheek. Tears were shining in the corners of her eyes. He went inside and sent her a couple of text messages to say goodnight, to see if she was okay. Come next morning, she must have been sleeping still after the shock of last night's events, while he watched the highlights of Saturday's football and sat waiting for a message.

When it finally came, it wasn't what he expected. It was longer than most text messages and, though signed with an x, seemed colder.

Fergus, I don't think we should see each other for a while, the message began. *I'm going up to my parents' house for a few days, then maybe a couple more days with old friends in the Lake District.*

By this stage, the dykes at the back of his eyes had been broken, rupturing as violently as on the morning after the accident. The same set of boiling waterfalls began to bubble and then erupt.

Sometimes you just need time alone to get your head together.

He got down on his knees on the carpet as the dye became liquid. *Say hello to Lance for me and maybe we'll all get in touch again when I get back*, she said. *For now I want to be left alone. Katy X.*

But what exactly was the equation of that X? It could be nothing or it could be everything. It could be a sign of friendship or female politeness. It could be a legacy of old habits, or a casual, customary act.

The X of the olden days or the X of social media? A gentle kiss? On the cheek or on the lips? A passionate kiss or a simple peck? One between lovers or between friends? Or, as he feared, a goodbye kiss?

Regardless, he texted her back with a double x but she didn't reply. Feeling a terrifying emptiness, he realised the whirlwind was over.

13
Cold Comforts

After the storm passed and she was gone, Fergus was fighting a flood, caught up in a whirlpool and drowning. Holding his hand out in desperation, he felt there was nobody to help him, especially not the one person who a week ago seemed destined to be the one he'd be with forevermore.

As nights got colder he missed her voice in the seconds before he fell asleep, and her soft presence set against the morning darkness.

He was in a cold, grim place from which there was no escape.

'Like Halifax,' Lance suggested after getting out of hospital.
'Where's that?'
'Up north,' he replied. 'Near Huddersfield actually.'
'And what's that got to do with anything?'
'You're driving there,' his friend surprised him.
'Why would I want to drive to Halifax?'
'Because I can't and Charlton have a Cup game on Sunday.'

At first, he protested. Though not as far away as Hartlepool, the former mill town at the outset of Charlton's travels back to 1947 was halfway up the torso of England.

Finally, he relented. On the Saturday afternoon, they set out from London in bright sunshine. As they passed through the Midlands, clouds accumulated like heaps of falling leaves on the hard shoulders.

'I'd love to take the back roads, see bits of the country.'
'Stick to the motorways, or you'll never get us there.'

They reached their destination in the darkness of the evening, booked into a guesthouse, had dinner, and checked out the pubs of this town. The architecture spoke of a place that had been rich once upon a time, with the names of companies and building societies scripted into high stone walls that seemed to have no use for the upper storeys these days.

'Because of immigration,' implied a friend-seeking racist they met in a pub, who expressed other thoughts less politely.

'Isn't it more to do with the decline of traditional industries?' Fergus mused, thinking of how Belfast suffered the same fate without having any Kashmiri factory workers to blame.

They drank, ate, and talked to the locals all night long.

'This is the great thing about away games,' Lance said. 'You get to see the country, learn stuff they never teach you in school.'

Huddersfield, for example, was less than half a dozen miles away. Former poet laureate Ted Hughes came from a village close by, where his wife Sylvia Plath was buried, and the 1980s TV wrestling star Big Daddy was born here.

'Always rains, but we've plenty o' people with suntans,' grumbled another friendly racist they met as the night wore on.

Going outside, into the rainy, soot-blackened streets, they found a place where some of those people with suntans ran a great curry shop. They ordered, then laughed with the guys behind the counter when Fergus said he was Irish. Then they paid, ate, and talked cricket for a while.

Then it was bedtime. He sent another drunken text to Katy.

'I'm in Halifax,' he said, 'for a football match xx.'

This past week, she had only replied once, telling him that the use of a double x was crossing boundaries. He was putting pressure on her. Falling asleep, he hoped she wouldn't get angry. Then again, her flashes of anger suggested she still cared, and the thought of that aroused him.

But when he awoke on the Sunday morning, head hurting, breath stinking of curry, there was no response. If he had sent her a message saying '*Help, I'm drowning*' she would have let him die in the night.

Going to the window, pulling back the curtains on a foggy, frosty morning, he felt like he was in a foreign country. Breakfast time, and then a trip to the Shay Stadium, where he would forget about Katy as *his* team, from the south, faced a hardy non-league, northern outfit.

Ted Hughes might have been born a few miles down the road, but there was very little poetry on show as they reached a stadium encased in a smoky fog and surrounded by the bare trees of premature winter.

'Mostly reserves,' said Lance as he read the team sheet.

Once again, since the *Paint Pot* game, Alonso wasn't playing.

'Strange,' Fergus breathed steam, 'how you can have such high hopes for someone and nothing comes of them in the end.'

'Fuckin' freezing,' Lance changed the subject.

'Where's the wee man with the whisky flask when you need him?'

'This is all part of tradition though,' the Londoner assured him. 'Getting through the winter's what makes you a supporter.'

It's not sunny days at home. It's dark afternoons in Burnley, Bolton, Blackburn, Sheffield, Stoke and Scunthorpe. Of course, from late December onwards, the south of England's not so different.

'Like last year's cup game, the coldest ever.'

That was a second round match against Luton Town, on a December afternoon, just a few weeks after he had returned from Afghanistan.

'England was blanketed in snow,' he explained, 'from Sam Bartram's country, up north, right down to the coast of Kent.' He paused, laughing. 'Even Sam had icicles hanging off the end of his nose.'

As he said this, Fergus's mind drifted off the coast of time. The Thames in sunshine, a feast of wine and cheese, a fresh romance.

'Snow so deep, coaches and trains couldn't get in,' Lance carried on as today's players emerged onto the frosty grass for their warm-up. 'We'd no more than a few thousand in the whole stadium.'

Down on the pitch, he said, it was cold enough to freeze the balls off a brass goalie. During the game, the air stung his eyes so much it was like watching through a screen of glass. At least Charlton started well, scoring after only six minutes and going into the half-time tea break leading by two goals to one, thanks to a Johnnie Jackson strike.

'But the second half was so cold, I was almost delirious,' he carried on. 'The game started to drift, and so did my mind.'

'I know the feeling,' mused the Irishman.

'At one point I was almost hallucinating,' he said.

Holding onto a coffee cup for dear life, as if it was a hot water bottle, he could feel the raw cold in his bones. Back in the army they had taught him how to deal with weather extremes and how to understand frostbite.

First, he said, you feel so cold you think you're going to die. Then you start to get so hot you want to take all your clothes off. That's when you know you've crossed boundaries and you're sinking into madness.

'It was the middle of the second half,' he added, 'when I started to get so cold that I felt the first trickle of warmth.'

He paused to applaud the players as they finished their warm-up.

'Remember, I'm just back from Afghanistan. I've been cooped up in a hospital with broken air conditioning all summer and winter,' he said. 'I'm looking down on the pitch, getting colder and colder, teeth chattering like there's a *Punch & Judy* show going on in my head.'

It was cold here too, and grey. Fergus wondered if the same dark clouds had spread treacle on the hills all the way to Huddersfield. He might get a text message at any moment, inviting him there.

'Then suddenly, on the left side of the pitch, Kyel Reid takes a pass.' His voice was getting animated now, bringing sunshine to the scene. 'Immediately he's the only thing in the world that's not grey.'

Rising up sharp as the sword on the club shield, the young winger took the ball on the tip of his white boots. Frost glittered on the pine-green stubble at his feet as he turned, racing towards the goal. All Lance could see was the white streak of a No. 11 on his back, and all he could hear was supporters breathing hard, then stopping in anticipation.

'One of my favourite players,' he remarked, 'but like a lot of guys at this level, he can be great one minute and drift away the next.'

The crowd were on their feet. They wanted greatness, not drifting. Charlton were 2-1 up but it was their non-league opponents who had spent most of this half on the attack. After going through the motions for so long they needed a moment of magic, and their number 11 was the man who might deliver it. For a split second in the communal imagination of 8,000 fans huddled in the cold, Kyel Reid was suspended in a Maracanã moment, like the one when John Barnes scored a classic goal against Brazil a quarter of a century before.

He had the ball at his feet, running down the line in a long lazy dribble that brought back memories of 1984.

'This was like sips of hot whisky from a hip flask, little drips of heat stinging your tongue and slipping down the back of your throat,' said Lance, 'and slowly setting your guts on fire.'

And it was. For a few seconds, Fergus could forget Katy Prunty. Kyel Reid's carnival moment was about to come. He was shimmying, seeming to race and dawdle at the same time like Barnes ghosting through the Brazilian defence in the heat of Rio. He was hardly moving but somehow stayed ahead of the chasing pack, hanging on one elbow in mid-flow as he swayed towards the corner flag on the edge of the North Stand.

'You're crying out for him to come on, give us a shot o' medicine for the cold,' his teeth chattered, shivery as an addict. 'And you can feel that precious whisky getting hotter in your belly, as the defenders close down on the number eleven, and you're hoping, against hope, there's a way through.'

But there wasn't, as a big ugly Luton centre-half got in the way.

'There was going to be no Maracanã moment, no high end to the day. The ball goes wide, and gets lost somewhere in an empty North Stand. You're at a Cup game in the cold and that's all you've got.'

He paused, glancing forwards at the sight of today's kick-off. 'But that's when you know you're addicted, hopelessly addicted to following a team who always put ice in the Christmas whisky.'

'At least they take us places,' the Irishman laughed. 'I've driven to Halifax without a licence and ended up with a stopover in Rio.'

Down on the pitch, you got a sense that today was going to be more ice than whisky once again, and this made him wonder why they keep coming back for more, these addicted red men.

For him, this was curiosity and the chance to travel somewhere new. For them and for Lance, it was a religion full of habits and rituals, stories and anecdotes which went back to their grandfathers' times.

'Like the 7-6 classic against Huddersfield,' he explained while the first half passed sluggish as the clouds knitted overhead. 'That's one of those games where we got more whisky than ice.'

'Big score,' Fergus remarked. 'Were you there?'

He laughed. 'It was Christmas 1957. The pitch was a mud-bath. Bill Shankly was in charge of Huddersfield, and we'd a guy up front called Johnny Summers.'

'Another of the stories your grandfather told you?'

He nodded. 'Yes, he was there. But then so was anybody you ask, even though the official crowd was only about 12,000, and half of those left to do their shopping when we found ourselves 5-1 down.'

Then suddenly, in the midst of the story, they missed a first goal. Matt Taylor, centre-half, had headed an opener in the 40th minute.

After the celebrations died down, Lance carried on with his story. 'Then the 100,000 fans who claimed they watched the game saw something they'd never expected, a Christmas miracle in SE7.'

Maybe there was hope for the same happening with Katy.

'Johnny Summers started to play like a man who knew he hadn't long left in this world,' he said with glazed eyes, as if he had known him personally, as a member of Charlton's extended family.

'What happened to him?'

'Died of cancer at the age of thirty four, a few years after.'

'That's sad,' Fergus said. 'Makes you see what's important.'

'Yes, and glad that he had one perfect day in his football lifetime,' Lance added. 'He scored five goals and created the winner too.'

Fergus wondered if there had been any of Katy's ancestors on the Huddersfield side, down for the day, sitting in the south stand above the sodden, moor-black pitch.

His friend's laughter brought him back to the present. 'And maybe the funniest thing of all, there's an urban legend that as Bill Shankly left the Valley, he swore under his breath…'

Lance paused, and then attempted a Scottish accent. '*I never want to see another bloody team in red for as long as ah live.*'

The Irishman tried to laugh at the joke about Liverpool FC's legendary manager, but other thoughts clouded his head as the half-time whistle sounded, and he checked his phone for a text message.

'Nothing,' he realised, seeing the empty screen.

There was nothing for the whole of the second half either, which drifted past without any goals until three came in the final minutes, started off by Johnnie Jackson and finishing with a 4-0 victory.

The drive home was a quiet affair in the darkening day, and still there was no sign of text messages, even when they arrived back in London.

'You'd think she'd ask if I was okay; see how the journey went.'

'Sometimes people close chapters of their life, they put up boundaries and there's just no going back,' his friend consoled him. 'You've still got your job, your friends, and football too.'

'Where's next on our travels?' He tried to forget her.

'A tube ride across the city to Brentford,' Lance replied, 'and then at the end of the month, a home game against Huddersfield.'

'Great, bloody great, there's just no escaping her.'

'It's a couple of weeks away,' his passenger assured him as they hit the slow traffic of London's tunnels, crawling towards Greenwich. 'Look, you're not going to forget about her but you'll find ways to deal with it, to shut her out of your thoughts as she's doing with you.'

This wasn't the time to tell his Irish friend that she had come to see him in the hospital, on the evening before she caught a train to Huddersfield. She had stayed no more than fifteen or twenty minutes, fearing that Fergus would see her there. Besides, they hardly knew each other and hadn't much to talk about. She had brought him grapes and a magazine – about music, not football, because she said she didn't like football.

'Is that because you don't like crowds?' he asked.

'No,' she said, 'I don't like people sitting around watching silly games and silly boys getting paid silly amounts of pounds, when there's such serious stuff they could be doing with their lives.'

'Fergus likes football, and he's doing good things with sport and education,' he argued, 'and I like football, and I fought a war.'

She looked at him then with frosty eyes, as if composing arguments against that too, but changed her mind and softened.

'You've been through an awful lot with that tattoo.'

'Keeps me safe,' he said, wondering why she noticed it, why she was looking at his body, half-stripped in the hospital bed. Turning it to the light, he explained more. 'It's kind of like having a Saint Christopher badge on the dashboard of a car. Looks after me in my travels.'

She reached out then and touched it, just for a second, before a nurse passed by with a trolley and she withdrew her fingers from the sword, saying goodbye and leaving the room as suddenly as she had come in.

Before he could say bye, she was gone, leaving behind something more than grapes and a magazine – a rush of testosterone and the stabbing hunger of a cactus tree in a desert. Maybe it was the drip in his arm, the loss of blood, the shock of all that had happened, but for the next couple of days, a dry physical desire stayed with him.

Since then, they had talked on Facebook once or twice, though she wouldn't follow him on Twitter because of his constant references to football and friends from the army, she said, when there were a million causes in the world she wanted to keep up with. The chat, of course, was mostly about Fergus, snippets from her side of the story. She said that they didn't really know each other and had always been too different.

'I think he's old-fashioned,' she said. 'Looking for the kind of girl you're not going to find nowadays, especially not in this city.'

He would get tired of this, make an excuse, stop talking to her and go back on the football forums, with far less weight attached to the banter.

'Maybe *they* deserve each other,' he would try to convince himself. 'They're both mysterious, like they're holding something back.'

But he hadn't time to figure out what that was, because he had work to do clearing up the site of his community garden. He had spent hours drawing up plans, making designs, ripping down the old wilderness.

'Best thing of all,' he told Katy on Facebook, 'is getting to know people. I've been living here a year and this is the first time I've got to know my neighbours, like the Somalians across the way.'

'What about the man you guys call Merlin?' she asked.

'He's never volunteered,' Lance messaged back. 'But the boy has come to a few of our clear-up sessions, helping to dig space for a mini-orchard, and then a pond where we hope to keep some frogs.'

'Bees and butterflies would be nice,' she changed the subject.

'One step at a time,' he told her. 'You'll see some changes in the garden when you're back in town. When are you coming back?'

Again she changed the subject. 'So how's Merlin's boy?'

'Interested in him?' he jested. 'Fergus will be jealous.'

'He's got no reason, and he's got no right.'

'I was only teasing,' he typed quickly back. 'The boy's okay, but doesn't say much. Comes slouched in his hoodie, does the job he's asked to do, and then goes.' There was something else strange he hadn't thought of before. 'Seems to spend his time working with young kids and an old Chinese couple who don't speak much English.'

'He's a mystery,' she said. 'Just like FS.'

Again she was talking about Fergus, using his initials.

'Gotta go,' Lance wrote. 'Paperwork to be done.'

'Okay,' she replied. 'Talk again some time.'

'Sure :)' he agreed and left with a smile.

After chats like this, he tried not to go on social media for a while. Talking becomes addictive, and he had seen the suffering in Fergus's withdrawal symptoms. Besides, it was hard to catch a tube across the city, watch the Brentford game and come home feeling like a traitor. Suddenly, he was the one resisting old feelings for Katy Prunty.

Come the Huddersfield match at the end of the month, he hadn't spoken to her for a few days and it seemed Fergus was cured too. Instead of going over old ground, he had concentrated on the present.

First, he took a more active interest in the community garden. Enlisting the help of Omar, his colleague, and some of the boys, he spent a couple of evenings a week overseeing clearances and planting. At night, he read books and watched old films borrowed from the library on the history of the Charlton Athletic Football Club.

He found pictures of Johnny Summers and the laced-up orange ball with which he had almost scored a double hat-trick against Huddersfield.

'These days they keep it in the club's trophy cabinets.'

'Jesus Christ,' Lance said when he passed on the information, 'you're starting to know more about my own club than I do.'

Come the last Monday night of November when Huddersfield's footballers arrived in town, they brought the weather with them. Finding himself back inside a bricked-in bubble of pain, Fergus fought hard to forget this was Katy's town, and to concentrate on the game.

Down in the Valley, under the floodlights, live on TV, the red men faced the biggest test of their season so far. Huddersfield, in second place, hadn't been beaten in a league game since December 2010, securing 25 victories and 18 draws in that period of time. In doing so, they had broken Nottingham Forest's run of 42 games unbeaten under Brian Clough's management in the 1970s, and were now gunning for Arsenal's all-time record of 49 games unbeaten in 2003 to 2004.

All talk before the match was about Huddersfield and the record. They had become torch bearers for the Football League, offering its greatest chance to outshine the Premiership for almost two decades.

'As if they've forgotten *we* exist,' home supporters grumbled. 'Huddersfield, Huddersfield, that's all you hear.'

Fergus understood the feeling all too well. Even the hungry seagulls, going to roost on the shells of the Thames Barrier, cried out her name.

'Knock 'em off their perch!' someone shouted as the game began.

Sure enough, they bossed the opening couple of minutes. Solly and Wiggins, surging forwards from full back, kept his mind off Katy Prunty and those eyes soft-blue as the shirts and flags in Jimmy Seed's stand.

Down on the touchline, Chris Powell stood emotionless, dressed in his usual club tie and smart attire. You can tell a lot about a man's character by the way he conducts himself in times of pressure.

'He always carries himself so humbly and so graciously,' Fergus mused, but a few seconds later the shell was about to crack.

As Danny Green sent in a free kick from the east, Charlton's valiant French knight rose towards the ball. Another header, another goal.

'One-nil to Charlton,' the choir sang.

Huddersfield's record was on the ropes, after no more than 23 minutes, and Chrissie Powell was suddenly dancing on the sidelines, fists clenched, tie wavering, and teeth gleaming in satisfied relief.

The crowd chanted the scorer's name, 'Yann Kermorgant!'

Fergus wondered what they were saying in the TV studios now. Were Katy's family watching the game, half a dozen miles from Halifax? Were they football people? Supporters of their local team?

'I don't know anything about her,' he concluded.

The floodlights were a blur at this stage, a screen onto which he could project his memories, then dissect, deconstruct and demonise them. But again, as he found himself caught in a whirlpool of emotion, his players reached out a rescuing arm and saved him from drowning.

Chris Powell was smiling again. Lee Clark, in the opposing dugouts, was fuming. The red men cut open their defence from a throw, and struck home a second goal of the evening. Charlton's management team were already in a huddle by the time the ball reached the net.

'Two-nil!' the stadium announcer hollered, but everybody from here to Greenwich already knew as the volcano erupted.

'Half-time,' said Lance when the whistle blew.

'Let's get a beer,' he suggested.

One became two to drown out the cold before a walk back down the steps for the second half. Now it was a case of Charlton holding out long enough to deny Huddersfield the chance of their record.

'*We beat your team two-nil x*,' he texted Katy as whole hours seemed to pass before the game finally ended and three sides of the stadium breathed relief, in communion, as celebrations began.

'I'm going to watch this all over again later tonight,' Lance said as they made their way out. 'I recorded it on the net.'

'I'd join you, but too much work in the morning,' Fergus replied as he felt a sudden buzz from the phone against his groin.

At once, he looked for the text message.

Sure enough it was Katy, but not at all what he had expected to see.

'*Stop fucking contacting me,*' screamed the first line.

Instantly, he stopped dead as a drowned man.

'What's wrong?' Lance asked.

'You go ahead,' he told his friend as he began to scroll his way through the message. 'I'll catch up with you at the station.'

Looking down at the screen, he finally sensed what it must be like when a landmine explodes out of nowhere. It's not like a car crash.

When you're behind the wheel, you've always got to keep the expectancy that something could go wrong, outside your own control.

But this was cruel and unexpected. '*You're harassing me, Fergus,*' she wrote with a vengeance. '*If you don't stop this now, I'm going to the police to say you won't leave me alone.*'

Seeing these words, he felt a shudder of terror run through him with such force that his heart began to race and his head began to ache.

He didn't get migraines but he thought they must be like this, when your skull's on fire and your brain's pulsing, trying to douse the flames. Not from fear, but from absolute severance. After all they had shared, how could she say such a thing? Would she see it through? Would she get him sent back to prison, even if he had never told her he had been there?

She had said she loved him, and she had allowed him inside her castle walls, but everything was no more than fiction.

'Forget about her,' Lance argued, when he caught up with him. 'You've no choice after this. She's dead to you.'

Like Lucy, he thought, and then told Lance the story of the joyride for the first time as they made their way back to the apartments. When it was done, he went to his room, made himself sick in the toilet, and texted Omar to say he was taking the next few days off work.

It would take a while to get over the shock of what he had learned. If he was drowning, she wouldn't just refuse to hold out her hand. She would take him by the throat and push him deeper into the whirlpool.

He would sweat her fever out. 'So long, Chelsea girl.'

14
Plastic Holly

Summer seemed long ago on the Saturday of the next Cup match when Carlisle came to town once more and lost 2–0 on a frosty afternoon. There were no Maracanã moments to warm the blood, only the promise of a third-round tie with Fulham, further down the Thames.

'Everything gets damp and dreary in December,' he had warned his team of gardeners. 'One more weekend, then it's shutdown.'

As frost seeped out of the nights, the ground became tenacious as a 3rd division centre-half, and the grass stopped growing. To assemble his troops, he dropped leaflets through doors.

'Saturday, 10 a.m., last clear-up before Xmas,' they said.

Strangely, after the first drop, he had a couple of unexpected volunteers. Tuesday afternoon, alone in his flat, he heard knuckles knock on his silence.

'Too early for Fergus.'

These days he worked late to forget Katy. *His* secret Facebook friend. What if it was her when he went to the door?

But when he got there, the faces that greeted him were very different. Two girls. One from Somalia, another from the same coast.

'No,' he self-corrected, 'they used to be from Africa.'

'We're from over there. We want to help.'

'Sure,' he agreed, studying them more closely.

The speaker was tall and slim. She wore a headscarf. The smaller girl beside her was less shy. She was shiny-eyed, curly-headed and smiley.

She squeaked excitedly. 'Can we give out letters?'

Next thing he knows, they've stepped inside, unaware you don't do these things in London, like they're part of the same tribe. They've gone straight to the printer where they paw over fresh leaflets.

'Careful,' he warned. 'The ink's not going to be dry on those.'

'Sorry,' they reply in chorus, but he's the one feeling sorry.

He hadn't been good with kids since the bomb, because they ask too many questions, and ask them too directly. But the least he could do was to be hospitable. They seemed like nice kids, even if he had never expected to be this close to a female in a headscarf ever again.

'Do you want some juice?' he asked.

They nodded and he gave away two glasses of his hangover rations, letting them sit down at the table to drink it. Sure enough, they asked dozens of questions, some of them about his injuries. Usually, when he talked about the blast he felt a certain kind of shame.

'I lost half my leg,' he admitted.

'And what about your finger?'

He held out his hand in front of the little rabbit-eyed girl. 'No, I didn't lose that in the war. I lost that as a teenager in a fight.'

For a second, he almost said something he would have regretted. They didn't need to know the colour of the boys who had mugged him.

'Don't walk through parks alone at night.'

'Can we see it?' they asked.

'See what?'

'Your leg,' answered the girl in the headscarf.

Again, he didn't tell them what went through his head. Aside from doctors and nurses, nobody back home got to see his prosthesis. Sometimes, lying in bed, he imagined the scene of showing it for the first time to a woman as you're getting ready to sleep with her. Usually, these past months, the woman in the scene was Katy Prunty.

'I don't normally do this,' he said as he began to roll the leg of his trousers up over the prosthesis. 'But since you're dropping leaflets...'

'Wow,' they said, staring intently at the memento he still found hard to look at himself. 'Can you run as fast as those athletes on TV?'

'I can hardly walk in the bloody thing,' he laughed, noticing the shock in their eyes as he swore, 'so it's nice of you to help.'

When they had gone, he decided to take a drive into Eltham, to pick up some materials from the garden store. On the way, as he passed the shadow of trees in every second window, he thought of sparks broken off a communal fire. Through the Torino's windscreen he caught snapshots of Santa Claus, lights flashing as insistently as those of paparazzi, and figures of snowmen creeping up gable walls as stealthy as cat burglars.

South London's streets seemed a long way from the summer's riots. Sure, once or twice, you caught flashes of memory. Boarded-up windows, 'Wanted' posters, tales of capture and whispers of turf wars still being fought by teenagers wearing different shades of shoelaces.

Reaching Eltham, he saw the high street was a world away from the night of right-wing extremists hijacking Operation Red Man. Strange, he thought, how everybody got caught up in paranoia and empty rage.

Though it had become colder by twenty degrees, sparkly lights warmed the mood. Drifting down the street, browsing a few windows as he passed, he caught the garden store before it closed, and collected what he wanted.

Getting home, he saw there was no sign of Fergus. Katy was there, though. Not in the flesh. Just in cyberspace, where they still met.

'Hello,' she said on Skype. 'Are you there, Lance?'

There was no harm in answering, just for a minute. 'Yeah.'

But one minute worked itself into two. Then five, ten, an hour. Getting deeper into discussion, he ignored a couple of knocks on the door. Perhaps it was Fergus or the girls who had finished their task.

After a while, they switched to camera. Drank a couple of beers together, cyber beers, as he told her the story of his new friends.

'They asked to see my leg,' he said as he looked into her eyes on the screen. She lay on her bed in front of the computer. 'You know, it's strange but they've cured me more than those counsellors in the Ministry of Defence.'

'Would you show it to me?' Katy asked suddenly.

Immediately he felt embarrassed. 'That's different.'

'Why?' she asked, pulling the duvet around herself.

'You're a grown-up, I suppose. And you're a woman.'

'I don't know whether or not I should be offended.'

'Okay,' he said, standing up to take the plunge.

'You're taking off your trousers!' she exclaimed.

He paused. 'Do you want to see it or not?'

She nodded, sipping her beer, trying to act only half-interested. Dropping his jeans to the floor, he positioned his leg in front of the camera, watching her eyes as she watched him doing so.

Again she sipped her beer. 'First I've seen in the flesh.'

'Except it's not flesh,' he said. 'You realise that very quick.'

Like the first time you walk too hard, too fast, too much, and you end up with poppies of blood coming through your trousers at the kneecap, from where the raw bone's pressing up against the prosthesis.

'Another beer?' she asked, as if not knowing what else to say.

'Sure,' he said, becoming the one watching her again.

By now she seemed the more intoxicated, drinking bottles of Yorkshire ale from the fridge in her parents' house. She was getting sleepy; once or twice she almost drifted off as he talked of gardening.

'What did it feel like?' she asked, struggling to stay awake.

'Showing you my war wounds,' he presumed.

She nodded, giving up on the fight of finishing her beer.

'Felt naked,' he admitted. 'You've seen parts of me I've never shown any other woman, never even admitted to myself.'

'I'm tired,' she answered. 'I'm going to fall asleep soon.'

'Okay,' he replied, trying not to seem disappointed.

'Will you stay with me until I'm asleep?' she asked.

'Sure,' he replied, watching her as she began to get ready for bed, removing her upper garments, replacing them with a nightdress, giving him a glimpse, for no more than a few seconds, of her second layer.

'Guess we're even,' she said, as she lay down on the pillows. 'You've shown me your nakedness, and seen something back in return.'

'Suppose we are,' he answered, stunned by the speed of it.

'It's just a body, not what's inside us.'

'A beautiful body,' he mumbled under his breath.

'Goodnight Lance,' she whispered; closing her eyes.

Then she was gone, turning out the light and drifting into dreams, staying as a grainy blue silhouette in the glare of the computer until the screen saver flickered on, and she faded into a dark sea of snores.

As everything turned gradually black, he whispered. 'Goodnight.'

The sight of her naked body would stay with him for hours, days, weeks, maybe a whole lifetime. He couldn't shake the thought out of his head, regardless of how hard he tried.

Speaking again the next evening, sober and for a shorter span of time, they never mentioned what had happened the night before. Maybe she was right. It was only their bodies they had shared. He had seen as little of her true self as in those days of staring towards her lighted window from a distance. Her naked body was no more of her entire being than his was an artificial limb.

'Gardening tomorrow,' he told her, wishing she was there.

'You two boys, don't get frostbite.'

As she said this, he could see she was thinking of Fergus again, and of all the reasons she had left London. Soon after this the conversation finished. But come the next day, he couldn't shake pictures of naked flesh out of his head as the first volunteers began to arrive. The two girls turned up with their brothers and sisters at the crack of dawn; bright-eyed and chattering. Shortly after, he caught sight of his friend's red head and face, the same colour from a hangover.

'You brought none of your boys today?'

'They'll be back after Christmas.'

'Right,' Lance instigated. 'Let's get started.'

The ground was bone-dry after weeks of frost. Crystallised.

'You'd swear you were striking stone,' the Irishman said.

For the first time, Lance felt uneasy in his company. Subconsciously, that was why he had stationed him at the far end of the garden, but his voice kept coming back into focus every time he struck the ground.

A new voice interjected. 'Excuse me.'

Lance turned to face someone taller, with skin as dark as soil in shadow. It was the man he had nicknamed 'Merlin'. Close up, the bike-riding master of secret potions seemed more athletic than from a distance.

'Can my kid join you again?'

His words were slow, his narrow lips hardly moving.

'Of course,' Lance replied as he turned to the boy.

As always, the youth said nothing, brown eyes staring from a shaven scalp, and forehead shiny as a two-pence coin. Today, the lower half of his face was covered in the cannons of an Arsenal scarf.

'They're doing okay this season.'

The boy's eyes smiled at Lance's attempts to break the ice.

'Loves the Gunners,' his guardian spoke once more.

'I'm a Charlton man,' Lance stated, before sensing impatience.

Merlin hadn't come here to discuss football. That much was clear in his expression. He wanted to leave the boy with the group and get back to whatever he did, in private, with his potions and spells.

'You can help the girls,' Lance suggested as the young Arsenal fan shivered in the cold. Then he melted into the body of volunteers.

There was a lot of work to be done: beds to be laid and planted with bulbs for the spring, fences to be secured against cats and foxes, boxes to be made from old railway sleepers he had gotten for free. He had assigned this task to Fergus, who had a flair for carpentry, and again felt guilty as he watched him working with faithful speed and passion. Time passed quickly on these afternoons, with hours melting into beads of frost in the rationed sunshine. Every so often they would take a break from stones and splinters, stopping for tea. But the Irishman worked on, brushing off a cold sweat, determined to finish the job.

'I've done something good here,' Lance tried to assuage his guilt as he listened to a Chinese couple's laughter and the excited chatter of girls working alongside Merlin's boy masked in a football scarf.

He had created a sense of community where there wasn't one before. Maybe this was the government's vision of 'the Big Society', but the former soldier's motives were personal, not political.

Needing a cause to help him get out of bed in the mornings, he had found it in the most unlikely of places. The abandoned and untended jungle outside his window had become a community gardening space. These people knew one another's names for the first time.

'Going to get dark soon,' he heard somebody say.

'Almost finished,' Fergus followed up through a cloud of wood shavings as he smoothed the last edgings of his creations.

Across the way, they could hear Chapel bells echoing above the cobbled courtyards of the Old Royal Naval College. Counting the strokes, seeing sunset on the river, Lance realised it was four o'clock.

All afternoon he hadn't thought about football. Or Katy's flesh, flirtations and Facebook. His team were playing lowly Walsall.

It would have been half-time by now, up there in the Midlands. He could have gone, but there was a greater urgency in the gardening project.

Packing up his tools shortly after four, he felt this was the right decision. Seeing people go home happy, talking about what they had done and their hopes for spring, he didn't really care about today's result.

'Besides,' he assured Fergus, 'we're as good as promoted.'

Historically, Bourdin's ghost might have a nasty habit of emergence after Christmas, but this team was good enough to see the battle through. Even on bleak days in the middle of December, they held firm. When he went to his room alone and switched on the TV, the game had finished a goal apiece, and Charlton remained top of the league.

'Let's see how Arsenal got on.'

One-nil victory at home to Everton, with a goal from the Dutch striker Robin Van Persie on the afternoon of their 125th anniversary. Assuming his support wasn't cosmetic, Merlin's boy would be happy. Next time, maybe next month, they could have a chat about football.

Between now and then, there was another road trip. This time he was heading westwards, through landscapes where autumn's freckles had changed to a dirty brown sludge. England has fewer forests, Fergus always said. It's a land of glass and not mountains, he argued, but on the drive to Yeovil this whole country seemed to be made of trees.

The Irishman was using Christmas to drown his last feelings for Katy.

'I've two choices,' he'd said. 'Go to the pub, get blind drunk.'

He had paused then, sinking towards temptation.

'Or I can go out and do something useful.'

He had opted for the latter, again thanks to his boys.

'I'm going to help feed the homeless on Christmas Day,' he had explained as they went on their separate ways. 'And I hope you have a good time up in Bristol with your mates from the army.'

He had said he was travelling there after the Yeovil game was done. Actually, he wasn't. But it was best for his friend to believe that he was. While Fergus was working in his soup kitchen, he had other plans.

One evening on Facebook, he told Katy he could come up to see her before New Year, to spend a night in Yorkshire maybe. She had agreed. He felt like a traitor, conscious of Fergus's suffering. You could sense his terrible pangs of loss and feel the silences which consumed him.

Working in the kitchen was his methadone for a dead addiction, like those electronic cigarettes that give you nicotine but not the warm smoke. Without the garden to work on, he had found another worthy cause. Anything would have done to help him forget, and he didn't need to know that his best friend was stealing his girl from under his nose. Besides, she wasn't *his*, and it wasn't a lie about his army mates.

He had agreed to meet some of them on the day before the game, the very same day when Fergus was rising at the crack of dawn, heading out to help the hungry and homeless, as if healing all the world's troubles.

Getting to Yeovil at the end of a drive across the thighs of England, he found a bed-and-breakfast motel, at half London's prices. There he settled in for the night, talking to Katy on Skype once again.

She had just returned from a walk across the moors, after cooking chilli for supper, and was still wrapped up in layers as she sat down, red-faced, by the computer. Slowly, she unpeeled a thick orange scarf and then her coat, saying that her fingers were numb from the cold outside, but burning under the fingernails from chopping up *local* Kashmiri peppers.

Seeing her remove the first layer of herself, he wished she would show him more. He wanted her to strip off the sweater and jeans, but she didn't even take off her Wellington boots. Seeming more tense than before, she was like a body mummified.

'Are you sure we're doing the right thing?'

'Do you feel guilty?' he asked.

Questions were easier than answers. 'You?'

'A little, but we're doing nothing wrong.'

'Not yet,' she agreed. 'This talking, whatever else we've done, it's only fiction, but if it becomes flesh then it's something else.'

'I know,' he admitted. 'These past months Fergus has been like a brother to me, and I'm stabbing him in the back. I think he loves you, and if he knew about us it would destroy him.'

'He thinks he loves me, and maybe he does in some ways,' Katy's voice was soft but sharp as a paper cut, 'but he doesn't know me.'

'Do I,' he asked, 'know you?'

She changed the subject as she would always do. It was a couple of days to Christmas, she noted, and then a couple of days later they could meet, if they should, for she was starting to get cold feet. But he hadn't time for games or wasting emotions after what he had gone through.

'We meet,' he insisted, 'or we stop these conversations.'

'I'll think about it,' she said. 'Don't ever shout at me again, and remember you don't own me just because you've seen me naked.'

'It's only fiction,' he reminded her, 'not flesh.'

But then, as if to blur the boundaries between fiction and flesh, she brought him back to the place they'd visited a few nights before, transporting the computer across the room to where she lay down, peeling off her clothes as she slipped beneath the duvet. This time, touching herself as he watched, she led him gradually downwards through glass, across mountainous boundaries, reaching secret valleys where the speed intensified to a dizzying haste. Seeing her moan and sigh, it was as if he too could feel the chilli, coming loose from beneath her fingernails, and spreading out in a slow trickle through her flesh and across the borders of hardware, into the open continent of cyberspace. It was as if they were entangled in a network of cables in a place far beneath the sea, losing themselves in a stir of red-hot waves dyed in chilli powder.

Several times, she threatened to turn off the camera. Reaching out to touch her image on the screen, he begged her not to. He had never done anything like this before, with a real person behind the computer screen.

Listening to her sighs, seeing the look in her eyes, he felt sensations of boiling desire poured through him, forceful as the sound of match day. For the first time since the explosion, he could feel a tingling in the nerves of his shattered kneecap and recall the toes he didn't have. Though it was impossible, he was sure he could feel tingling down there too as his desire and the red volcano reached eruption.

'Enjoy that?' she asked when it was over.

'Yes, I certainly did,' he answered, struggling to stay awake, feeling like they were evens now as she held tight to her power over him, whispering that she was going to watch him as he fell asleep.

When he woke in the morning, she was gone, and the feeling was gone from his prosthesis too, but he was happy because he was going to meet his army mates. They would spend Christmas together, since they didn't want the fuss and the effort of being around their families.

'I know that sounds crazy,' they agreed, 'but seeing everybody together, happy, celebrating, brings back all these bad memories.'

You realise what you've lost and what you might never have again. Maybe with Katy he would find it. The others hadn't been so lucky.

One had seen his marriage collapse because he was screaming instead of his new-born baby at night. Another had tried suicide, even though the doctors certified that he wasn't depressed.

Others punched walls, smashed up kitchens, heard landmines all the time, and found themselves stuck in moments from the past, as unable to remember yesterday as they were unable to forget every detail of war.

In the meantime, Fergus helped the bedraggled and the bearded, weathered old men and addicts with hard-luck stories. This was his Christmas cause. Every so often the Irishman would send text messages and updates, each one prickly as a stomach full of holly leaves.

He made it through Christmas day with the help of conversations and beer. Katy's time was spent with her parents. After last night they needed a break from each other, even if this was nothing more than fiction.

On Boxing Day, he rose and made his way through the town towards Yeovil's old-fashioned West Country stadium. It was exactly what you would have expected from a rapidly-risen former non-league team.

At the start, thoughts of Katy served as his whisky on a cold day. Very soon, he didn't need artificial sustenance.

Amongst a faithful band of travelling supporters he found himself singing the usual away songs as the game got off to a blazing start.

'Yeovil's a shithole, I want to go home,' they sang, in the same way that opposition supporters taunted Charlton when they visited SE7.

'But actually,' he thought to himself, 'I'm going to Huddersfield.'

Distracted, gazing towards vitreous spaces in the clouds, the former soldier found himself lost in memories from a few nights before. Again, he could feel a tingling in his toes, an anticipation of what was to come in the days ahead, and that seemed more important than anything taking place on the pitch below. Through all his years of following football, nothing had ever taken his mind off the game this way.

He was thinking of her layers and getting beneath them the way a plough might cut through soil, seeing more than just the surface.

That though was beautiful, the most perfect body he had ever known. He had never known it before, never understood when people asked '*what's your type*', as if there's one. He was thinking of this, recalling every detail as the clouds foamed past. Then, moments later, the two worlds intersected. The heavy sighs and moans around him signalled a score for Yeovil, by a kid on loan from Tottenham Hotspur.

Soon after, the sighs turned into cries of delight as the visitors equalised. Suddenly, he could feel a red tide of heat going through him like mulled wine. Come the second half, the home team in green and white went ahead once more, sending their fans into cider-drunken celebrations, singing '*where's your shithole now?*'

Not for long though. This wasn't the Charlton of seasons past. Bourdin's ghost hadn't followed them on their journeys west.

Two goals, one from a Kermorgant free-kick, sent the travelling supporters home happy as 3-2 winners.

'Eight points clear at the top of the league,' he texted Fergus.

'Good,' the Irishman said and then fished for more information. 'When are you back?' Again, he tasted holly leaves as he read on. 'Now that all the feeding's done, it's getting boring here without you.'

'A few days,' he replied. 'A few more sleeps :).'

In truth, he was going to Huddersfield after one more sleep.

15
Northern Detour

Driving up from the West Country, he watched England's roads become small spheres of colour as he moved through darkness towards the north, following the moon as if it was Katy swimming through the night sky. Hedgerows gleamed in green orbs created by the headlamps. Bare trees and black thorns glistened. Reflections of stars danced like silverfish amongst the straight lines of cats' eyes, dug surface-deep in tarmac.

Night-swimming England's Midlands, he was far from London's December days, wrapped up in ragged bandages of mist like Fergus's beggars in the soup kitchen, fighting numbing cold, gnawing hunger. Not wanting to think of this, he recalled the game as he drove.

Bright colours on the pitch as darkness came. Standing in an open terrace, with cold fingers of air creeping through the windshields. Floodlights turning the pitch fierce green as darkness deepened.

Supporters screaming abuse at the goalkeeper as Yann Kermorgant curled his free kick towards the concrete steps of the away end.

Singing songs of celebration afterwards. Having one beer, sleeping it off in the guesthouse for a couple of hours, then wakening, packing up, handing in his keys and heading out of town at midnight.

'300 miles to Huddersfield,' the satellite navigation system announced from its centre-field position on the Torino's dashboard.

He preferred to drive in the night, on roads emptied of traffic. Travelling the 3rd division for half a season, he felt he had crossed the same portion of England. This was a good league for away supporters, even if the grounds weren't the greatest. You got to see places, and most people never get to see their country as a whole, catching only snapshots and fragments on television or through train windows. They don't get to drive its roads and know its landscapes, to feel like it's a part of them and they're a part of it, whatever *it* may be.

'I don't feel such an attachment to place,' Katy said a dozen hours after his drive had ended and he had reached his destination. He had sought out a hotel room then asked her where they would meet in the evening.

She had suggested a pub, on a hill, with a view stretching as far as Derbyshire, and the whole of Huddersfield, alight. Lights loosened from stony highlands towards a rollercoaster of terraced streets. Then a patch of floodlit green, a soft-blue oasis framed in a set of arches dipping inwards like gulls at full wingspan swooping down to the sea.

'That's where the football team plays.'

The stadium was stylish and modern unlike Yeovil's or Charlton's. He was impressed with this and the beauty of his company. Tonight, dressed in white, she was fluorescent as those arches, so much like a snowperson he feared she'd melt as they bought drinks, and took a seat by the fire.

Colour filled her cheeks at the mention of computer conversations, the way tongues of flame crackled through gaps in the burning logs. Sipping on a glass of wine, she told him stories of Huddersfield.

He told her stories from Afghanistan. Looking deep into her eyes as she listened, he noticed her pupils become as marble-blue as healing wells. She said that even though she hated wars, for some reason he gave her clarity.

'You make me feel protected,' she suggested.

Yet she wanted to depend on nobody, least of all on a soldier.

'Used to be a soldier,' he clarified then moved to kiss her.

But as he leaned across, she pulled away as if she wasn't ready for that. Going back to talking, he couldn't make sense of all her contradictions. She shrugged her shoulders, bouncing her gaze off the wine glass and the reflections of fire caught in its curves. As if neither could make sense of what had gone before or what was still to come between them. There was nothing else to do but go to the bar, order another drink, come back, sit down together, sharing blue stares and awkward silences, hoping there was some way of breaking each other's shells.

Gradually as the night wore on, the lights reduced on the hillsides, the fire died and the drinks took effect, the shells began to soften. At first almost imperceptibly, a hairline crack, and then a sudden fracture. He had been describing the drive north, and she leaned in closer to listen.

'Underneath the soldier there's a poet,' she whispered, then paused. 'I'm starting to regret not kissing you, now.'

'There's still time,' he said, feeling sharp pain as he spoke, as if a fragment of eggshell was trapped beneath his fingernails.

Again he leaned close, and this time she didn't refuse. Suddenly, he was kissing the woman he might have been put on this planet to meet, if there was more to life than simply random chance.

The wine had melted the fireguard of her eyes, as he leaned close. Though soft, her mouth was cold as dough. Like the kiss was detached from the rest of her body, not coming from her heart. Still, he had waited for this a long time and wasn't going to lose it.

'Want to come to my hotel?' he asked afterwards.

'What would Fergus make of that proposition?'

He didn't want to think of Fergus. 'I don't know.'

'Okay,' she said, and then asked the barman to call a cab.

The journey was a slow, ever-darkening downhill drive. Trying not to think of Fergus, he looked at the woman beside him, white as a banshee, radiant as the last lights of farms on the hillside. Taking her hand in his, he kissed her again in the back of the cab.

The driver, an elderly Sikh, looked bemused in the presence of young love as they pulled up outside Lance's hotel, right in the centre of town. Quickly they got out, paid the fare, and made their way inside. Once upstairs, after a fight with a stubborn key-card, they found themselves alone, or half-alone, because Fergus was a ghostly presence inside Lance's head, and possibly Katy's too, though he dared not ask her about it.

The room, which was going to be the first where they made love, was a double en-suite with a bed the colour of Valentine red and chocolate brown. On the sideboard, by the customary TV and coffee tray, they discovered a complimentary bowl of fruit and bottles of champagne you could buy. The silence was such that they needed the sounds of both. She peeled the fruit as he uncorked the champagne and filled the glasses.

Without speaking, they faced off on the edge of the bed, letting hands drift across the fruit, until they interlocked in the middle. She picked a grape off the bunch, laughing, feeding him from her hands.

He started to do the same, but crushed the fruit against her cheek, letting the juice run down her skin. Very soon, they'd fallen about the place, smearing each other's upper bodies in juices, sharing bites from the same apple, and then drinks straight from the bottle, becoming more giddy, passionate, and intoxicated with every swallow.

Then she rose suddenly, dressing down in the middle of the room. He stood up to do the same, more conscious of his prosthesis than any other part of his body, as her pupils turned into blue fire once more.

Stepping backwards, feeling awkward, he found the bed, turned away from Katy's gaze, pulled the chocolate covers over, and prepared to remove the artificial leg before she got in beside him.

'No,' she said, as if keeping it on aroused her.

Getting in beside him, she lifted his hands away from his kneecap, raising them up towards the grapes of her bosom. When he closed his eyes to strengthen all his other senses, for a few seconds she felt as cool and smooth as apple skin, sounded of sighs, tasted of champagne and turned ever more fragrant from the fermentation of desire.

He had never thought a woman would find him attractive ever again, not to mention push herself against the prosthesis as if every touch aroused her another droplet more. This was more than he had ever imagined, swimming in the tides of her desire, fighting to forget the betrayal of his friend, concentrating on the blue snatches of her eyes and the sting of her fingers floating, bobbing, clinging as jellyfish.

Sobbing, soaping, smearing, sipping, sighing into one another's bodies, the fruit bowl changed to pulp, and then seeds of pain inside their bellies, from which they needed relief, but couldn't let go of.

Finally, as the ache reached a bottleneck, she allowed him inside. Here she seemed different. Silent but suffering, screaming within. Several times he pushed against her without reaction, as if she had suddenly gone numb from pins and needles, punch-drunk on fruit, until the seeds of pain shot out of him and the suffering concluded.

He tried to make conversation. 'Better than technology?'

'Sure,' she replied, 'but I'm already feeling guilty.'

'Fergus,' he presumed, thinking of his friend as a dead weight coming between them, as she sat up and began to dress.

Suddenly the room felt cold, as if frostbite had crept down from the castle hill where they had spent the evening. The fires of the pub and the lights of the leaping dolphin's stadium were suddenly extinguished.

Only the shandy glow of a bedside lamp remained.

'Perhaps we shouldn't have done this.'

Sensing shame in her voice, he protested. 'It's okay.'

'Fergus is a nice guy,' she said softly. 'Doesn't deserve this.'

'He's a man the same as me,' he argued. 'He's no saint.'

She turned her body on the pillows so she was facing him again with curious eyes. 'What do you mean by that?'

'I can't say,' he told her. 'It's not my place.'

'You've started saying it,' she pursued.

He wasn't going to labour the point. 'Forget it.'

'If you won't talk to me, I'll go.'

'Don't go,' he pleaded as her eyes demanded answers.

'Why did you say that Fergus is no saint?'

'Because he was in prison. Because when he was a teenager, he was the driver of a stolen car that killed his girlfriend.'

'The gang,' she whispered inexplicably.

'They weren't a gang,' he told her. 'Just kids from a small town messing around, and one of them died after a police car chase.'

Katy rose from the bed. 'I've got to go.'

'Stay the night,' he reached out to her.

She was already up, moving towards the door.

'Don't ever tell anyone about this,' she wagged a finger.

'Wait,' he called after her, struggling to rise.

By the time he found his footing, she was gone. She had hurried down the stairs and out into the silvered streets of her northern mill town. High above the lines of grey buildings, a stone lion prowled.

If he could see the streets from such a height, there might have been a chance of finding her. As it was, the darkness had swallowed her up. When he tried calling her on the phone, she wouldn't answer. There was nothing to do but go back to bed and lie down as if in a fever.

'I'm going home in the morning,' he swore.

Getting through an almighty hangover, he kept to his word. Assuaging guilt and rage, he got in the Torino and drove to London. This time the roads were busier, cased in black ice, while the countryside was crystallised in frost. Along the way, he stopped off in Sheffield and ate lunch, thinking about the rest of the season.

Next month, his team played both of Sheffield's football clubs. Away, one Saturday, at Wednesday. Home, the next, to United. If they took four points from those two games, possibly even two, they would get promoted, regardless of bad women and Bourdin's ghost.

Thinking of this, he drove on. Past bare trees and into the early darkness that stretched a few minutes more since his trip to Yeovil. Reaching London, he felt that only frost in the air signified the season.

He parked the Torino, slipped inside, turned on no lights and went to bed, to sweat some more out of his system. When morning came, his head was clear for the first time in months. He rose early, worked a couple of hours, checked out the state of his gardens, walked by the river, came back and summoned the courage to find Fergus.

'Working with the homeless was amazing,' the Irishman said. 'So busy, there wasn't time to think of anything else, anybody else.'

'That's good. So you've got *her* out of your system?'

Fergus didn't want to discuss that. 'How was your trip?'

'Fine,' he replied, not wanting to discuss parts of that either. 'Winning at Yeovil on Boxing Day was great.'

'What's next on the agenda?'

'Away to Orient,' he answered. 'Live on TV, New Year's Eve.'

The days passed slowly until the game, with no news from Katy. Saturday evening, as the final hours of 2011 approached, Charlton's league leaders travelled east across the Thames to Olympic country.

There, in the back streets of Leyton, one tube stop from Stratford, they found Orient's Brisbane Road stadium. Just down the road, London was preparing to host the 'Games of the Triple X Olympiad'.

Very soon, the eyes of the world would focus upon this forgotten corner of England's capital. There would be a frenzy for a fortnight, Lance presumed, before everybody cleared off and the grounds emptied.

'They're going to give the stadium to a football club,' he told Fergus as they settled down in front of the television, 'and that's probably not going to be Orient, even if they're the most local.'

'Tottenham Hotspur or West Ham United, isn't it?'

'Yeah, somebody bigger, less local, more fashionable.'

This was a new age of gentrification for east London, he explained, where there had to be collateral damage in the name of progress, regardless of sentiment. These days, nobody wanted to be held back by the past. There was no room for the foolish, romantic stories his grandfather used to tell. Many of Orient's players from long ago fought and died for the Footballer's Battalion in The Somme Offensive during World War One.

Like so many generations of Londoners before and since, they sacrificed their lives for their country – and got back what exactly?

'A wreath of poppies, a couple o' medals and a team they'll eventually call Stratford Olympic kicking a ball across their graves.'

With every day that passed, bulldozers steered closer to Brisbane Road in the headlamps of seven values named as respect, excellence, friendship, courage, determination, inspiration and quality. If a Premier League club moved into that stadium a couple of years from now, Leyton Orient FC would face a hell of a fight to survive.

Maybe this was why they started tonight's match with passion. Wearing red, they went at the task as eager as lovers in a hotel room. Charlton, in white away strip, struggled to get going.

'Wake up lads!' Lance barked.

But instead of waking up, the visitors showed signs of half-sleep. Six minutes into the game, Ben Hamer came rushing off his line, hitting the ball with his armpit outside the box. Instantly, the referee flashed red against the darkness of Leytonstone's back streets.

Dazed, Charlton had to reshuffle in the face of change. Twenty minutes later the home team scored, after a spell of domination, and held onto a deserved lead for the rest of the game, no matter how loudly the armchair supporters screamed and swore.

'It's a long way to East London,' said Fergus. 'They're not going to hear us with all the dozers and diggers over there, these days.'

'Beaten on New Year's Eve,' Lance grumbled as the game ended. 'Still we're going into Olympic year top o' the league.'

Despite the defeat, there was no point spending the night indoors.

'I've spent far too many New Year's Eves inside.'

'We'll go on a good old Greenwich pub crawl.'

Like a couple of sailors from bygone days, they made their way through the grounds of the Naval College, passing the sight of the Painted Hall in all its imperial glory, and the sound of Chapel bells ringing out across the cobblestones, before reaching a riverside tavern. There, settling by a fireside, they looked out on the Thames.

'Seems long since the riots,' said the Irishman, gazing across at fireworks rising up through London's festive village lights.

Lance agreed that it was, as he looked to the firelight, wondering if this was a time for honesty, as his friend had wondered in the past. It had taken time, but he had shared the story of his imprisonment.

Enacting a double betrayal, Lance had shared that story with Katy. He had been thinking with his balls, not his conscience.

'Supposing I told him, what'd he do?'

Maybe he would have, if things hadn't changed so radically when he got back from the toilets and found Fergus staring down at his phone.

'Look,' he said as he passed it across. 'It's from her.'

Lance shivered and his heart raced as he whispered the words *Hello. Saw Charlton playing football on TV and thought of you.*

Suddenly his heart was thumping so much it was going to punch a hole through his chest and take years off his life if it didn't stop.

You think you're cured of something. You tell yourself you're over it, that the whole thing meant nothing, and then you're caught in a moment of confrontation which brings it all flooding back again.

Feeling like he was trapped in a tunnel with somebody he wanted to avoid, Lance read on, trying to blink in the light to assist his bleary, blinded pupils. '*Hope you had a happy Xmas. Happy New Year. X.*' Hands shaking, he gave the phone back to Fergus. 'What are you going to do?'

'Nothing,' Fergus answered. 'I'm not even going to reply.'

'So you've finally shaken her off then?'

Lance fought hard to conceal the crackle in his voice and the riotous emotions passing through his skull as he thought of Katy. His head was on fire, as if with a migraine, and he felt a raw terror he had known only twice before – in the seconds after the IED explosion and in the days beyond as he faced the knowledge of amputation.

'I'm tired of playing games,' the red-headed man spoke insistently. 'Only ones I want to see from now on are those involving Charlton.'

'Here's to Sheffield then,' Lance raised his glass.

'To Sheffield's defeat,' his friend corrected him.

Tired of women's games, Lance thought football seemed far simpler.

By the time the bells of 2012 sounded, they were both merrily drunk. She could stay in Huddersfield for all he cared, and he hoped Fergus felt the same way, for seeing her text message was hard enough. Hearing her voice again could cost his heart whole decades.

Lance's resolution for the New Year was simple and twofold: watching Charlton win promotion and finishing the garden.

'We've got to do it now,' he said, like his life depended on it, as they wandered back through the College in the moonlight.

Getting into bed, Lance wished he had never taken the detour north.

'Takes a long time to get over riots,' he thought.

16
Blades of Truth

Cold daylight, sharp as a Turkish barber's razor, marked the start of the New Year as Fergus walked through the college grounds seeking out breakfast in a silent village where almost everything was closed. He made his way down to the river and its pubs, the source of his hangover from the night before, holding tight to the railings, looking across at the glass frontage of Canary Wharf, and missing mountains again.

It had been a good night, though no matter where you are you should be able to make New Year's Eve good. Watching the ambivalent tide of mid-morning, he felt seagulls whine in his head. Memories of the night before, mixed with memories of long-decayed first Januarys past, came at him in rushes. He could see flames atop the face of his own reflection in the Thames.

These were fires on the head of a traitor, a hypocrite, a straw man. Despite all his insistence and protestations, he had conceded defeat. Shortly after midnight, going to the toilets, he had found her on the wall; fungus getting inside his head, growing on the yeast of his thoughts.

'Did you see the picture of Marilyn Monroe in the toilets?' Lance had asked earlier that night, before he had noticed.

There was a time when she had been his alone, the mysterious woman across the way who occupied a fictional space in their chatter. He was welcome to her, as was every other man.

'We've no interest in her world of horses and hockey,' they both agreed. 'She probably even went to public school.'

They should have known the cold steel truth all along. Chelsea girls and Charlton boys don't mix. But despite this, despite having all this knowledge and choosing to ignore her, he had found himself fish-hooked by the glassy smile of an actress on the toilet walls. Forgetting all he had said before, he got subsumed in a wave of nostalgia and texted: '*Happy New Year.*'

Standing by the river, he regretted it, feeling as if he was the man in charge of the Thames Barrier, who had opened the shells just a little too wide, and allowed more water than was healthy into the stream. Wanting to dyke his feelings, he turned back towards the college, hoping she wouldn't answer, and she hadn't so far, which was good. Passing the Painted Hall, peeping inside, he caught flashes of ambivalence in the faces upon this historical pastiche, an ironic indifference to the passage of time in the place where it all began.

Time's footsteps quickened after he found a solitary café open and sponged his stomach in waves of grease from an Atlantic breakfast. Almost before he knew it, days had passed without any reply and he had travelled across the city, reaching a Chelsea girl's heartland. Though there was no countryside, no sign of stables nor hockey sticks, on the train he caught sight of young ladies with tennis racquets and thought of how she would look in the same pristine white costume.

Getting inside Craven Cottage, he thought the same again. Fulham's players happened to be wearing the same colours, which worsened the situation, as they shone fluorescent against the grass, warming up for their FA Cup 3rd round home tie against Charlton.

Lance had managed to secure tickets for this London derby, and they had fine seats in the cold heights of the away end inside a small, homely ground, even closer to the River Thames than their own.

Last time, against Orient, the team in white started badly. Today, cheered on by thousands, they were back in their familiar red strip, though, as Lance pointed out, they had worn white shirts when they won the Cup in 1947. These days, the best they could hope for was getting through the opening rounds and maybe causing a shock along the way, against opponents such as these, two divisions higher.

Eight minutes into the game, dreams of a shock subsided as Fulham's American striker Clint Dempsey ghosted goalwards. A few seconds later, the whites were in a huddle, the reds behind, their hands on their hips, trudging back to the halfway line. Momentarily, the away end had fallen so silent you could hear the river whispering in its flow towards Putney Bridge. Seconds later the action resumed, the songs and the eagerness too, as the red men began to put up a fight. Kermorgant came close to scoring, while Wright-Phillips, his partner in crime, made a series of dashes towards goal.

By half-time there was renewed hope as they queued for chips amongst the masses and got them just as the game was starting again. They ate, cheered, watched their men battling, waited for an equaliser and caught signs of its coming, before Clint Dempsey pounced again. Two more followed in quick succession as he claimed a hat trick.

'Where did that come from?' Lance wondered as they exited the Cottage for the long slow tramp back towards Putney. 'Eighty minutes gone, we looked good for a draw.'

'Maybe that's what's great about football,' Fergus supposed.

His friend wasn't happy. 'Losing four nil?'

'No, I mean never knowing what to expect.'

A few evenings later, as he was standing by the window, something else challenged his expectations. As darkness gathered, he caught sight of a woman's silhouette on a bicycle set against the Thames.

'Katy,' he thought aloud.

She was back in London, shaking up his emotions like a pebble caught in a spinning top of uncertainty. His first thought was to rush down there, say hello, ask what she was doing.

Hearing echoes of the word 'harassment', he hesitated.

This time though, she was the one doing the chasing. Some minutes later, as a knock came to the door and his chest thumped, he had reached a crossroads with his head and heart deciphering different routes.

The heart, though gentler, won in the end as he opened the door, saw her standing there and uttered a faint 'Hello.'

She replied with the same as she stepped inside, dressed in black, and accepted his offer of a coffee, a tea, or whatever she preferred. Coffee, she decided, and he whipped up a flat white at the speed of a barista. Then, as he passed it across, he asked her what she was doing back.

'Aren't you glad to see me?' she wondered.

For once, he soldered his gaze so his eyes revealed no truth.

She hardened too. 'I'm back to pack my things and go for good.' Lifting her blue-green eyes to the ceiling, she sipped as she spoke. 'Perhaps I shouldn't have come raking up old ground.'

'The ground's gone hard,' he skirted around the subject.

'I know,' she said. 'I've seen Lance's garden.'

'It's going to be very different in the spring.'

'Shame I won't be around to see it, but it's for the best.'

He slurped his coffee. 'Suppose so.'

'You can send me flowers as a souvenir.'

Anger ruptured in his windpipe, rising suddenly upwards.

'To give you more evidence of harassment?'

Her eyes dilated, gemstone-blue. Her voice was emotional.

'That was my way of protecting myself.'

'From what? Somebody loving you?'

'I thought you were in a gang,' she protested.

'And so what if I was?'

She needed to get off her high middle-class horse and recognise that not everybody had the chances in life she had got.

'It's not the worst thing in the world,' he insisted, crossing the floor to refuel with caffeine, thinking of his boys in Deptford.

'All our sufferings seem small compared to those of others,' she suggested. 'But I know about yours. Lance told me, accidentally.'

'About what?' he asked, though he already knew.

'The stolen car,' she confirmed, 'the crash, the girl.'

'Lance should stick to talking football and gardens.'

She brushed aside his opinion. 'Since I know your secrets, there's something you need to know to understand me better.'

This was a different, more honest Katy than the one he had known, or hadn't. Bowing her head to the empty coffee cup, she was preparing to speak, but couldn't, afflicted by a sudden emotional dyslexia. Watching her, he was touched and confused. Time had evaporated, becoming as meaningless for them as the ghosts of Greenwich.

Finally she broke the haunting silence. 'One time, you asked me about the dark-haired girl I used to be.' He remembered and nodded. 'Who was she? Where did she go to? Why don't I keep pictures?'

Intrigued, he kept nodding as her voice fell to a whisper.

'She went away to a very dark place, one night in the winter.'

He didn't understand. He had no idea where this was leading.

'She was eighteen, starting out in college, out for the night with a new friend she had made, coming home not so late after a few drinks. They're taking pictures and they're laughing, dreaming almost.'

Her pupils darkened. The lines around her eyes deepened.

'Suddenly there's a noise. They snap out of a dream and find themselves in the shadows of a high-rise estate.'

He had a terrible sense of foreboding about where this was headed.

'Together, they get this feeling like when you're crossing a field in the countryside and you suddenly realise there's a bull in the middle.'

Again he nodded, having known, experienced such a thing.

'Except there's a whole herd of young bulls in this field.'

'Oh Jesus,' he thought, reaching out to touch her.

She pulled away, rising up, crossing to the window.

'Suddenly they're stone cold sober, not laughing anymore, trying to get out of there before the bulls catch up with them.

But it's hopeless because there's too many, and they don't know the territory.'

He rose up to go beside her, to turn her face around and look into her eyes, dry as stone walls, as she continued with the dark girl's story.

'They try to run, but they're lost in a stone maze, looking for lights, doors they can knock on to say they're being chased and need shelter, but this is London, where every house belongs to a stranger.'

She was trembling, staring out on the very same lights.

'Soon they're cornered, surrounded by bulls.'

'You don't have to tell me everything.'

She was in a world of her own, deep in the darkness.

'They're helpless, and there's no point fighting,' she whispered, 'as they're taken down through the maze towards warehouses. When they finally reach one, it's a former slaughterhouse.'

Still he saw no tears, just resolute anger, a sense of injustice.

'When they get there, they're stripped down to their underwear, mocked, judged, and the gang's laughing like it's some sick computer game and they're about to fill their memory sticks with the hard drive of someone else's life.'

'I get the picture,' he wanted to say.

'They're taken downstairs into separate rooms.'

'How many?' he wondered. 'How many memory sticks?'

'That dark-haired girl, she feels like she's going to die.'

He tried to reach out again. 'Wasn't your fault.'

This time as she turned around, she became that girl.

'When we got to the room, the smell of death was worse.'

She lifted her eyes to the ceiling. 'Above them there was a lighting system and a pulley for transporting carcasses into boats on the riverside.' Her voice fell to a whisper, through clenched teeth. 'My first thought was that this was where I'd end up when they were done with me. Already, from the sounds of laughing and sobbing and different kinds of rage, I could tell they'd started on my friend down the corridor.'

She clenched her fists, pushing them hard against the glass.

'But I wasn't going to end up the same way, poisoned with their viruses,' she spoke through panes. 'At that second, needing to be smarter than ever before, my brain worked. I'll dance for you, I said. Stand back and watch, I told them.'

They did, she added, expecting nothing else of a *bitch*.

'Then, as they stood distracted, at a distance, I grabbed the ropes holding the pulley in place.' She drummed her knuckles together, reliving the scene. 'The whole thing was rickety so the lighting system and the trolleys for dead cattle came crashing down on top of them like one of those horrible castration devices I remember seeing farmers using on cattle and sheep when I was a little girl, and being glad that I wasn't a boy. But this time I was happy at the thought of the life being crushed out of them in the jaws of that clamp.'

'Good for you,' he said, thrilled by her victory.

'Good?' she wondered.

He listened as she forced her way out through a broken window, fleeing the former slaughterhouse, running from the echo of young bulls caged, suffering, and chastened beneath sheets of rigging.

'I ran to the river, leaving my friend behind.'

She was the one who suffered as Katy struggled to trust the world enough to approach an all-night grocery and call the police.

'Killed?' he asked, but she shook her head.

'They smashed her emotions, and she never forgave me.'

As if still running away, Katy paused to catch breath.

'Worst for her, I guess, was that only three were caught.'

'The ones hospitalised by your rope trick?'

'Yes, that's a nice way of putting it,' she surmised. 'So, we've both got our ghosts, Fergus, girls who won't get out of our minds.'

This time, as he reached out, she buried her head in his chest.

'Maybe you should stay. Just for the night.'

'Okay,' she agreed. 'I'd like that.'

She said she felt dirty and needed a shower.

'Sure,' he replied and gave her fresh towels, wondering if he knew her more, or less, as she made her way to the bathroom.

When she was gone and he heard the water running, he sat down, head in hands, and started crying. Maybe she was doing the same, feeling minutes evaporate, as she stayed there for aeons.

By the time she came out again, he had made her a bed on the settee. There was no more talk of young bulls and slaughterhouses in the days that followed. She decided to stick around London for a while. She did explain though how the dark-haired girl had turned blonde.

'Overnight I decided to change. Besides, it was at the end of the court case. You're shaken up and paranoid for a long time after, especially when you see the short sentences they're given.'

Newly blonde, she had never gone back to black.

'I told myself that no man would ever hurt me again.'

They could have her flesh, she added, but not what was inside.

'The past's like a first tattoo,' he supposed. 'No matter how many times you try to cover it over, it keeps coming back to the surface.'

They would stay friends for now, they agreed.

'That's good,' Lance said when he heard the news on Saturday. They met in the corridor as he was setting out for Sheffield, where Charlton faced Wednesday. 'Friendship's important.'

'How did she know though?' Fergus wanted to ask.

Why did she know about Lucy, the joyride and his time in prison? His friend was in a hurry, and the Torino's windscreen needed defrosting, so he would get no answers until after the game.

Even half a day later, when Lance returned, he talked about nothing except the game. By then, he had caught the highlights on TV. Hillsborough, entrenched in history, was a boiling cauldron of anticipation as 27,000 supporters filled two thirds of its capacity. The noise, Lance claimed, was so intense, so deafening they must have heard it in Huddersfield, thirty miles down the road from the Steel City.

'How's he such an expert on Yorkshire all of a sudden?'

But there wasn't time to ask as he described the opening minutes. Wednesday, solid as a knife block, took the fight to Charlton.

'They were physical, but the ref was having none of it.'

With 26 minutes gone, he awarded Charlton a free kick.

'Johnnie Jackson steps up and we're all praying.'

Fergus could picture the scene of a deep-freeze day when supporters dream of a Maracanã moment, a real-life Roy-of-the-Rovers story.

'He's making slow, steady moves towards the ball.'

He could sense a knot of tension in the away end.

'He's about to strike. Everybody's hanging on their seats...' Suddenly he rose out of the chair he was sitting on, buried his head in his hands with a cry of woe and exultation at the same time. 'Just as he's about to hit it, some bastard comes into the stadium late.'

Now, he seemed to be crying and laughing at the same time.

'He's blocking my view, stumbling half-pissed in front o' me.'

'Oh, God no,' Fergus sympathised.

'Yeah, and then there's a mighty roar,' his friend continued. 'Johnnie's scored a screamer, as close as anything Hillsborough's going to get to Cristiano Ronaldo in these 3rd division days and I'm the only fucker in the stadium who didn't get to see it. Still, we won.'

They had survived a second-half siege as the day turned gradually from blue to black and the clock slowed to a snail's pace.

Finally, when the whistle came, Charlton's players danced an exhausted conga towards the away end. Chris Powell stood amongst his men; arms aloft, teeth blazing, thanking the fans for their faith.

'If we beat Sheffield United a week from now,' Lance enthused, 'we could be ten points clear by the end of the month. But then again this is Charlton, not Melchester Rovers. We don't do fairytale endings.'

'We don't need fairytales,' Fergus thought.

If you do, go and support Manchester United. Take the easy choice. Support a team where you don't get hurt so often. Like fantasising over pictures of movie stars in magazines instead of chasing real girls. Wanting them always to be sexy and polished under the spotlights.

Katy Prunty had stripped off all her polish and allowed him to see what was underneath, but they hadn't touched, hadn't kissed. She was staying for a few weeks, she said, and then she would move back home.

These evenings were a special season when they could be together. Soon she would go and he would be left with Omar, his boys and community gardening on Wednesday afternoons, even if there was little you could do on gloomy days in the depths of January.

The nights were full of shimmering frosts after she would come and talk for a while in his room and then go again, as if she were a ghost of Greenwich. Sometimes, before sleeping, they would wrap up and walk amongst ghosts down by the Painted Hall or by the riverside.

There, as midnight's fog smothered the lights of London's villages and Canary Wharf's sparkling towers, they could have been wandering lost in the middle of nowhere, in South Armagh's dark mountains.

'No wonder people imagine ghosts,' he said.

'The only ghosts,' she suggested, 'are inside us.'

'It's true,' he agreed as he thought of how they were helping each other exorcise the ghosts which had haunted them for so long. 'But they make for good stories, selling Greenwich to tourists.'

'Yes, and Greenwich is pretty good at capturing ghosts,' she said. 'Everyone from King Henry's wives to Jack the Ripper's victims. There's even stories of him as a mad genius from Blackheath.'

Before he had time to reply, something stirred in the shadows. Jack perhaps, they both thought at the same time as their eyes connected briefly, catching sparkles of old habits and feelings. He would have leaned close if she had given him encouragement. He would have kissed her for the first time in months and done so gladly, but Jack's figure had assumed a solid form, moving through the mists.

'You gave us a fright,' she spoke first.

As always, the boy mumbled, 'Sorry.'

She looked into his eyes, shining like headlamps. 'It's okay.'

'Was seeing my mom,' he spoke sadly.

'Where does she live?' Fergus wondered.

'Flats,' the boy gave little away, but he seemed lonesome.

'You should come to the gardening Wednesdays.'

Again he mumbled. 'Prefer Saturdays.'

'Don't you like the company of other boys?'

'Don't care,' he said and turned to go.

'Wait,' Fergus caught his arm.

'Let go,' he screeched in a high-pitched voice.

Then he was gone, another mystery of the night.

'I was only trying to help.'

'Sometimes you can try too hard,' Katy said. 'There's something not right about Merlin's boy, but it's not any of our business.'

She was right. They had their own lives to lead, and she needed somebody to accompany her to a fashion show on Friday night.

'With the Shoreditch crowd again,' he presumed.

'Yes,' she answered. 'Don't you like them?'

'I do, but I feel out of place.'

'Like me at a football game.'

'Maybe that's the trade-off,' he suggested.

'Oh come on, you can't be serious.'

'Yes, I go to your fashion show, you come to the football.'

'There's no comparison,' she protested. 'Drinking wine in the company of pretty girls, inside in the warmth, versus sitting outside amongst thugs, drunk on beer, screaming abuse at each other?'

'That's not what football's like,' he argued. 'You'll see.'

'I'll come if I can read my book.'

'That'd be an insult, like reading during a West End show.'

'Why? Is *the Phantom of the Opera* playing? Or *Priscilla*?' Pausing, she laughed. 'Players roll around like drama queens anyway.'

'Fuck, you really do hate football.'

'Yes, which part of this didn't you get before? I could spell it out for you, letter by letter. I H-A-T-E-F-O-O-T-B-A-L-L – full stop.'

'What did football ever do to you?' he wondered.

'Nothing to me, nothing for me,' she replied.

'Okay then, we'll forget my suggestion.'

'No, I'll go to prove a point,' she softened unexpectedly.

'We'll go Saturday after the community gardening.'

Again, he could have kissed her but didn't. Same as Friday night, the fashion show in the historic Bishopsgate Library. There, as they wandered the dusty aisles between cases and shelves, several times they leaned close as if losing their footing, intoxicated by the fragrance of words and the feel of antiquarian books on their fingertips.

'If you want a book for tomorrow, there's plenty here.'

She shook her head, smiled and spoke softly.

'I'll be too busy looking out for the phantom.'

All through the show and on the way home, he could smell Bishopsgate Library, in traces of paper off her skin, and wine on her breath, staying so strong it was still with him in the morning. Regardless of his hangover and the pleasure of lying on the pillow remembering, he rose at sunrise for some gardening.

It was so cold outside that there were no spiders in the ground. Instead, the gardens teemed with another species. Human beings from different parts of the world, working together, broken up into teams. Merlin's boy was amongst them, and the young Somalians.

Lance worked with the boy, showing him plans for the orchard.

'Along this side, we'll have fruit trees a year or two from now.'

The boy, who had bright eyes, looked and listened through a hoodie. Their head gardener was thinking long-term, planning for the future. So was Fergus as hours passed and the game approached.

Lance kept on working as if he had lost track of time.

'Aren't you coming? It's almost two.'

'Might give it a miss today,' he said, unusually.

'But it's the biggest game of the season so far,' Fergus was stunned. 'Even Katy's going today. You can sit with us.'

But he was insistent. 'You go ahead without me.'

Fergus packed up his gardening gloves. 'Okay.'

After a quick wash, he raced to the station, caught a train and made his way towards the statue where he had first kissed Katy Prunty.

She was sitting on the base by Sam Bartram's boots.

'All ready?' he asked and she said that she was.

Slowly, they made their way inside to the East Stand after queuing up and buying tickets on a day that was busier than usual.

'About 20,000 people here,' he supposed.

'Like a full house in a theatre,' she said nervously.

She would have preferred the Saturday matinee to this, and she had a choice of books in her bag but was prepared to give football a chance.

'It's a frosty afternoon,' he said, searching for their place.

She sniffled in agreement, edging towards the cold steam of the centre circle, and their ringside seats. As she surveyed the Valley, her eyes had the glaze of someone in a foreign country for the first time. The Jimmy Seed Stand was far from the Grand Circle of West End theatres. There would be no phantoms swinging in on chandeliers – just shirtless Sheffield fans with moon heads and bellies as big as Jupiter.

'They're such a northern stereotype,' she grumbled.

Still, she had always supposed football inhabited a galaxy of stereotypes. Before he had time to answer, the players were out on the pitch and 'Red Robin' sounded across the PA system. Everybody rose to their feet at this stage except Katy, who stayed small down there.

The tension was about to abate as the players assumed positions. Seconds later, the whistle sounded. Saturday's matinee had started.

'The Sheffield players seem bigger,' she observed.

'Yes,' he agreed, 'and they're more physical.'

This was going to be a wrestling match as much as a football game. Steeling themselves for battle, they tried to outmuscle the home side. They were sending the ball down the flanks, up to their centre forwards. One of those, a young Welshman, had been in the news for a rape charge. Charlton's supporters weren't going to forgive and forget.

'She said no!' they sermonised from the North Stand, trying to unsettle him every time he touched the ball. 'Oh she said no!'

'What's that about?' Katy asked.

Fergus felt uncomfortable. 'I'll explain later.'

'Tell me now,' she demanded, sensing its meaning.

'Wait,' he insisted as the game drew back their attention.

'The Dutchman's down!' shouted a wiry old lady as United's full back clattered Danny Hollands to the ground. 'Free kick?'

'Yes!' Three sides of the stadium spoke then erupted into a chant. 'No one whacks 'em like Jackson!'

Fergus thought back to Lance's story of how he had missed the goal a week ago when Wednesday and Saturday intersected in Sheffield.

This free kick was from the same angle, but a few yards further out.

'Give us another Ronaldo moment,' he pleaded to his team captain, wishing Lance was here to see it. 'Come on Johnnie boy.'

Surely it was too much to hope for, he thought as he struck the leather in the direction of naked beer guts conspiring to distract him with catcalls. They wobbled, bounced, made faces out of nipples and belly buttons.

Johnnie, lean as Svevo's last cigarette, didn't give a damn.

The rest of the stadium, including Katie and the players, sighed as one.

Slowly, surely, the ball travelled towards the goal, taking an eternity to cross the thirty yards and few inches between the highs and lows of success and failure. Most likely, it would skim the crossbar, come back out, get whacked down the other end and they would score.

That, after all, was Charlton. They didn't do fairy stories, or comic-book endings. No, the Valley was like Kansas in

The Wizard of Oz and better times always remained nothing more than a distant dream over the rainbow. Today, as always, the hot smoke of hope would go cold very quick.

'No!' he already anticipated the outcome as the ball curled towards the crossbar.

But everyone else was shouting 'yay-asssss!' and celebrating with bear-hugs, including the manager and his team of assistants down on the sidelines.

'One-nil to the reds. Johnnie Jackson scores,' boomed the PA orchestrator, loud as the Wizard of Oz.

Two weeks in a row, the captain had scored with a magical strike.

'If only Lance was here to see it,' he said to Katy as everybody started hugging everyone else around them and he chose her.

It was strange choosing gardening over football, as if he had lost his faith, going through some kind of late-twenties search for meaning. Perhaps it was a delayed symptom of his post-traumatic stress.

Whatever the reason, there was no time to think of it now.

Sheffield's wrestlers were fighting hard and dirty as Giant Haystacks, trying to get back into the match.

'Hold to half-time,' Fergus prayed, and a Red God listened.

As darkness gathered and the whistle sounded, they took a break for tea, and Katy quizzed him on the song directed at the centre forward.

First, he was reluctant to tell her after what she'd gone through.

Eventually he relented, fearing she might start reading her book.

She rolled her eyes. 'Classy game, classy players.'

Hopefully come the second half she'd see a more positive side of the beautiful game; the passion, camaraderie, and Maracanã moments.

As soon as United stepped on the field, the songs started again. The referee's whistle sounded and the physical battle resumed.

'They're the best visiting team I've seen all season.'

'The only teams I've seen in a lifetime,' she joked.

Down on the pitch, the sustained pressure was no laughing matter, as the afternoon darkened and grew colder. Everything in their arsenal, United pushed on the Charlton defence, as fans breathed steam, punched the air, and spilled tea in the melee.

Stiff purple clouds suddenly began to race against the setting sun. Shots rained in on Ben Hamer's goal like arrows in a medieval battle, as Chrissie Powell galvanised his legions from the sideline. Minutes later, as the two sets of players clashed swords in the centre of the field, cards flashed yellow, then red, as the game turned unruly.

'Christmas was a bloody month ago!' screamed supporters.

Worst of all, there was five minutes of injury time.

'No, bloody no!' yelped a bulldog of a man as United's centre forward broke through on goal with seconds remaining.

'Phew,' the home audience sighed as his shot sailed over the bar.

Ben Hamer took a long time to collect the ball, counting down the seconds until the whistle sounded amid a mighty surge of relief.

'We won,' Fergus lip-synched the words of every fan.

The whole stadium had erupted to the moods of a gospel concert. Chrissie Powell was leaping and dancing on the touchline, enacting a two-fisted arch-backed jump into the air, the way he used to leap to the sky after his victories as a player. It was like he'd been holding these feelings inside for months, waiting for a moment such as this.

Suddenly, he was rising like a gospel singer towards Heaven. It was the jump of a man driven by higher belief, by love, by ambition, and faith that there's triumph at the end of every tunnel of black woe.

Then he faded down a white tunnel, paused, changed his mind, and came back again for a second leap of celebration and then a third. They'd seen something special this afternoon, a man of reticence and humility baring his soul to the audience, on the afternoon when they *knew* they'd won promotion.

In the midst of it all, Katy was pressed tight against Fergus. Turning around, her eyes reflected powdery udders of cloud, and a mascara trail of jet lines.

'Looks like it's going to snow,' she whispered, pushing so close it was as if the whole weight of the crowd had pressed against his body in that moment.

The sky was reddish purple as methylated spirits above the Valley when she raised her eyes towards it, as if Svevo or James Joyce himself had scripted the scene. The first flakes of the winter would soon fall, covering the parks and gardens in layers of snow, then slush. Covering the two islands he inhabited, one in his heart, and one with his body, where he stood beside Katy; getting high on the silver foil of floodlights reflected in her eyes. At that moment, she leaned forward, connecting the heart to the rest of his body. He was as close to her lips as his team stood on the threshold of promotion, seven points clear at the division's summit. The show was almost over and for once Charlton might script a comic-book ending. There seemed no choice but to seal the moment with a kiss.

'Guess I'm staying,' she said, when the bubble burst some tens of seconds later, pinpricked by *Valley, Floyd Road*. 'Tonight, and after.'

17
Valentine Bouquets

Seeing them back together had been insufferable at the start. Like during those nights after the landmine exploded, he would suddenly waken from surreal dreams, feeling a sharp recoil of absence and then emptiness. Sometimes he avoided the sight of them. Other times, he went out of his way to see them, from a distance, searching for signs or reactions; weighed down, way down, like a deep-sea diver fishing for oysters.

'If the world knew,' he thought. 'If Fergus knew.'

But despite what she had done, he cared enough to hold his tongue. Besides, this was a different state to that of being crippled in the dead of night. Before, caught up in sheets of heat and stench, he felt there was no escape.

'I've got the garden to take care of now.'

This was his consolation; a dream of green fields at the end of a dark tunnel, a small extension of himself which he was going to shape into London's finest garden, regardless of the plentiful competition.

'Kew Gardens or the Chelsea Flower Show won't compare,' he told those who came to help him through the cold days of midwinter.

In February's frost, numbers dropped to a faithful few. Even Fergus's boys from Deptford, and Omar, their teacher, stopped coming. They promised they would return when the weather got better.

'This is England, not flaming Africa,' he wanted to say. 'There might be no more sunshine till the football season's over.'

But these days he was more polite, relying on help from the Somali girls who had brought along a pretty, older cousin, and on Merlin's boy, who seemed to avoid that girl, as if too shy to talk with her.

Lately, he had been coming more often.

On Saturday mornings, he would be there first, tending to the perennials and making sure there was no damage done in the night, as happened sometimes.

'Stupid kids throwing their rubbish everywhere.'

So long as it was just litter, he didn't mind. Once though, late at night, somebody lit a fire and sat around it drinking cans of beer as if there weren't enough decent pubs down by the riverside. He had shouted through his window, but by the time he got down they had scarpered. Like teenage Taliban staggering into the shadows.

These days, Fergus didn't help so much. He would spend his weekends hanging out with Katy's Shoreditch crowd, preferring posh pubs, poetry nights and West End shows to football.

Still, they had been to the Sheffield game. He knew because he had gone out of his way to avoid them, slipping anonymously into the North West Stand so there was a whole pitch's distance between them.

A few days before Valentine's, the Irishman turned up at his door. 'We're going up to Huddersfield for the weekend.'

'Meeting the parents,' he supposed. 'It must be serious.'

'It is,' Fergus answered. 'We might move in together, too.'

'Great. Next thing I hear, you'll be having babies.'

'Come on,' his friend protested. 'One step at a time.'

'Exactly. Just as with my garden.'

'How's it coming along?' Fergus's interest was genuine.

He was okay. Katy was the bitch, dividing them in this way.

'Going to do a lot of work this weekend. Charley's helping.'

'Who's Charley?'

'Merlin's boy,' he answered.

'So he's finally spoken enough to tell you his name?'

'Yeah, between conversations about Arsenal.'

'Seems like you've made a friend then.'

'I don't need a friend, I need a woman,' he told the Irishman in the doorway. 'There's a Somali girl who comes to help but she's young.'

'Her father might have something to say about it too,' Fergus laughed, throwing a playful, ex-boxer's punch towards his ribs.

'Sure,' he agreed. The mood softened and he asked his friend inside for a beer, the first time they had had a drink together in ages.

Except that those times had blown up in his face like Bourdin's bomb. Things could never go back to the way they had been, like those riotous nights of forming friendships as London's villages burned.

Katy changed everything; a rucksack of secrets in his skull.

'See you when you're back from Huddersfield.'

'I'll keep you updated.' Fergus spoke things he didn't want to hear. 'When I'm back in town, we'll all go out together.'

'Sure,' Lance said and closed the door tight.

While they headed off on the train to Huddersfield to stay at her parents' house with public school photos, horses and hockey medals, he would spend Valentine's Night at the Valley, watching a midweek game against Milton Keynes Dons. MK Dons, the least bloody romantic team in the country after what they had done to Wimbledon.

Lately there hadn't been much football because of bad weather. Great for Fergus and Katy, throwing snowballs at each other like a couple of kids, but more punishment for broken hearts and gardens.

One morning he found a rose outside his door.

'A yellow rose wrapped up in silver paper.'

'Who left it?' asked the boy he had happened to meet down by the riverside, where he went walking at the end of his day's duties.

'Dunno,' he admitted. 'Not who I want it to be, probably.'

'Who'd you want it to be?'

He spoke out through his Arsenal hoodie, down to the Thames. Maybe sometimes a man needs to get things off his chest.

'Have you ever seen the girl who lives across the way?' he asked the boy who turned his head slightly towards the light. 'The blonde one who's kind of pretty like Marilyn Monroe?'

'Marilyn Monroe's not pretty.'

'Everybody's different, I suppose, the way they see pretty.'

Again he changed the subject. 'Ain't she the red man's?'

'Don't think she'd see things that way, but maybe she is.'

'So you're trying to steal your friend's woman?'

He had turned his head away from the blueing darkness, towards the beam of streetlamps on smooth, oaken skin. Suddenly he looked as angry as the kids on the streets from summer's battles in Lewisham.

'That's such bad faith, man.'

'No,' he fought disapproval in the boy's glittering coal-black eyes. 'When you're sixteen or seventeen, it's easy to say that.'

'So I know nothing just because I'm a god-damned kid.'

'No, you're smart,' he tried to assure the boy.

'Fuck you,' the boy said, 'you're like the rest of them.'

Sadness fogged his voice as Lance put a hand on the boy's shoulder. Suddenly, just for a second, he noticed how quickly the boy's skin turned a pure shade of orange under the streetlamp. His eyes reflected fire as he tilted his face sideways, catching a streak of light on his nose and then the corners of his angry mouth.

'I'm not a bad guy,' Lance insisted.

'But you love your friend's woman, right?'

'You can't help who you love,' he argued.

The boy's hoodie was down at his shoulders, and his cropped hair glistened dark as freshly-laid tarmac. The bones in his neck had too many hollows; his pout was too sensitive for a boy.

Lance looked at his shoelaces.

Then suddenly he heard an echo so soft it seemed to be coming from the other side of the river. 'You can't help who you love.'

Looking towards the water, he thought of Katy's rose once more. Closing his eyes, he breathed in the imaginary scent of her love. She had fought with Fergus in Huddersfield and realised he was *the one*. Right about now, she was on her way back to London; so fast it was like she was travelling on one of those bullet trains they have in Japan.

He could see her holding a book, perhaps the book Fergus said she brought to the Sheffield game and hadn't read. Suddenly, despite the cold rising off the river's surface, he sensed the breath of her anticipation and felt her fingers moving, making a cradle of her hands. His flesh was made of paper and his words resided in her head.

'Love me.' The words came unexpectedly.

Other words followed before he had time to react to the first.

A hot breeze flooded his eardrum. 'I want to kiss you.'

Before he had time to turn, the words changed to action.

'What the hell!' Lance exclaimed, feeling the boy's mouth pressing against his cheek, and a damp patch flowering, burning.

Pushing him away, turning around, he stumbled on his bad leg.

'Sorry,' the boy said, his eyes teary, and turned to run.

By the time he had found his balance, the kid was gone, and he wasn't sure what to make of the whole scene. More than ever now, he was convinced there was something dodgy about that Merlin, and his sorcery.

'Paedo,' he told himself.

He would have reported this to the police, if it hadn't been for that kiss.

'It was nothing though, and nobody saw it.'

It was best to forget the whole thing, go to the game and tell nobody, not even Fergus. He had gotten good at keeping secrets from his friends. Slipping into the red heart of the crowd, he thought that the noise and the passion of the East Stand would soon drown out the memories, even if it was harder to erase the kiss, no matter how many times he rubbed the team scarf against his cheek on the train journey to Charlton.

Getting there, he had this strange fear they would all see through him. Grabbing a pre-match meal of fish and chips, he looked around at the lonely men and the lucky bastards who were part of couples out on a date. Maybe if Katy and Fergus were here with him he would feel less alone. Though he had done nothing wrong, he couldn't shake off feelings of dirt. They were reflected in the brown crust of the pitch below, after weeks of frost.

The game started with its usual spark of songs and chants.

'Come on, Charlton!' yelled the whisky-flask man.

These were famished people. There hadn't been much football in recent weeks. Maybe that was why he couldn't concentrate, like Svevo's first cigarette after a long abstention.

Even at the Sheffield game, through the haze of knowing Katy was there with Fergus, he had never taken his eyes off the action for a second. Here, feeling traces of that kiss eating into his cheek like gangrene, he didn't seem able to concentrate more than a minute at a time.

He would see something like 4:32 on the clock, lift his head just for a second, drift back to the riverside, wondering if there was anything he had done to encourage the boy, and then tell himself 'no'.

His eyes back on the game, he would see 5:55 all of a sudden. Then he would lose his sense of time once more and would not realise what was happening.

'Off, off!' bodies sprang up in the seats around him.

Last man sitting, he hadn't seen the referee's flash of red towards the MK Dons centre half, and the reason why he had awarded a penalty.

Too embarrassed to ask, he watched his captain preparing to shoot. Seconds later, the ever reliable Johnnie Jackson had the ball in the net. This time, unlike at both Sheffield games, the view was perfect.

First time round, it had been the fault of some piss-head. Second time – Katy's, because if she hadn't gone, he would have been in the East Stand. Instead he had to watch from a more restricted angle in the North West, but all that was forgotten now amidst these songs of love.

'Top o' the league, champions by Easter.'

The whisky man raised a toast. 'To Valentine's night at the Valley.'

The more the game brewed, the less he brooded on the boy. Come Charlton's second goal, he was hardly losing a moment's concentration. Not even when the momentum faded and the visitors pulled a goal back in the second half, leaving the final score at two goals to one.

'It's as sure as can be,' the whisky man assured those around him as they made their way out of the ground. 'Just another couple o' wins and we're going back to where we belong, the higher divisions.'

Lance was going back too, after a stopover in one of the pubs where bloggers gather before and after games to discuss their thoughts. Tonight, everyone's mood was much the same as the whisky man's.

'Here's to the Holy Grail,' they raised their glasses.

'And a piss-up on promotion day,' someone added.

'A piss-up on promotion day!' the bloggers chorused.

That piss-up on promotion day was shining brightly in his mind as he caught a fast late-night 180 back towards Greenwich. It was growing more clouded as the domes of the Naval College came into focus.

Sensations of burning came back to his cheek as he got off the dartboard bus and walked slowly towards the river and the flats.

Getting closer, he could hear a commotion.

'Teenage Taliban,' he thought to himself.

There was a lot of laughter. He could hear three or four different voices. Getting concerned, he quickened his pace. He could see shadows loitering.

'Wait a minute, one of them's got a spray can.'

Little bastards, covering the walls in graffiti. He had to stop them. Suddenly the night of the fireworks flashed through his mind. This time round, he wasn't going to get stabbed. Like in the army, when you're out on patrol in hostile territory, you get the bad guys before they get you.

If you hesitate, you're going to end up dead. This enemy was stoned, unaware of his presence, as he grabbed a lump of loose wood from a railway sleeper's remains.

Stepping out of the shadows, before they even noticed, he swung his weapon, with one target in mind. Taking them by surprise, he got exactly what he'd wanted. A precise thump, a crack of bone, a screech of stunned agony, and a crushed canister tumbling to the ground.

'Not so smart now, Van Goff,' he said, and then as one stepped towards him he cried out, 'come on Picasso.'

He was big, and confident. 'I'm not Pic .... aaahh.'

Before he could finish, half a scissor cut through his shoulder, clipping him backwards into the arms of his accomplices.

'Maybe someone else fancies being Picasso then, huh?'

'This guy's crazy,' they muttered to each other, as he edged towards them, wielding his stick high and straight as Charlton's five o'clock sword.

'I'm a trained soldier. I know how to kill.'

Legally he couldn't, but he'd nothing to lose. Below them, the boy who held the canister was on his knees, clutching broken knuckles. Bare finger bones blazed white as the College on the riverside.

'We didn't mean no harm,' they whimpered.

'Okay, one's enough to teach a lesson.'

Fraternally, they protested at first, and then decided to run.

In a flash, they were gone, leaving him alone with Van Goff.

'You came into my garden,' said the former soldier, raising his weapon high as an executioner performing a medieval decapitation, 'spraying your senseless shit all over everything.'

He was back in Afghanistan, acting out a role reversal, punishing the invader. Soiling this land was like cutting out his heart, leaving him with nothing to live for. All he could see was a scrawl of nicknames and swear words, above broken planters and ripped-up flower beds.

He'd do gaol for the statement he was about to make.

'Please, we didn't mean no harm.'

'You're a slug,' Lance growled, stepping closer as the boy shrivelled up in a salt of fear. 'No, you're worse than a slug. They destroy gardens because they're hungry, and it's their nature. But you, you ....'

'Please don't kill me,' the boy pleaded. 'I'll go.'

Tightening his hold on the weapon, Lance felt no mercy as he surveyed the damaged gardens. 'Go where? Some other place where you'll do vandalism? Is this all you've got to offer to the world?'

Again the graffiti artist held up the bare bones of his hand, as if enacting Hamlet's graveside scene. 'Please mister, I need a doctor.'

'You're going to wreck no more gardens.'

Raising his weapon in the air, this was payback.

But just as it was falling, he heard a shout. 'No.'

Somebody rushed up from behind, pushing him out of the way before he'd struck the sobbing figure beneath. Suddenly he'd lost his footing, dislocated his prosthesis, and lay helpless on the ground.

'What were you going to do?' boomed an angry voice.

Looking up, a bald, bearded skull came into focus.

Slowly, he raised himself up. 'Defending my territory.'

'If you're in prison, you can't look after your garden.'

'This country sent me to the desert to kill people,' he laughed. 'They'll not send me to prison for stopping crime in my own streets?'

'They will. That's how the law works.'

'I'm bleeding, mister. I'm suffering.'

'This young man needs help,' Merlin suggested, 'but we can't take him to a hospital because they'll ask us too many questions.' He spoke in a commanding, cultured tone. 'I'm not a doctor, but I am a trainee pharmacist, so I should be able to patch him up.'

Suddenly Lance felt guilty. 'Is there anything I can do?'

'No, you've done enough damage for one night.'

Leaving Merlin with the boy, Lance headed back to his flat. There, though he knew he shouldn't, he took solace in

Facebook, looking up Katy's pictures of her good time in Huddersfield with Fergus.

Surfing, stalking, reminiscing and regretting, he felt time passed fast. Around midnight, a knock came on the door. Fearing arrest, he felt relieved when he opened it and saw Merlin standing in the corridor, clutching some kind of book. As always, he seemed serious.

'We need to talk.'

'Come in. Don't suppose you want a drink?'

'Water will do. I don't need anything stronger.'

'I do, after all that's happened.'

'Quite a night with young boys.'

'Look, I know what I did there was wrong.'

'Yes, it was,' Merlin showed no mercy. 'But that boy's patched up.' He paused, sipping from his tumbler. 'Charley's not so easy to fix.'

'I haven't done any harm, but I understand.'

'No, you don't have a fucking clue,' Merlin swore, which was out of character. 'Do you remember the London riots?'

'How could anybody forget them?'

Their legacy was still in the news every day, *Wanted* posters in the windows, and burned out spaces where there used to be shops.

'Nobody should know this,' the pharmacist leaned close as if to reveal secrets of himself or others, 'but you're caught up in it.'

His knee twitched as it used to do after first getting the prosthesis. Unable to control the spasms, his leg pecked the underside of the table. His face was smithed hot as the seconds after Charley kissed him.

'What am I caught up in? Do I want to know?'

'This,' he spoke solemnly, as he placed his book on the table.

'A scrapbook?'

It was full of cuttings from during and after the riots. He could see stories of rage that had engulfed his city in the summer before, some colour, others black and white, some tabloid, others broadsheet. Combinations of fact, opinion, analysis, statistics, and pictures.

'Take a look at the faces,' Merlin interrupted a moment where he had got lost in a fog of images from the burning streets of Lewisham.

'*Gallery of shame*,' said a headline above a crew of teens.

'See that one,' Merlin said, placing his finger on a boy's face.

He was about seventeen, good-looking, with the confident pose and figure you might find in profiles of players in a match programme.

This still wasn't making sense. 'What about him?'

'Remember the shooting in the Church in Greenwich?'

'Yeah,' he recalled. 'The night Fergus first met Katy.'

'What?' Merlin asked, confused and impatient.

'Nothing. Just a night of gangs and guns.'

'Yes, and this was the boy shot as he sang in the choir.'

'No way,' said Lance, lifting the book up into the light.

He could have been any one of Fergus's boys, a teenager gunned down on streets that lead to Deptford, giving praise to Jesus Christ.

This cocksure boy, in a track suit top, with one pierced ear was the body covered over, under sheets of rain, dead as Marilyn Monroe.

Merlin though had no time for his reminiscing. 'Look at this one.'

'The girl with dreadlocks?'

'Yes, she's got a link to that boy's shooting,' his guest informed him. 'They were both witnesses to a murder during the riots.'

'So that's why the boy got shot on our doorstep?'

'Yes, and there's more trouble the same doorstep.'

'They're going to come back and shoot somebody else?'

'Charley,' Merlin's answer filled the room like a gunshot.

Suddenly stolen kisses on the cheek shrank in comparison.

'What's Charley got to with any of this?'

'Witness to the first murder, and I'm a family friend through volunteering in a shelter that looks after girls who get cut in Africa.'

'Cut? So they've got AIDS or something?'

'Female genital mutilation,' the pharmacist corrected his ignorance. 'Barbaric practice we're trying to stop.' He raised sober eyes, searching Lance's to see that he could trust him. 'You see, Charley could have suffered the same fate if it wasn't for this country, this city.'

'You mean, they'd have cut off his ....'

Merlin's eyes swirled to piteous disbelief.

'Take a closer look at the picture.'

He leaned in. 'The gallery of shame?'

'Don't you recognise anyone there?'

He shook his head, as Merlin put a thumb across a girl's scalp.

'Imagine this young lady without the dreadlocks.'

Looking closer, her lineaments started to take shape into Charley's.

'Impossible,' he exhaled shock and relief in the same breath.

The feel of her kiss, and a landmine went through him in reverse.

'She's in disguise, because of threats on her life,' Merlin clarified as he pulled his thumb away, and closed the scrapbook's cover on the girl with dreadlocks, 'and I'm providing a safe-house.'

This was a lot of information to take in. More too, as he explained how she'd come to the country as a child, after the death of her father, and been a good girl, kind to her mother, when she was young.

'But she got in bad company and made mistakes.'

'I didn't touch her if that's what you think.'

'Lance,' her guardian cut into his protestations of innocence, 'this isn't about you, or me. It's about Charley. She's got a price on her head, offered by the same gang who shoot boys dead in God's house.'

Suddenly, this was more serious than a kiss by the riverside. Thinking back to the scrapbook's gallery of shame, half-relieved that she was a girl, the soldier found himself back on the edge of someone else's war.

18
Ghosts on Greenwich Park Benches

Crossing England, leaving one home, returning to another, they caught the first stirrings of spring through their carriage window; new life and lambs fighting the cold, buds on the branches, and blades of grass pushing through stubble sharp as the sword in Charlton's badge. Getting back to Greenwich, they found a world of stone that never changes through the seasons; iced-white, frozen in time.

Suddenly Fergus missed the countryside of the days before. Taking refuge on a bench in the park, they watched February suns dissolve like ecstasy tablets in green lemonade. Thirstily, they swallowed, getting high on the serotonin of memories percolated through a tinderbox of trees, in shadow, guarding the Observatory's orange fire.

'Huddersfield was good.'

'What's your favourite part?' Katy wondered, as if some presence of the past lingered in leafy flakes of light on the tea-black tree bark.

'There's too many to name at once,' he admitted as she rested her head on his shoulder, dark and natural as the turf of the moors. 'Watching you riding a horse for the first time, seeing how much you love them. More than people I guess.' She grunted a sign of truth. 'Sylvia Plath's grave, after climbing a hill forever, riding an old steam engine to where the Brontes lived, drunken nights in an Irish Centre or the pub on Castle Hill, and touring the stadium.'

'Of course,' she laughed. 'There's always football.'

'And the night you went back to black,' he added.

'Marilyn's gone, I guess. There's just me left.'

'That'll do for me,' he told her as another sun slipped away, leaving a crescent of incandescence on the contours of Observatory Hill; distinctive as the arches of Huddersfield's football stadium.

Katy spoke, puncturing his thoughts. 'Seen Lance lately?'

'I have,' he said, 'but there's something different about him.'

He sensed concern in her mannerisms. 'In what way?'

'It's strange. He's made friends with Merlin.'

'Sounds like a touch of jealousy there,' she teased.

'That's just different to the Lance I used to know.'

Looking up at the Observatory darkening, he recalled stories of Martial Bourdin's ghost and those crazy summer nights of seeing streets burn and protests hijacked by the English Defence League.

'At least I understood what was in his head back then.'

Back from Afghanistan, he was angry and pouring it out.

'These days he's silent, sneaking about the place.'

'His garden's coming along well.'

'Yeah, but he works at strange times.'

You could see him out there at midnight, working with Merlin's boy. There would just be the two of them, digging, planting, pruning. Hiding in shadows, out of the lamplight, as if wanting nobody to see them.

'Maybe it's the graffiti attack,' she suggested.

'Maybe,' Fergus agreed.

While they were sitting snug together, the world around them slowly turned black. That's when they realised that the gates closed at sunset. They found themselves locked in for the night, staying in a hotel of spiders, squirrels, red deer and scrawny foxes scurrying through the darkness. First, they passed time by fantasising that their bench was magical. Anyone in history could step out of the Observatory, sit down beside them for five minutes and share a conversation.

'Anyone,' she suggested, 'from dead ancestors to celebrities.'

'Martial Bourdin,' he supposed as he got into the spirit of the game. 'I'd ask him what he was doing that evening over a hundred years ago, and if it's true that his ghost still comes back to haunt Charlton.'

'The suffragettes,' Katy said. 'My Gran and Marilyn Monroe.'

'My father,' he said softly. 'Lucy, who died in our joyride, Johnny Summers who scored those goals against Huddersfield, and maybe a cigarette with Svevo, even though I don't smoke.'

'Charlton again,' she laughed as a fox stirred in the undergrowth, torching brambles with yellow eyes. 'Since it's Greenwich, I suppose it'd be good to hear the stories of Henry's six wives as well.'

Watching out for foxes, they fell into silence as the lights of London's villages came gradually to life. Though the night was clear, they felt cold and spooked by the park's open spaces, so they took shelter by the side of the building Bourdin had tried to bomb.

There they made beds out of branches, in each other's arms.

Some hours later, drifting in and out of sleep, Katy shivered then sprang up suddenly in the starlight to make an announcement. 'Fergus, I've decided who I'm meeting on that bench.'

'Yeah,' he said sleepily, 'who?'

'The boys who attacked us,' she said confidently. 'They're going to face me and all their ghosts, and they're going to be dressed up as women, by the suffragettes, and sent into King Henry's court where they have to strip and dance for drunken Tudors, and Queen Boudicca's daughters, under threat of being sent like young bulls to a cattle crush if they refuse.'

'What about our kids?' Fergus asked. 'Yours? Mine?'

'Nah,' she said. 'The future's no fun if you know it.'

'Okay,' he said. 'We'll stick to ancestors.'

She had sentenced her ghosts to humiliation. The night was new and young above a park as black as the curls of Bourdin's last smoke.

19
The Shadow of Bourdin

'Sam Bartram, Charlton's FA Cup team of '47, and my grandfather,' Lance suggested when Fergus proposed a strange pastime one evening. 'Or God perhaps, right here in Greenwich Park.'

'Ask him if there'll ever be a united Ireland.'

'Or when Charlton get to play United again.'

'Anyway,' he diversified, 'how's things?'

They hadn't been great, on the football field or off it.

'We lost at home to Colchester, Tuesday.'

It was one of those beautiful night games where white moths are fluttering against the silvery glare of floodlights and you can taste the promise of summer in the creeping heat of twilight's glorious lilac.

After twenty eight games his team had 64 points, a goal difference of +33 and a real chance to smash all the records ever set in the 3rd division. Charlton of course had never done happy endings.

Maybe that was why the Valley was half-empty on a mild night at the start of March as Bourdin's shadow came back into focus like a bad dream. If Charlton had Svevo, Colchester United's literary symbol came in the form of Wordsworth. Anthony Wordsworth, a left-sided midfielder, one of the best in the division, alongside Johnnie Jackson.

Almost instantly he scythed through the home defence, angling his body like a pen on parchment, preparing to shoot. The ball floated in echoes of the Dale Stephens oeuvre from earlier in the season.

Almost without breaking sweat, he had scripted the opening scene.

'It was a great goal but early days,' Lance said. 'There was nothing to worry about. We'd come back before the half was done. We'd get promoted and buy players as good as Wordsworth in the summer, to make our own poetry in the 2nd division next year.'

If Colchester didn't want to lose their star players, maybe they had to get promoted too. Aware of this, they fought for a place in the play-offs.

Hard as the visitors fought, Charlton pushed back, struggling for an equaliser. 'But it was as if every man was constipated.'

There was no way through. Then, with 75 minutes on the clock, a short, sharp sting determined the course of the night's ending.

Ben Hamer, safe as a lighthouse between the sticks for most of the season, lost concentration as he toed the ball for a clearance.

'Wake up and watch out!' screamed the supporters in agony as their goalie wandered hopelessly out of position, unaware of an attacker coming at him with the speed of a wasp.

If Wordsworth's opening goal was poetry, this was comic farce. Hamer was forced into a reckless clearance. Without any height on it, the ball deflected off the wasp's boot and towards the empty goal.

'One of those nights,' Lance supposed. 'We've lost our home record, but we've a good chance to bounce back again at the weekend.'

They would face the Magpies from Nottinghamshire – the world's oldest professional football club – whose black-and-white stripes had inspired Italy's Juventus to adopt the same colours and abandon their original *pink* jerseys a century before. Notts County were on a five-game winning streak, buzzing on the edge of the play-offs.

'You'll be going to the match,' Fergus supposed.

'Maybe,' Lance mumbled. 'We'll see.'

'Surely you're not losing your faith?'

'Maybe,' he lied again. 'Scared we'll mess up and spend another winter playing Rochdale and Yeovil.'

'You can't throw this away,' Fergus assured him.

But he couldn't be so certain about this, or anything else that was happening in his life right now, as he gazed out across the soft green expanse of the park in the evening light. Down on the river, the boats looked the same as they had done for as long as he had been coming to these heights in the park, but Charley's problems had changed everything, and lately he had spent a lot of time in her company. There was nothing physical between them now the teenage crush had passed. Besides, having barely passed seventeen, she was more than a decade younger than him.

He would often joke. 'We barely speak the same language.'

Sometimes she found that funny, sometimes not. She liked to hear stories of Afghanistan, as if they relieved her withdrawal symptoms from the world of guns and gangsters she had left behind.

'I ain't no saint,' she boasted. And she wasn't.

She had been a member of a gang somewhere out by Selhurst, home of Crystal Palace, Charlton's former landlords.

'This really is enemy territory for you,' he would say, out of earshot of Merlin who watched them like a hawk and couldn't stomach their making light of a very serious situation.

The boy she had been with, or one of the boys, shot somebody.

'At random, in the head,' her guardian said.

Charley got caught on CCTV, running from the scene.

'The police arrested her and held her for days,' Merlin had explained. 'First she said nothing, and then as she got scared she told them everything she knew, and the boys got arrested too.'

Charley saw it differently. 'They beat me up, made me snitch, made me break the code.' Alone after the betrayal of her friends, she felt trapped. 'What am I going to do, where am I going to run to?'

Working together with Lance in the garden, she had a purpose to her days.

'Can't go to school, can't go out, can't do nuthin' till the trial's over, and then what am I going to do?' she would ask. 'Everybody hates a snitch, and every gang from here to Jamaica's going to hate me.'

'You don't have to be part of gangs,' he would tell her.

'There's not much else in this city.'

'There's other kinds of gangs,' he had supposed. He had an idea. 'Couldn't you come with me to a football match one Saturday?'

'No way,' Merlin said at first. Then he relented.

This was why he couldn't talk to Fergus about the County game, couldn't give his reasons for going there with Merlin and *the boy*.

'Maybe you'll come house-hunting with me?'

'House-hunting?' Lance echoed his friend's words.

'Yeah, I'm looking at a few places tomorrow.'

'Where? And why aren't you taking Katy?'

'It's a surprise,' the Irishman answered. 'I'm looking at a place for us to move into, and where else but Charlton?'

'Renting or buying?'

'Omar says they're going to make my contract permanent, so I've looked into getting a mortgage and buying my own place,' he said. 'Seems like both of us are going to be Charlton Men.'

'That's cool,' Lance lied again.

Even though his strongest desires for Katy had passed like the last days of a fever, he wouldn't be human if there wasn't some relic of emotion lingering in his heart whenever he thought of her.

'We'll go tomorrow evening, a place called Kashmir Road.'

'Close to the street where I grew up.'

'Where you said they've a family of Afghans now.'

'Don't want to think about it.'

Strangely, as the next day passed, curiosity burgeoned. Catching a train to Charlton then ascending Church Lane, going past the Jacobean house, Lance had a desire to see the place he had grown up in.

Almost unconsciously, they took a detour. There, in the streets off Cherry Orchard, they found a brown brick house dressed in ivy, with a ginger man mowing the lawn and a teenage girl in a room upstairs, putting on make-up.

'Not an Afghan in sight,' Fergus teased.

'I used to live here,' Lance said to the man, who switched off the machine and offered the chance to come inside.

He shook his head, preferring closure on the past.

'It'd be like going into your ex-girlfriend's room where she's sleeping with somebody else,' he thought to himself.

So they moved on towards Fergus's house, or the house that was possibly going to become his home, over time. There, he might settle down with Katy, and stamp their shared identity on the place, with cats, dogs, garden gnomes, and kids who'd speak in Charlton accents.

At least, that was Fergus's dream, fuelled by ignorance.

What would he do if he found out about Huddersfield?

There was no time to dwell on an answer though. They had come to the red-brick house with a green door, which Fergus knocked upon.

A slim middle-class man answered, letting them inside, leading them through a pastel hallway into cosy rooms and then a garden gleaming Irish-emerald. This, for Fergus, seemed the most important thing.

'Grew up in the countryside,' he told the slim man as he surveyed a narrow space populated with a shed, a greenhouse and a neatly-planted line of rose bushes and fruit trees, all bare and out of season.

This was perfect, he added, closing his eyes to breathe in the scents, echoes of past history and stories yet to be written. He would grow apples and plums, make jams and crumbles in the summer, and down at the bottom of the garden, where there were palm trees, he would clear a space for decking under the shade, to drink beer on summer nights.

His world would be out upon this fragment of English soil which was going to be an Irishman's, and Katy's country would be inside. Shaking hands with the owner, he had decided to put in an offer. His head was full of dreams and the house already his as they made their way down Kashmir Road, past cats coming out on the prowl at dusk, as if to thank the great cat in the sky for the warming days.

'So will I see you Saturday?' Fergus asked as a black-and-white kitten strolled by, sporting Notts County colours.

'Possibly,' Lance added to a division of lies spreading slowly down from Huddersfield to the tail end of Nottinghamshire.

Come Saturday, he would make an excuse. Maybe, if the weather was bad, he could hide inside a heavy anorak. Unfortunately, the forecast promised a sunny afternoon, and so he chose to avoid his friend, pretending that it was because he had been too busy sorting out the details of the purchase.

It was strange going to a football match with a teenage girl.

'I'm coming too,' Merlin said, as if acting as a chaperone.

'Okay,' Lance agreed. 'I'm taking the Torino today.'

That way, there was less chance of bumping into Fergus.

'If he finds out,' he explained to his passengers, 'then he's going to tell Katy, and we're not going to be able to keep a lid on this thing.'

Her guardian spoke insistently. 'You've no choice.'

Charley was excited and Merlin was worried as they reached the stadium, parked the car and made their way inside. Since he had a season ticket, they would have to sit a few seats apart in the East Stand.

'It's all white people,' Charley said about the crowd.

Lance laughed, then pointed down to the pitch and whispered. 'Yeah, but see their manager. The main man's black.'

Seeing this, she relaxed and began to applaud with the crowd.

Before the kick-off, an advertisement for season tickets blasted out. 'Buy them before Easter, get them cheaper!'

Mantras resonated. 'Chrissie Powell's men are we!'

If Charlton won this match, they would be virtually guaranteed that the Championship circus would roll into town next season. Colchester's win had been a fluke. This was a sunny day, not a drop of mist rolling in from the dark river that reflected the pastel-blue sky. The scene was set. A great burst of enthusiasm from 17,000 spectators welcomed the teams out of the tunnel. County kicked off, shooting into the North Stand, and thankfully there was no sign of Fergus.

'Come on, Charlton, get stuck in!' came the cry.

But straight from the off, they looked dead on their feet. It was as if half of them hadn't come out of the dressing room. Where was the poetry in motion from the autumn and winter, the fireworks against Preston or the fighting spirit on the road at Yeovil?

Come on, he thought to himself, *give us a Maracanã moment for Charley's sake and for the sake of selling tickets for next season. The more we sell, the more chance of signing up guys like Wordsworth who'd provide the poetry for another promotion charge.*

'Come on, lads!' he called out to the players.

They had the supporters' fate in their hands.

'But if the hands that hold us are Hamer's…'

The visitors had scored with a bastard child of Colchester's two goals on Tuesday. Alan Judge, County's Irish midfielder, found himself in space thirty yards out with no defenders close by. Momentarily, he was free and loose as Ireland's legendary Liam Brady during his brief spell at Juventus. Charlton's men stayed away as if he carried an infectious cough, watching him tee up a shot that whooped hopefully towards goal. Wondering if he could catch anything this far out, Ben Hamer dived hopelessly to the right. The ball slipped by, like a knife going through butter.

Football's a cruel game; the moods of its supporters are so arbitrary.

'Useless, get him off!' The fans slated the keeper whose name they had happily chanted on so many afternoons since September past.

'They're running us ragged,' moaned a man with his face in his palms as Judge broke through the defence once again.

'Two-nil!' Charley called across. 'I thought *you* were good.'

By half-time, it was 4, with 3 goals from their centre forward.

During the break, there were no announcements, no attempts to sell season tickets, only stunned silence in the stadium.

The whisky man vented his fury. 'Never walked out on a match in all my life, not even in bad times, but this is going to be the first.'

The others were more optimistic. 'Weren't we 5-1 behind to Huddersfield in the classic of '57?'

Answers came thick and fast, together and alone.

'A ten-point lead won't be long disappearing,' said the men congregated around TV screens, checking on the day's other results. 'Three bad games and it's down to nothing.'

Voices of fear and doom thundered all the way from the back of the North Stand down to the side of the river and the mighty flood barrier. 'If we lose this there's no coming back. We'd be destroyed.'

'We'll face a tough Easter,' prophesised an old man who had seen it all before. 'We've hard games coming up, especially Huddersfield.'

The only thing they could get out of today was some pride. Chris Powell needed to inoculate passion into this team of second-rate season ticket salesmen. As supporters returned to their seats for the second half, they hoped for a remake of Huddersfield '57.

It would be a miracle if they rescued a point from this, but a few minutes into the restart there was a glimpse of hope. Wagstaff, always a man of extremes, steered a perfect cross into the flight path of Wright-Phillips. As the ball was coming in across the face of the North Stand, the Brockley Pelé started his ascent, positioning his body for an overhead kick. The disbelievers looked on, expecting nothing. He would fall flat on his backside in a perfect metaphor for today's performance.

But no. Echoes of 1957 stirred in SE7.

'He's scored!' the voices rose up.

At least one man wanted to sell season tickets. Minutes later he was back in the box, returning the favour for Scott Wagstaff to score with a glancing header. 4-2, and the stadium was rocking.

Whatever Chris Powell said at half-time, it had worked. They had finally woken up, as if they had been invigorated with strong black coffee.

This was the Charlton he had watched and followed across the country in the months before. These were echoes of the team that had graced autumn afternoons in a stadium ablaze with expectation.

To a man, and even to a woman, with Charley screaming too, they willed them on to keep the momentum going. As they pushed forwards, Chrissie Powell waved his fists, his shirt collar open and his tie flapping in the breeze. But as time passed, the players tired. Charley wasn't going to see a classic. The game petered out into a 4-2 defeat.

'You lost,' Merlin spoke emotionless at the end.

'But we fought well,' Charley protested.

Feeling emotional, she was forgetting to use the deep voice she usually affected in the presence of other people to keep up the pretence of being a boy. Chastised by her guardian's eyes, she fell silent as they made their way through the turnstiles of the East Stand, towards the car park, where they mingled with those from the more middle-class West.

Suddenly Lance caught sight of Fergus and Katy amongst the day's departing spectators. Hurriedly, hoping they wouldn't notice, even though he had caught a sudden snapshot of Katy's eyes, he got inside the Torino, telling the others to do the same, crouching low until the crowds had passed.

Driving home, he couldn't help feeling the game was up.

20
Lessons from a Northern Town

Huddersfield's stadium was electric-blue from a distance on the train journey into the town where Fergus had decided to spend the night before Charlton's latest game. He had caught the train from Kings Cross after finishing work around five, leaving clear instructions for tomorrow.

'Your boys should come at about ten,' he had explained to Omar. 'Lance will be there. He's not going to the game.'

'A dozen or so might come along,' his colleague predicted.

'That's good,' Fergus said. 'It's the big spring clean-up.'

The Somali girls had been putting up posters all week and pushing leaflets through letterboxes, rousing enthusiasm in the community.

This Saturday's crowd was expected to be bigger than ever; there were going to be as many bodies in the community garden as in the away end of Huddersfield's ground. Since the game against the Magpies, things had improved slightly.

The red men captured a hard-earned point in Scunthorpe and then a three-nil midweek victory over Yeovil Town at the Valley.

'You drove there at Christmas,' Fergus recalled.

'Yes. Six goals in one season. Good going.'

Lately, Lance had been distracted. Looking out the window at England's army greens pushing through the loosed pinafore of winter, Fergus was distracted too. Villages manned in steeples, nameplates of stations, and trees whirled in and out of view, intersected with words and memories like glass, sunlight and liquid silk.

'There are two kinds of people in the world,' Katy sometimes argued. 'Those who see spiders as their greatest enemies in the whole universe, and then the rest of you who act like they're invisible.'

As he watched the magnificent handless construction of a spider's house in the constantly changing country of the window's top corner, the voices in his thoughts shifted southwards. It had been a strange day, a bad one at work, where he had almost fought with one of his boys, maybe from the stress of trying to purchase a home in this country.

'Paperwork and lies,' Omar defined it.

He had gone to the pub alone, wanting to forget. Besides, even if she had known about the house, Katy was out with the Shoreditch crowd.

'I'm going to surprise her with the news,' he would announce to everyone except her, 'after coming back from Huddersfield.'

He thought about this as he sipped his pint alone in a pub in Charlton Village, beneath a canvas print of 1947's FA Cup heroes. Raising a glass to Sam Bartram, they had much in common.

The giant goalie married a local girl too, just down the road in Our Lady of Grace Catholic Church, and then played a game against Middlesbrough on the same afternoon. Maybe, if Katy accepted his proposal, they could have their reception at the Valley, and she could carry a bouquet up the aisle in the shape of an FA Cup.

Some chance! - he had thought to himself - *She still hates football, even if she's agreed to come to the odd game.*

Shortly after this he wandered home. It was on the walk from the train station back towards the gardens that he caught sight of something shocking. Lance was standing by the river, looking out on the lights of Canary Wharf, close to someone else's shadow.

First he thought it was a girl, then saw the familiar Arsenal hoodie. He recognised Merlin's boy. Since that day at the Notts County game when Katy said she saw them getting in the car together, there had been something curiously secretive going on, and he didn't understand it.

Instead of saying anything, he stood in the shadows and watched, silent and cunning as a spider. The boy took out a cigarette, held it up between his long fingers and fumbled in his pockets for a match.

'You shouldn't smoke so much,' Lance said compassionately.

The boy mumbled something under his hood, looking up into the streetlights that torched his eyes phosphorous-bright.

Suddenly Lance reached across, put his arms around the boy, pulled him towards his chest, forgetting the public space just for a second.

'No way,' Fergus mumbled, stumbling in the darkness.

Lance turned and caught sight of him.

'I don't want to know,' Fergus turned away.

Giving chase, Lance hobbled after him.

'I really don't want to know,' he insisted.

His friend wouldn't stop banging the door until he answered.

'It's not what you think,' he protested. 'Let me explain.'

After a few seconds he relented. It was the secrecy he didn't like. Deceit's a harder thing to forgive than the crime itself.

'We saw you together after the County game,' he told his friend, setting the tone for truth. 'Katy's got sharp eyes.'

Lance shivered when Fergus said this. 'Where is she?'

'Some launch for an art book,' Fergus answered.

'What I'm about to tell you I don't want her to know.'

'I can't keep secrets from the woman I want to marry,' Fergus argued.

Lance shivered again. 'It's for the greater good.'

'I hate deceit more than anything.'

'Fine,' Lance replied, weighing up whether or not to share the story. 'I'll tell you what's going on, and you decide the rest.'

Looking into the spider's web, whole and glistening, Fergus wondered if Katy's tiny enemy stored secrets away from his soulmate. Possibly, but nothing as big as this sorry tale of guns, gangs and gender.

The train was pulling into Huddersfield's neoclassical station, as fine a piece of architecture as anything created by his travelling companion. Fergus had a busy night ahead of him before Charlton's busy tomorrow.

He booked into a hotel across from the station, unpacked his bag and ate dinner. When that was done, he phoned Katy's parents to arrange a meeting over breakfast. He would have been happy to meet them anywhere, but they suggested going out to the house, since his request sounded serious.

His nerves tingling, he took a walk through the undulating streets of Katy's town so as to get to know her better – the girl she was, the teenager, sister, daughter and shadow of his future wife.

As darkness gathered, rain fell and the walk was done, he caught a bus back and forth through the countryside to pass the time.

Then he returned to the hotel, lay down and waited for morning. Rising early, he caught a taxi out to Katy's parents' farmhouse.

There, he asked if it was okay for them to move in together, giving hints that this was a precursor to engagement and marriage.

'Well, we can't speak for our daughter,' her mother said, as if they found it too quaint, too orthodox for him to be asking their approval. 'Obviously, if she's happy we'd give our blessing.'

He remembered then that he was in England and not Ireland, free from the cell of a culture that offers both comfort and constraint.

They poured fresh tea, served up the eggs and bacon, and then changed to talk of horses, let loose from the stables after the winter. Then they drove him back to town for the day's football.

He browsed the shops before making his way towards the white arches of the stadium, which like Charlton's rested in a small valley. There, a good-sized crowd was gathering, mostly home supporters who showed no animosity towards the few figures in red scarves and jerseys.

Not even when he slipped inside the club superstore and bought himself a gnome, to take pride of place in his new garden, when those agents finally got around to sorting out the last of the paperwork.

'Great atmosphere,' he texted Katy, who had known he was going to the game but did not know he was taking a detour to see her parents.

The atmosphere stayed in place as he made his way inside the stadium, to the away end, which was like a blue boat floating on the same sea of army greens that he had observed from the train window.

Though he had enjoyed the journey, he was going home a different way. He had booked a supporters' coach to take him back to Charlton.

Standing amongst those same supporters, waiting for the game to start, he felt he was part of something – a tribe, a community.

'Can you hear the home team sing?'

'We can't hear a fucking thing,' the red men sniped.

'Huddersfield's a shithole. We wanna go home.'

Good-humoured banter rifled through his eardrums as he willed the game to start, willed his team to victory and wished to see Katy's face tonight or tomorrow when he shared his plans for the future.

Sure enough, minutes later the teams were on the pitch. Huddersfield's blue and white stripes blazed against the baize as they played towards the away end at high speed in the opening minutes.

'We broke your bloody record!' somebody shouted down in the direction of Jordan Rhodes, the 3rd division's top scoring striker. 'Couldn't get past us in your 44th game!'

Deep down though, they would have loved to see the likes of him breaking records with a sword on his badge, instead of a Yorkshire terrier.

Twice in the opening ten minutes, young Rhodes, on the edge of breaking his club's post-war scoring record, came close to revenge. Then his team broke forwards again, sending the ball to the left. Out on the far edge of the penalty box, there was no danger, until the attacker tried to cut inside. As he did so, Darel Russell, a new midfielder on loan from Preston North End until the close of the season, stuck out his leg. The man in stripes was on the ground, the referee had pointed to the spot. The away fans were on their feet, screaming blue murder.

Thanks to a reckless challenge from Charlton's No.37, Jordan Rhodes stepped up and scored No.35 of the season, disregarding baying behind the goal. Now the home side could sit back and defend.

'No chance we'll see a 7-6 classic,' the fans agreed.

Those chances were further lessened in the second half when Russell, centre stage once more, found himself on the floor after a challenge. Red rage clouded his judgement and he kicked out in retaliation.

As a melee followed, fans bayed to the referee, 'Send them off!'

The men in stripes had manhandled at least two of the Charlton players. Yes, the red was coming out. The away supporters clapped. Then stopped suddenly, realising it was Darel Russell with his head in his hands. He was being sent off whilst the Huddersfield players involved in the melee were staying on the pitch.

'The ref's a Yorkshireman!' cried the travelling fans. 'Get out yer cloth cap and slippers, and sit with the home supporters!'

After the sending off, against a team so defensively organised, there was no way back. Huddersfield counted down the clock to a 1-0 win, but things weren't so bad despite the defeat to 12 Yorkshire men.

'Thirty nine games gone, seven to go, and eight points clear,' supporters enthused as they made their way towards the coach, 'we'd have taken that in our stocking from Santa at Christmas.'

Getting on board and settling into his seat, Fergus thought of the community garden, wondering how many of Omar's boys had come along. Things would be shaping up nicely by the time he got back to London.

'Goodbye Huddersfield,' he thought as the arches of the stadium began to recede when the coach pulled out of the car park.

He was wondering whether he would see them again next season.

Some teenage boys in the back seats answered his thoughts as they taunted home supporters through the open windows. 'We'll never see you again! You're staying in Division 3!'

Then, as the coach edged through a weight of match-day traffic towards the town centre, the mood changed suddenly, violently. Almost like the rupture between bad dreams.

'Goodbye yah cunts, goodbye!' they screamed.

'Wait a minute,' he thought, 'there's no need for this.'

It'll die down, surely. They're pissed, angry, over-exuberant.

'Bastards, cunts, faggots!' the insults thickened to a broth of vitriol as drunken, coke-eyed teenagers beat their bodies against the glass like bumblebees in an airless room, maddened by suffocation, fighting to get outside at the fathers walking their kids home after the game. 'Bunch of fucking northern bastard paedophiles!'

Come on, somebody's going to stop this, somebody with authority and an accent like theirs. The driver maybe, or the old couples or the man whose daughter's sitting beside the very windows they're screaming out of, like she's deaf or she's not even there.

It's getting worse. 'Your father's your brother, your sister's your mother, all the dirty northern families are fucking one another!'

Jesus Christ, this was worse than 'the Shankill and the Falls'.

'Isn't it? Am I the only one thinks this is wrong?'

Was this normal on journeys to English football games? Were these boys only voicing the thoughts of every supporter in the coach? If not, then why the hell didn't they try to stop it?

Coming through an Asian neighbourhood on the town's outskirts, they catapulted V signs in the direction of a Sikh taxi driver, openly cavorting their own incestuous ignorance. 'Hey, I thought Bin Laden was dead, but he's walking around the streets of Huddersfield!'

Soon, though not soon enough, they were in the countryside, where at least nobody could hear them as they scoffed about

Emmerdale, the sight of chickens and the size of a horse's penis behind a hedge.

Then, as quickly as their rage had erupted, they fell silent.

Once again, you could hear the hum of the engine and the voices on the radio, where analysts discussed the afternoon's football results. Yorkshire had slipped into darkness as the bus buzzed through scattered groves of light, down motorways towards London's orchard.

When they reached Charlton, hours after service-stopovers, Katy was waiting by the station, to catch a train together to Greenwich.

'As long as I live,' he promised as they stopped for a drink at the men of 1947's pub, 'I'm never going to another game.'

'It's football,' she said, expecting nothing else.

'It was your home town,' he said sadly.

'There's more to Huddersfield than football.'

'More to Charlton too,' he said as he surveyed the faces of good, decent men who had given their lives to this place and this sport. 'Society's changed a lot since the days of Sam Bartram.'

'So quaint,' she said, taking on the face of her mother.

'I'm buying a house here,' he said suddenly.

She seemed surprised. 'Okay.'

He reached out to touch her hand. 'For us.'

'Us?'

Her eyes moved towards the men of '47.

She was looking at them in a way he had never seen her look at anything before, as if considering time's passage, how they seemed so old and out of date, even if the trophy they carried stayed shiny and silver.

'Yes, I want us to live together.'

'And leave my little flat?'

'Yes, whenever you're ready.'

'Tell me about the house,' she said, biting her lower lip the way people do when they're scared to dream. 'Paint me a picture.'

'Okay,' he began as he held tight to her hand, 'it's got three bedrooms, a bathroom we'll recreate with an ocean theme, a kitchen facing a garden full of palms and fruit trees, and a space for growing our own herbs and vegetables. On sunny days you'll be able to open the door and feel the breezes as you're baking, and the fragrance of fruit's going to take you away to the Mediterranean.'

'Makes Charlton sound exotic,' she whispered.

'Anywhere can be exotic if you want it to be.'

'We'll lie out on the grass, reading books and sunbathing,' she whispered, suddenly caught up in the web of shared dreams, 'and then look up at the trees, counting apples, making plans for *our* baking.'

Suddenly she paused, turning back towards the picture, seeking some reaction from the men of '47 which he couldn't decipher.

She spoke slowly. 'And then it crumbles.'

'What crumbles?' he wondered.

'The dream,' she said. 'There's something I have to tell you. It's about Lance and things that happened in Huddersfield.'

'Lance?' he echoed. Things were starting to make sense.

This was answering some of the riddles of Christmas. Always, in the back of his mind, he had had questions about Lance's travels at that time.

'Fergus, I love you. You give me more clarity and security than anyone's ever done, and I feel closer to you than to any other person on this planet. I tried to build a castle around my heart but you got inside every layer. Then along the way I made a terrible mistake.'

Then she went on and broke his heart, disentangling the web.

Deceit, in its purest form, pulled the rug from under his desires.

21
The Fires of Friendship

There was only one way to describe how Fergus seemed when he came banging, thumping, kicking on the door in the middle of the night. Heartbroken. Worse. He had the crazy nothing-to-lose eyes of a dying smack addict facing the dealer who had provided the fatal, final shot. There was going to be no methadone to calm him down, as if he already felt tumescent shudders of death creeping through his insides.

If Lance hadn't opened the door, in a few seconds everybody in the place would have wakened and somebody would have called the police.

'You bastard,' he spoke through a colander of emotion.

Seeing the shadow of tears, Lance understood.

'You slept with *my* Katy.'

'Don't do this out here.'

'So they don't know what the hero gardener's really like?'

'I don't give a damn about that.'

'How many friends did you shoot in the back on the battlefield?'

'I know you're upset...'

'Upset?' Fergus roared. 'Don't they say all's fair in love and war?'

'People have kids, they're sleeping. Don't do this out here.'

Already he could hear doors opening behind other doors.

'If you weren't a cripple and I wasn't a boxer, I'd...'

'Hey,' Lance was starting to feel angry too. 'You don't own *her*.'

'No, but I love her,' Fergus raised his fists and replied through clenched teeth, 'and you knew that and you still…oh fuck.'

'This was when you weren't with her,' Lance fought back as he watched his friend spin around and punch the air. 'I liked her first.'

'You liked her, and I loved her,' Fergus's voice boomed off the walls and down the stairs. 'You're a treacherous bastard. Pity they didn't blow both legs off you when they had the chance in Afghanistan.'

That was it. If the Irishman wanted a fight, then he would give him one. Edging forwards, swinging out a fist, Lance threw a punch in Fergus's direction. Having been a fighter, his target knew how to duck out of the way.

Hitting nothingness instead of a red head, Lance tumbled forwards, collapsing to the ground at his friend's feet.

For a second he could see what was going through the Irishman's green eyes – the temptation to kick an opponent when he was down. Despite his anger, there was enough of the gentleman boxer left in Fergus for him to reach out a hand and help Lance up. Then, without making eye contact, he turned around, saying farewell to their friendship.

'Fergus,' Lance called after him but got no response.

Going back inside, he wouldn't be able to sleep.

'Flaming Irish,' he thought aloud.

He had the right to say that since he had their blood in his veins, even if they couldn't see it the way you see black ancestry, for example. Pouring himself a whisky, he looked out on the dark Thames.

It had started out as a good day, before beginning a horrible evolution. Omar brought enough boys to make a football team, and this whisky as a sign of appreciation. Those boys seeded, hacked, hewed, pruned, pared and prepared all morning, hardly stopping for a break. Then, as the afternoon wore on, Charley came to join them.

'I have to go,' she said shortly after.

As she left, he noticed a group of boys whispering, asking questions. The cute Somali teenager pointed up towards

Merlin's window. Hours later, Charley's guardian came to the door. That's why when he had first heard the knocking, he was afraid of who he would find on the other side.

'Those boys,' Merlin said, 'they know who she is.'

'How?' Lance wanted to know.

'Word of mouth,' Merlin said. 'London's a smaller place, when it's all carved up into a map that's shared between gangs.'

Every borough had its own colours, and not just in its shoelaces. They had found Charley and she was no longer safe.

'At least the trial's only a month away.'

'Nervous month for you, and nervous month for Charlton, but these things pass quickly and it's all going to be okay.' Lance tried to offer comfort. 'Before you know it, we'll be watching another game.'

The man of science had no time for games or football. 'This isn't *Roy of the Rovers*. These gangs don't do happy endings.'

Sipping his whisky now, Lance thought everything seemed to have darkened. Even the lights of London's villages, across the river, appeared as foreboding as those first nights when he had forged a friendship with Fergus.

He supposed that was gone now, as the last mouthful of tonight's whisky burned like a Chinese lantern in his stomach. He looked out at the dark space of the room he had once called Marilyn's.

'I loved her just as much,' he spoke into the shadows. 'English love's as good as Irish love, and loving a football team's a whole lot safer.'

A few days later, he renewed his season ticket. Signing up for another year of highs and lows, expectations, dreams, failures; traversing the map of a different division, seeing sunny days and blankets of rain beneath the floodlights on stormy Saturdays. Games cancelled due to blizzards, wonder goals, own goals, no goals, the colours of jerseys, match programmes, and B&Bs in towns he had never been to before.

'370 quid,' said the girl behind the counter.

She had eyes as bright as beads, and a 'Help for Heroes' box stood beside her.

'Good value for a year's entertainment,' he said as he donated a couple of pound coins to the charity, to spite Fergus.

The Irishman had shown his true colours. Getting blown up was no joke. When he regretted the loss of a friendship and felt a creeping sense of apology for his wrongs, all he had to do was replay those words at full volume in the jukebox of his thoughts.

First, he didn't know how to react. Now he did. He was furious, and working in the garden calmed his fury. Planting herbs and vegetables, he trowelled raw wounds in the earth; then shaped bandages around seeds glistening like shrapnel in the spring sunshine.

The days passed fast on the way to the weekend. Fergus too passed from a distance and in corridors. Like the ghosts of the Naval College, they moved by without speaking; eye contact brushed aside with a downward glance. He guessed it was the same for Katy, though she was staying with friends in Shoreditch. He had found that out on Facebook. You learn a lot about someone from their digital presence.

Those nights of cybersex seemed as long ago as the opening fixtures of a different season. Games against Bournemouth, under blue skies, compared to the grim chill of Lancashire's mill towns in winter.

Saturday came eventually; a home game with Orient flying the flag for East London and escaping the shadow of Stratford Olympic.

'Come on, you reds!' the crowd surged.

Sitting in his old familiar seat, soon he forgot everything as the home side attacked from the start, driving forwards like a wasps' nest disturbed. This was Charlton in full flow, the way they had played in earlier parts of the season. With 7 minutes gone, Stephens combined with Wiggins, who set up Wagstaff to stroke home the opening goal.

His boys were coming together like eleven newly-discovered elements in a periodic table, taking him back to the blue skies of the season's start, then on a whirlwind tour through autumn and winter's highlights. DS1 floated above the baize with the ease of a red admiral. BWP had a penalty turned down. YK teased defenders as if incarnating Katy's eyes.

There was humour too. Charlton's lighthouse between the sticks, back to his best, tempted repeats of history. As the half ended, Leon Cort, rising high as a fisherman's rod to meet a corner, punched the bloody fink into Orient's goal with such force you would swear he was playing volleyball.

'We've had a Brockley Pelé and a flying Dutchman,' joked a Scotsman a few seats away as the goal was disallowed and the half ended, 'and now we've a Southwark Maradona to add to the list.'

Mikel Alonso was still missing but he had long since been forgotten as the teams returned for the second half. Fans expected more goals, they wanted more goals and needed more goals, but the game began to drift. After all the showboating, the Harlem globetrotting, there was only a single goal between the sides. Orient had changed tactics too, sensing that the referee had left his cards in his long trousers today.

'Lord sake, book some of them!' supporters demanded as Scott Wagstaff got chopped down in full flow on the East side. 'That's a bollocks-high agricultural tackle if I ever saw one.'

They had lost their momentum. They should have been three-nil up after 20 minutes and here they were on 70, facing the danger of a one-all draw. It wasn't even that Orient were attacking.

Things had got very pedestrian. This was old Charlton again.

'Give us a substitute!' the fans cried desperately.

Finally the man on the touchline relented, sending on a loan player called Danny N'Guessan in place of the Brockley Pelé, who had almost faded out of view in the second half, as he had a habit of doing.

'We're plodding our way to promotion,' Lance thought.

Then suddenly, as the shadow of Bourdin came back into view, the substitute rose high to power home a header, make it two-nil, send the stadium into a paroxysm of delight and give Charlton the three points.

'Six points clear of Sheffield United,' said the bloggers in the pub afterwards, 'and out of sight from the chasing pack.'

'If this was the Grand National,' they agreed, 'all we've got to do is run down that final straight and the trophy's ours.'

Six games to go, and most of the horses were out of the race. Only United, Wednesday and Huddersfield had any chance of catching up. He thought of this on the long walk home from Charlton, down the Woolwich Road and into Greenwich on a mild last night of March. While he was working out the possibilities and permutations, time passed quickly, and soon he reached the river, the flats and his empty bed.

Shortly after, he was dreaming of Afghanistan.

'Up ahead,' said the officer as they moved through a forest.

But he broke from the pack, going towards a clearing where a girl took his hand, leading him gently down a path to a tree house.

He could feel the gun hard between his legs, the weight of a rucksack, the touch and smell of leaves against his face. She began to climb a ladder to the house, starting out white and changing to black.

'Charley,' he thought, taking a step forward.

The undergrowth crackled like blackberries bursting on brambles. Juice came up through the roots, out on his boots the colour of blood. He's expecting an explosion as always.

But there's banging instead. 'Wake up, wake up!'

Somewhere between the tree house and the real world, he rises. There's a smell of smoke he remembers from dreams of Bourdin.

'Get up, get up for fuck's sake!'

It's in the real world. He's in the real world.

'The girl in the tree house is gone.'

This wasn't Afghanistan. The room smelled of a doused barbecue.

'Knocking. Somebody's knocking.'

Realising this, he rushed to the door.

'Coming, coming,' he said.

Getting closer, he saw the smoke thicken. He could hardly breathe but he hobbled on, fixing his prosthesis into place as he moved.

At the last second before it seemed like he was going to choke, he managed to reach the handle, pull the door open before collapsing. Coughing, spluttering, he could see boots again. Then faces, eyes shining down at him from between helmets and uniforms. Police officers and a fire-woman. Behind them, others were moving quickly down the stairs, getting out of the building and away from the smoke – black, oleaginous, all-consuming, paining his chest and stomach.

'Got to get out,' they said. 'There's a fire.'

Through the smoke it was hard to see. Tougher to breathe.

The fire-woman's voice soothed him. 'Rise up gently.'

While she was helping him down the stairs, he noticed that her blonde hair was dirty with soot. When they reached the bottom, she left him outside in the cool air.

Everybody was there – Somalis, Chinese, young professionals, families and even the ones he never saw, who never helped with the garden.

'What's wrong with him?' he asked, seeing Fergus's crouched body amongst those getting treated down along the riverside.

'That's the one who saved them,' the fire-woman replied.

Everything was a drunken, sleepy blur. 'Saved who?'

'The people in the room where the fire started,' she answered. 'He's the one who punched through the door and got his hands burnt.'

'Badly?' he asked, gripping the woman's arm.

Shivers of fear snaked through him as she pulled away.

'Sorry, I don't know. I've got to get back.'

Suddenly he realised that amongst all these people, there was no sign of the three most significant in his life – Charley, Katy or Merlin.

If Fergus was the one who saved them, then he had the answers. Catching his breath, Lance walked across towards the red-haired man.

'Come to fight me when I'm down?' he asked, raising up a pair of fists, freshly bandaged, wrapped up thick against his pain.

'Of course not,' Lance said. 'Just came to ask questions.' He paused as memories detonated. 'Whose flat was it?'

Fergus wouldn't look him in the eye. 'You don't know?'

'I was asleep, pissed after the Orient game.'

'Merlin's place,' he said, keeping his eyes to the ground.

Lance needed more than drip-feed. 'You saved them, right?'

'Yeah. I was up because I couldn't sleep,' he explained. 'I heard the crash, the bang, the explosion, whatever it was, and ran to the door.'

The word *explosion* resounded through Lance's thoughts.

'Petrol bomb thrown into the kitchen.'

'That's beside Charley's bedroom.'

'I know,' Fergus said, 'I had to go in there to get her out.'

'But she did get out? She's okay?'

'She's no worse than you or me.' The red-haired man soothed Lance's fears. 'Lucky there was more damage done to the kitchen than the people.'

'And Merlin?' Lance asked. 'How's he doing?'

'Shaken. He's strong. They'll both be okay.'

'Where are they now?' Lance spoke fast.

'Hospital,' Fergus turned his head away slowly.

'I'm going to see them,' Lance insisted.

'Will you do something for me first?'

'Sure,' Lance said. 'Under the circumstances.'

'Call Katy,' Fergus requested, holding up his big useless fists once more.

'Sure,' Lance agreed, since petrol bombs, burning kitchens and the ghost of summer's riots placed the feuds of a shared love affair in perspective. 'I still have her number somewhere on my phone.'

'I know,' Fergus sighed, finally looking Lance in the eye.

A Chelsea girl had come between them, but an Arsenal one was pulling them back together, slow and sure as whispers in the Thames.

22
Runaways

On Easter Sunday morning, Fergus dipped his burning hands in the Thames as a part of a ritual to cool the wounds and recall the past. There were parts of his life in Ireland he couldn't forget. Thoughts of palms, incense and healing rituals had returned in this holy week. Despite talking to Katy again, he hadn't quite forgiven her.

The house purchase, like his charred flesh, remained on ice.

Memories of the burning apartment came back in his dreams, as he had once been haunted by a joyride and a sea of fire, seared in sunset.

'This time,' he thought, 'there's a happier ending.'

Local papers had covered the story. *The Mercury* described him as punching through the door like the Incredible Hulk. It was a good feeling for a boxer to steal the headlines from footballers, for once.

Getting inside, seeing the flames crawling through the kitchen and out into the hallway, he had called out. Merlin, furthest from the smoke, was able to respond. Fumes as thick and dark as beeswax made it impossible for them to see anything but the whites of each other's eyes.

'Charley,' Merlin coughed and spluttered, pointing towards a small side room close to the kitchen, where fingers of flame had begun to creep across the paint, as on cars in Lewisham's streets a summer ago.

'You get out,' Fergus warned, for he had breathed too much smoke.

As Merlin hobbled away, as if on wooden legs, the red-haired man raced to Charley's door, kicking it and finding it locked.

Forgetting himself, he grabbed hold of the handle.

'Hell!' he cried out as pain went through him.

Feeling his flesh flare then melt, he was in pure 100 degree agony, but was driven to smash that lock, even if it was the last thing he did. Punching through the wood and his own pain, seeing flame in the corner of his eyes, adding to the burning ache he already felt, he smashed the lock with his fists and kicked through a path with his feet. Getting inside, he felt tongues of fire follow him. Charley was there on the bed, without sheets, a child in lingerie passed out from the fumes. Looking at her, you would wonder how she could ever have passed herself off as a boy; watery-eyed, smooth-skinned, long-limbed.

Crossing the floor, he swept her up in his arms and for a moment her sweat-glazed mahogany skin cooled his suffering as he caught glances from the faces of her guardian angels in the night, a gallery of Arsenal players, past and present. Some Irish from the '80s, which surprised him, but mostly black, from today, with fire in their eyes again drawing out memories of summer's riots as he raced past them.

Getting outside, into the hallway, putting her on the ground, he suddenly became conscious of his own pain once again. Looking down, he saw the blisters rising up in a violent froth of cloud out of one eye. Through the lens of the other, Merlin resuscitated Charley.

Waking up from the kiss of life to the sound of ambulance sirens, she seemed stunned, confused, struggling to say thanks, but unable.

They had taken her to the hospital, where she stayed under guard.

'She breathed in a lot of smoke,' the doctors said.

A few days later, he had gone to the hospital to see her along with Katy. Even if they weren't a couple, it was good to have her for company. Besides, it made Charley feel more at ease. Though still not so well, she was able to sit up, read magazines, eat sweets and talk football.

'Feels like I smoked forty cigarettes at once.' She laughed and then got serious. 'You saved my life, man.'

'Couldn't let a real football supporter die,' he had lightened the mood. 'Liked your posters of the Irish players. They brought back memories. Never thought anyone under thirty would know Liam Brady.'

'He was cute, but Frank Stapleton was better looking.'

Perhaps this was the return of the girl who'd got lost somewhere along the way, and was easier to find than the missing Katy Prunty who surfaced in his dreams and the waking world too. In the evenings, he'd spend hours wandering the streets of this place which he'd made his home; trying to make sense of being stabbed through the heart.

After learning the truth, he couldn't think of her name without seeing Lance, and feeling fumes of rage as he thought of them together in bed, always wondering what they'd done together and how many times. She said it was just once, in the flesh, and several times on the computer, which seemed even worse, even dirtier than the other option.

And if it was bad with her, it was ten times worse with him.

'Thanks for saving Charley's life,' Lance tried to normalise things a couple of days after the fire, but he had said nothing in response.

Even Merlin had tried to act as an intermediary, staying there while he found a new place. Lance was sorry, Merlin said, and wanted to sort things out when he got back from Oldham, where Charlton played on a stormy Good Friday. Sorrow though wouldn't take those images out of his head. He was happy to go for a drink with Katy down by the riverside on Saturday night, tell her about his chat with Merlin and even get nostalgic about the good times they had shared together.

'Maybe it's time for me to move on as well,' she tested.

'Yes,' he agreed. 'It's probably for the best.'

After he said this, she didn't contact him on the Sunday. He missed her voice, sensing that something was wrong from the start. Without her, he felt numb. But it wasn't enough just to want someone with all your heart, to feel as if without them you're half, not whole.

'You have to trust them,' he told himself, 'and if you're going to be with them for a lifetime, you can't not trust them for a lifetime.'

The hours passed slowly as he walked through Greenwich Park, past Blackheath, into the streets of Charlton, trying to make sense of all that had happened, playing Katy's words over, as if they were old records. The world and its occupants passed him by in a blur as he weighed up his relationships inside his head, as if enacting a courtroom drama.

'If you love someone, don't judge them,' Merlin had argued.

She was a woman alone when she went out with Lance. She had the right to sate her sexual desires with anyone of her choosing.

It wasn't his place to deny her the freedom to do so. Maybe trying to control her made him no better than those men who cut the girls in Africa so they could never know the power of possessing passion.

'But Lance, of all people,' he couldn't get out of his head.

Not so long ago, Lance was supposed to be his friend for life; alongside Omar and Katy, probably his only friend in England.

What would they do at dinner parties in the future? Imagine sitting at a table with the woman you love, and beside her there's someone else who has loved her too and has known her flesh in the same way.

The English, of course, were better at moving on from the past. Yet, despite all he was thinking, he wished she had sent him a goodnight text, just so he could see her words, as the last thing before he fell asleep.

There was no hum of the phone, no goodnight whisper.

His next contact with another person wouldn't come until the following afternoon, when Lance knocked unexpectedly on his door.

'I don't want to go to the football,' Fergus said immediately.

He had no interest in seeing the game against Walsall. Ever since that afternoon in Huddersfield, he had lost interest.

Like it said in that text in the Book of Corinthians, always used at weddings, about faith, hope and love, you've got to put childish things aside when you become a man.

'I'm not here about the football.'

'Oh,' Fergus said, wondering if it was about Katy.

'I'm here about Charley.'

'What about her?'

'She's gone.'

'Gone where?'

'We've no idea,' Lance admitted. 'She was getting discharged from the hospital and we were supposed to go pick her up, but when we got there she had already packed her bags and left.'

'Do you think she's in danger?'

'Maybe,' said his former friend.

'Are you going to look for her?'

Lance shook his head sadly. 'In this city, it'd be like looking for a needle in a haystack. She could be anywhere.'

'Okay, well, keep me posted.'

The words had come from his heart, not his head. Saying them, he saw hope glimmer in Lance's eyes for the salvation of their friendship.

'See you,' he said, and turned away for the game.

Fergus followed the match on the radio, since that wasn't cheating in his promise to never attend another game again. They won 1-0 with another goal from the loan player N'Guessan, staying well clear at the top of the division, and just a couple of points short of promotion.

Looking at the league table on Sky Sports News, Charlton seemed on top of the world, miles above both Sheffield teams. Not so long ago he was there too, but now twin blades of loneliness and homesickness stabbed his chest.

23
Journey's End

Twice in history, Charlton had been promoted in Carlisle, as if the long journey was a metaphor for the slog of a season's travels.

Lance thought of this as he drove the Torino through the Lake District, where miles of unspoiled countryside seemed paradisiacal after stuttering through hours of industrial landscapes.

It was good to be here in the fresh air, out of London, where things weren't so great on the day his team could seal promotion.

After more than a week there was no sign of Charley, and tension lingered between himself, Fergus and Katy. They still weren't a 100 per cent back together, but this time she hadn't sought refuge in anyone else's bed. Okay, that was bitter. But he was entitled to bitterness.

Everybody had forgotten about his feelings in all of this.

'I'm not just some dumb fuck addicted to football.'

By the time he got to Carlisle he was happy to zone out. Again, as often before, he would stay in a guesthouse and drive back tomorrow.

'Where's the nearest pub?' he asked a gaggle of exuberant boys wandering through the streets, draped in red flags and swords.

When they pointed him in the direction of a place that welcomed away supporters, he downed a pint of Cumbrian ale and then around two o'clock made his way to the ground. Almost 1000 supporters had made the trip up, down or sideways.

'They've flown the team in,' came the whispers on the terraces, sweeping across like wind from the Scottish Borders.

The scene was set for scripting history. Wherever Charley was, and Fergus too, he hoped they were following the game. There was, of course, no point texting, for he wouldn't reply; as much as he wanted to describe the scene of anticipation and the slow crawl of the half.

The second half was just as nerve-wracking. News filtered through of other scores. Both Sheffield teams were losing and then drawing.

'United have scored again,' someone moaned.

Then, with over 70 minutes on the clock, old friendships came to life. Bradley Wright-Phillips denied by a save, and then another a few minutes later denying his strike partner, Yann Kermorgant.

'C'mon Johnnie,' the red men yelled across the heads of stewards as their captain crossed the pitch to take the subsequent corner.

Sweet yet as sharp as the blade of free kicks piercing Sheffield steel, Jackson stroked the ball towards Dale Stephens' leonine presence. Heading it downwards, the Brockley Pelé scripted history.

A corner of Cumbria became Charlton's. 'It's in, it's in!'

Seeing Bradley bundle the ball across the line, suddenly Lance found himself caught up in a conga, crushed tight as a marsupial in his mother's pocket, yelping, hissing, laughing and screaming with joy.

'76 minutes, 76 minutes!' interjected a rare voice of doom.

Suddenly, the shadow of Bourdin came back to haunt them.

'This is Charlton, remember. They don't do happy endings.'

14 minutes to go, plus injury time. Then 13. Next 12. Ages after it's down to eleven, and it seems to take forever like the switching on of Christmas lights or the countdown on New Year's Eve. A whole season's coming down to this. 11 minutes to decide whether the Torino's going to traverse a higher division a season from now.

10 to go, and then it's an eternity until 9, while 8 seems as if it's never going to come, like somebody's turned off time

in the Observatory. Suddenly it's 7 and you get caught up in the action and it's 6, 5, 4…then time slows down again, as in those minutes before a job interview; hands sweating, doubts sinking in, mind going blank. 3's never going to come, and 2's the first minute you've ever known that seems to have 200 per cent's worth of seconds included in its passing. Suddenly it's 1, oh lovely 1, the loveliest 1 you've ever seen, the 1 you've been waiting for all your life, a perfect 60 becoming 50, 40, 30, 20, 10, and the guy down on the sidelines is lifting up the signal board for injury time.

'Five more minutes!' the roar goes up.

Unbelievable, like you've just spent 14 minutes rolling a giant rock up a hill, and some guy's just pushed it a third of the way back down.

'Sheffield games are over,' said a man with an i-phone.

You could taste the sweat in the suspense as he broke the scores. United had won, and Wednesday drawn.

'If we hold out for these few minutes, we're promoted.'

This was like straddling the meridian line on your naked testicles. One side's got darkness, representing the past, and the other's offering a starlight future back in England's higher divisions.

'Time's almost up!' the visiting choir protested.

Then sure enough, the whistle blew. Another conga started as the players formed a huddle, raising Chrissie Powell up to the grey sky. Though the heavens didn't part, the Holy Grail had been found.

A thousand bodies surged forwards, out past the frantic stewards who couldn't hold them back, as they forced a path onto the Cumbrian turf, where they ran to congratulate their heroes. Lance had seen nothing like this since the '80s, and it felt good, boys being boys, being bad, breaking the rules as officials tried to force them back off the pitch.

In the midst of red men leaping and running alongside the players, he stopped to text Fergus: *We did it. The red men bloody did it.*

They had invaded Carlisle with less than a thousand men and came away with victory, crushing thoughts of Martial

Bourdin under their chariot wheels in the process. They would go back to their seats, watch the troops celebrate, and then head out on the town for the evening.

He would get drunk with any red men spending the night in Cumbria, drunk and dizzy in a place where you could see the stars, closer to Scotland than the lights of London's villages. Then in the morning, he would drive home, following a text message from Fergus.

'I know the score. I followed the game on the radio,' he had written. 'They said there was a rowdy pitch invasion at the end.'

'If that was rowdy, I wish the army'd sent me to Carlisle.'

Getting back, he went to set the record straight. Talking about the invasion and then the football, they had reached a kind of truce.

Somewhere in the middle of the conversation, Fergus apologised. 'Shouldn't have said those things.'

'What's done's done.'

They each agreed to forgive and forget, ending their feud. Through the week they talked and Fergus helped out on the garden where able, with his hands still heavily bandaged. Come Saturday and a game against Wycombe Wanderers, Lance offered to buy him a ticket but he refused, saying that he was staying clear of football for a while.

Alone, Lance watched his team winning to secure the 3rd division title and move within reach of breaking the 100 point barrier for the season. The runaway leaders had reached 97, with two games still to play.

Strangely, every time he looked at the league table he felt sad, thinking of another runaway. Two weeks had passed and there was no sign of Charley, though they had heard rumours she had been seen right here in Greenwich, amongst all the ghosts of the seasons, centuries and summers past. Sometimes in the mornings, he would go to the park, sit on a bench and play the game Fergus had introduced him to, wishing she would rise up through a tunnel of time and step out of the Observatory.

24
Closing Layers

Greenwich, in moonlight, stood on the borders of spring and summer on those last cold nights of April when the football season came to an end. Charley hadn't returned, leaving Merlin sick with worry. Lance was worried too, though he had the distraction of a journey to Preston. It was Charlton's last away game of the season and a tradition of going in fancy dress. He had invited Fergus for the drive, but the Irishman refused. Still, they were talking again, even if traces of frost remained on the edges.

'So what's your costume then?'

'A Roman centurion,' he explained.

'Isn't that slightly premature?' Fergus laughed when he saw the golden tunic and helmet lined with horsehair. 'I mean, shouldn't you save the costume for when you actually reach the 100 point mark?'

'We'll make it,' Lance spoke self-assuredly.

On the evening of his drive north, they passed one another on the grounds of the Naval College, on Fergus's way home from work. He was swinging a briefcase with hands still wrapped as securely as Ben Hamer's.

'Good luck,' the Irishman said, 'and by the way, Katy reckons your centurion costume's going to be too cryptic for football fans.'

Regardless of what Katy Prunty thought, he made his way north to the steely clouds and quietude of another Lancashire mill town. Walking its streets, he thought of Charley, out there somewhere, alone. Going to bed without going for a drink, he prayed to God, as in Afghanistan on nights before a landmine devoured his faith.

Next morning as he rose early, ate breakfast and prepared his costume, he hoped Charley was able to eat. By now, if she was feral, her hair would have grown longer and she would have looked more like a girl.

'What would she make of this?' he wondered as he looked in the mirror, comparing himself to Marlon Brando in *Julius Caesar*.

He might never know if they didn't find her. He had to forget. Torturing himself over Charley, as he had over Katy, wasn't going to help. Of course she was younger and was never going to be more than a friend. Katy, on the other hand, had offered him a real possibility of romance, and that was gone now, even if she wasn't fully back with Fergus.

They had been spending a lot of time together, for two people who weren't a couple, though they didn't seem to share the same bed. Maybe there was some kissing. Did she touch herself for him on the computer? Start making love with a passion and then go cold suddenly?

These thoughts played in his head like echoes of songs on scratched CDs as he hobbled the streets of Preston towards Deepdale, at the north end of the town. Though the walk was long, painful, and though he should have driven, he was glad of the time spent thinking.

Reaching the stadium at two, making his way into the *Bill Shankly Kop*, realising this was another town associated with the great manager, he saw fancy dress costumes grace the terraces.

'Dangermouse, a female Smurf, Spiderman, Superman, Zippy from Rainbow, Elmo from Sesame Street,' he listed them out in his thoughts. 'There's even an Ugly Sister as a belle of the ball.'

If they hit 100 points today, she might get lucky. Personally he would have preferred to see Katy in the crowd, but that was never going to happen. When the game started, Charlton went on the attack from the off as thoughts of two women scissor-kicked through his mind. Very soon though, he forgot both. Peckham boy Danny Haynes had scored the opening goal, sending the hordes in fancy dress into a sudden huddle. Across the way, Dangermouse led a dance down to the edge of the pitch.

'We're going to get the 100 points!' the cry rose up.

Sure enough, it seemed more likely as a second goal came, from Danny N'Guessan, stirring up a salsa of one hundred costumes as those left behind in their seats sang, 'It's like watching Brazil.'

Come the second half though, momentum faded. Somewhere in the midst of Zippy, Elmo and all the rest, Martial Bourdin was lurking. Two late goals brought Preston level and left the team on 98 points, needing a win against Hartlepool on Saturday to smash the record.

'We blew it,' he moaned, returning home to the man who had been staying with him since the fire, 'but we've one last chance.'

'Hopefully everything turns out right in the end,' said the man whose real name was Mamadou, caught up in fear and worry. 'You guys get your hundred points, and the police find Charley before it's too late.'

'They will,' Lance insisted. 'Then we'll all go to the game together.'

The club promised something special for the season's grand finale. Throughout the week, rumours abounded as to possibilities. Some of the blogs spoke of the Red Arrows coming, dropping Chrissie Powell out of a plane into the centre of the pitch to lift the championship trophy.

'Too far-fetched,' Fergus said.

'Will you come?' Lance tried to peel off another layer of frost.

The Irishman shook his head. 'Katy's asked me to the theatre on Friday night, to see a show about Big Daddy and Giant Haystacks.'

'Saturday's another day,' Lance pushed the issue.

'To tell you the truth, I've been off football since Huddersfield.'

'One per cent of one per cent of Charlton fans,' Lance argued, 'shouldn't poison you against all the great things about the club.'

He rolled up his sleeve, showed the badge again, the sword rising up like a syringe and the word 'addicted' in bold lettering beneath it.

'I thought I was a Charlton fan,' Fergus spoke softly as he stared into the sword, 'but I can't forget, and I'm not so good at forgiving either.'

'Sometimes you've got to forget your pride,' Lance philosophised, 'put the past behind you, like I've had to do with Afghanistan, and listen to what your heart's saying instead o' your head.'

'Maybe,' Fergus said and left the conversation at that.

The rest of the week passed slowly, with rumours gathering pace and the moon waning more every night above the domes of Greenwich. Then suddenly, on the Friday night, as Fergus and Katy prepared to see their show, all changed.

They'd been leaving the apartments, heading down towards the riverside, when they saw Merlin, in a panic, heading towards the gates of the Royal Naval College, where there was a great deal of commotion. Passing them, Fergus recalled a night of two Gods and choosing wisdom over war.

'What's wrong?' they wondered. 'Should we see?'

'We could be late for the show,' Fergus suggested.

'What's five minutes here or there?' Katy asked.

Following Merlin, they came upon a scene of sirens.

'Like the night we met.'

'Yes,' Katy agreed, quickening their step.

A formation of police officers lined the steps of the Painted Hall as marksmen, nestled in the cupola, trained guns like film cameras on the doors and windows beneath. A couple, with loudhailers, tried to push back the crowd of bystanders and amateur paparazzi which stretched across the springing grass of the College lawn towards the Chapel.

At the front, they caught a flash of Lance's blonde head.

Merlin's too, bald and thrusting. 'I'm her guardian.'

'Charley,' Katy whispered. 'They've found her.'

'Yes,' Fergus supposed, 'but what's going on?'

Pushing their way to the front, they heard Merlin's voice.

'Let me through, let me talk to those boys.'

His pleas fell on deaf ears. 'They're armed and dangerous.'

'They're kids,' Merlin protested, 'playing games of gangsters.'

'Go back,' the officer said. 'They've already shot one man.'

'Who?' Fergus wondered as he approached his friend.

'An African security guard,' Lance explained as they resigned themselves to having to watch from outside, through a scrum of bodies. 'He came upon them as they had cornered Charley.'

'So wait a minute, she's in there?' Fergus tried to piece together the jigsaw of events unfolding in the rising, mid-spring moonlight.

'Yes, there's two boys holding her at gunpoint.'

'Poor girl,' Katy said. 'What do they hope to gain?'

'Who knows?' Merlin lamented. 'All we do know from the security guards is that they think she's been hiding in the College for weeks, moving between the basements and the domes like a ghost.'

'Did you see her?' Fergus wondered.

'No,' said Merlin. 'They're at the very back, holed up like cornered foxes, holding a gun to her head. She has nowhere left to run.'

'I'll call Omar and see if he can help,' Fergus suggested. 'They might be friends with the boys we work with. Maybe he can talk to them.'

By the time Omar arrived, the crowds, though swollen, had been pushed back closer to the riverside. The College grounds stood ghostly, their silence punctuated only by the conversation through loudhailers.

Stories seeping out into the night, from inside the hall, suggested that the boys had retreated as far back as possible, caught up in the wings of a historical pastiche, 17th century pornography for bored sailors.

Fergus thought of them inside there, hunkered down like squaddies in a foreign land, gazing up at kings, queens, mermen, drums, ships, cannons, muskets and the three golden lions in the far corner.

'Let me talk to them,' Omar begged the police.

'They're dangerous,' they repeated the mantra.

'I'm a teacher and a community activist.'

Finally they relented, opening the vestibule doorway, letting him go inside and climb towards the main hall's blaze of colour. Things happened slowly at first. They could hear his deep, restorative voice coming out of the loudhailer, through the windows of the building. Omar told the boys who he was and what he was doing there, suggesting that they give themselves up before things got worse.

'How could it get much worse?' Lance wondered, sceptical as always of approaches such as this, wishing he was able to go in there, take the fight to these teenagers as if they were part of the Taliban.

'Give him time,' Merlin pleaded in a gentle cadence.

Through the cracks of light in the doorway, they could see Omar's back set against the blood-red shades and shadows of the ceiling above. They could even make out the scene as far ahead as the archway adorned in the golden signs of the Zodiac, behind which the boys cowered.

'Stay back,' they must have said, for he stopped in his tracks.

Up on the roof, marksmen swung into action, before gesticulations from the officers below suggested they stay calm for now.

There was movement and sounds of muffled jackboots.

'What are they doing?' Katy wondered, tracking their movements around the sides and underneath the high, lead-grilled windows.

'Bringing the show to an end,' Fergus glanced at his watch.

'We've missed most of ours by now,' she whispered.

'I know,' he said, with one eye on her, one on the Painted Hall, and his thoughts deep in memories of Lance's words about sometimes listening to your heart instead of your head. 'But we can always go to the West End some weekend when this is over.'

'Or Charlton tomorrow,' she suggested. 'Lance says they're dropping the manager out of a plane. If that's true then it's going to feel like we're watching a scene from *The Wizard of Oz*.'

'We'll see,' he said, listening to his head, still proud, as his heart thumped from the sound of Omar's voice negotiating in the distance.

He was telling them to stop this now, to not cause a mess in such a fine, historic place, to be brave enough to let the girl go, put down their guns and try to make some history for themselves. They had made a mistake and done wrong, but the security guard wasn't dead. Even if they went to prison, they would get out one day and get another chance.

'Maybe,' Lance agreed, 'talking's the right way.'

'He's a good ambassador,' said Katy. 'Like Martin Luther King.'

'But look what happened to Martin Luther,' a scared voice reminded them. 'If the same happens to Charley, her mother's never going to forgive me. I was supposed to be looking out for her.'

The intermediary was moving closer, out of eyes' reach, towards the archway, as if to go right up, take their guns, rescue the hostage, and end this siege.

Standing on tiptoes, Fergus strained to catch images of the action; recalling his afternoon of refashioning the ceiling to a celebration of football. He had new heroes now, the Charlton Men of 2012.

Thinking of this, three lions flashed through his mind, blue and golden on the breast of Chris Powell on a night that he was better than Beckham in Lance's stories.

Crushed against Katy, he wondered if tomorrow's game would be as crowded as this; and what the zodiac might bring in the days ahead.

Daydreaming; the stars exploded suddenly, tossing the crowd sideways. The grounds of Greenwich shook, as if from the detonation of an *IED*.

Two landmines exploding at once, and their sounds overlapping – a sudden blast, a riot of screaming, and then a few seconds of haunting silence.

'What the hell?' Lance voiced everybody's concerns.

'Gunshots,' someone whispered. 'Two in quick succession.'

Resurfacing from the wave of shock, half-expecting to see Wren's majestic architecture reduced to rubble, the crowd surged forwards, then stopped; surrendering to the orders of police officers hardened by the summer's riots and the criticisms that followed.

This was no game, unlike the pitch invasion at Carlisle, but Lance was determined to get through, to see what had happened in the wake of those two gunshots which had left his eardrums numb.

'Was it Omar who got shot?' Fergus wondered.

'Or Charley?' Merlin asked as they fought their way alongside the police, behind a surge of marksmen, into the vestibule. 'But no, I heard her scream, so she can't be dead, maybe wounded.'

When they climbed the steps, the picture became clearer. As the police tried to keep them out, Lance shouted he was a soldier, Merlin – her guardian. They had to get inside to see what was going on, and eventually they did, passing under the moonlight coming through the dome, into the main hallway, and then towards the scene of chaos past the archway.

'Charley!' Merlin cried as he ran towards her.

She was on the ground, sobbing. Omar was above her, still alive. Beyond them, fresh blood glistened on the Hall's antique canvas, a new layer of colour on the gold, silver and sanguine celebration of war.

'The boys,' Katy sighed, 'they shot them both.'

'What happened?' Fergus asked, approaching Omar.

'Just like Tottenham,' he said, 'we're never going to know.'

One of them had lunged forward, the ringleader, due in court to be punished by Charley's evidence. Maybe he was going to hand over his weapon or maybe planning to strike out at the man in the middle.

'Whatever the truth,' Omar said, 'the police marksmen left nothing to chance. They shot through the side windows, hitting both.'

The siege was over. Charley's ordeal was too. There was nobody to give evidence against anymore, though there would always be gang members out there. She would always have to look over her shoulder, probably go to a new town, start university or something, and build a fresh life.

'It's possible,' Fergus told her when they all went back to Lance's afterwards to get her cleaned up and sorted out from the shock.

He had managed to make a fresh start in this place, and was soon going to make another, in the new house he was buying down the road in Charlton, which Charley started to talk about all of a sudden.

'Lance,' she said, 'it was your tattoo kept me going.'

As all eyes turned to her, she blushed then explained.

'I mean, thinking about it, the way you said it gave you hope.'

'Yeah, those times when I was in Afghanistan.'

'When they were holding me in the Painted Hall, I promised myself I'd see it again, like you always said you'd see Charlton again.'

'There you are,' he said, rolling up his sleeve.

'Cool,' she whispered. 'Guess I made it.'

'Coming to the game tomorrow?'

'Nah,' she said. 'Going back to being a girl.'

'Then that must make me a boy,' Katy made her laugh, 'because I'm going, we're going, to see the manager dropped out of a plane.'

'Enjoy,' she said, looking so tired, so hungry. It was time to stop talking football, time to make her a meal and let her sleep in a warm bed.

'Okay,' Fergus agreed as they left Lance's shortly before midnight, 'I'm going to start listening to my heart.'

His heart told him to share a hug in the doorway, ask Katy inside, make coffee even though it was late – her favourite flat white – leave her there drinking, go outside and pick her some freshly cut flowers. Then come back up, get down on one knee and be gracious enough to ask her if they could go back to how things used to be. Finally, ignoring the thoughts and voices screaming 'Lance', ask her to stay the night, as the last voice he heard before he slept, and the first he wakened to.

After a season's worth of games, it was time for Hartlepool.
'Last day,' Lance reminded them. 'Away team's fancy dress.'
'Smurfs,' Katy said when they got to the station.
'Hundreds,' Fergus remarked.

A year ago, at the very same end of season fixture, Hartlepool's fans turned up in Oompa-Loompa costumes of orange wigs and green face paint, looking like leftovers from a Saint Patrick's Day parade.

This time around they had come as blue-faced Belgians in beards, overalls and Roman caps, colonising London for the afternoon.

Getting inside the ground, they felt the mood was electric. Though the sky was grey, the terraces blazed London-bus red, aside from the Smurfs. Songs of celebration blasted out of the PA system, and then came the news which bloggers had been speculating about all week. Chrissie Powell wasn't dropping out of a plane, and it wasn't the Red Arrows.

Instead, the club had hired the British army's Red Devils to fly over the Valley at 120 miles per hour and drop parachutists from a height of seven and a half thousand feet, to land as close as possible to an X on the edge of the penalty box by the North Stand. Seconds later, before there was time to blink, the first soldier on a parachute floated into view above the hundreds of Smurfs. Swooping low, his heels seemed almost to touch their caps as he smothered them in a smoky red froth from the back of his parachute. Timing his descent to perfection, he skated over the centre circle and struck the X perfectly as he landed.

'Yes!' applause thundered from all four sides of the ground.

There were more coming, dispatched out of planes towards the mists rising off the Thames, blowing in a strange wind of change so different from the days of Bourdin or Svevo's last smoke.

An Irishman applauding the army, thought Lance.

By this stage the entire north side was a froth of smoke standing seven foot high. The voice of the announcer was rising to a goal-scoring crescendo. Half a dozen men had landed on the hallowed turf.

Soon the whole stadium was smothered in mist burning as red as the ink in Lance's tattoo; the Charlton dye was running through his veins, helping him recall when the colours had been new and shiny. Then he was in love and he had lost, as he was in love now and was losing all over again.

Rolling up his sleeve, kissing the badge, tasting his own skin, he called out to the only love that remained. 'Come on, Charlton!'

Fergus could feel the same colours deepening and congealing in his blood. With scarlet mists in the air, they had been transported to the Champions' League; enveloped in the smoky all-consuming atmosphere of watching big European games on TV. For a few minutes, they were travelling to Benefica's Estádio da Luz through the dissipating steam of fireworks, in a bus of 70,000 passengers.

As the steam rose, the sky above Floyd Road turned as mauve as a sunset, but the working day in Charlton wasn't done yet. Today's football was about to begin and give shape to a historic afternoon.

Things were dull at first, an anti-climax to the spectacle of celebration. Then after half an hour, Bourdin's ghost appeared.

'Johnnie Jackson's injured, going off.'

Two minutes later, Hartlepool took the lead. As the game dragged on, reaching 40, 50, then 60 minutes, the Smurfs held tight to a 1-0 scoreline, and the record wasn't on the agenda.

'At least we're champions,' Lance consoled himself.

He'd been waiting for this, since his last days of patrol in Afghanistan. Then, with 70 minutes on the clock, his mind drifted back there to battles with Norwich City and the Taliban, before Danny Hollands whipped him back to the present, galloping forward to discharge the ball into the net. The red men had equalised, transporting thousands to Benefica's Stadium of Light. Suddenly, 100 points was achievable.

'It'd be just my luck finishing on 99.'

'Keep the faith,' Katy said unexpectedly.

Minutes later, Danny Haynes, substitute, rose to meet a corner kick. Suddenly, the world slowed down on its axis, as the last bloody fink of the season brushed against the striker's forehead. Praying for happy endings, one last puff of Svevo's anticipation, nobody dared to breathe. Seasons past flashed through their minds, and promises of the future, as if 25,000 lives depended on the diagnosis of the dropping ball.

'Yes,' the red volcano loosed its rage.

The scorer turned on his heels, raced across goal, and skidded on his knees to the edge of the advertising hoarding. He'd have crashed through if Chris Powell hadn't raced down the touchline to jump into the arms of his history-maker. Fergus, Lance, and Katy were jumping too, three as one, as bad times were forgotten and friendships reborn.

Then, as they were still jumping, Yann Kermorgant scored a third from an impossible angle to seal the victory, so that even when Hartlepool pulled one back, Bourdin had no way through.

'We've done it,' Lance shouted, as the whistle sounded and the 101 point record was theirs forever, written into the history of his addiction.

'Yes. *We've* done it,' Fergus echoed.

It was time for celebration, and a rendition of *Valley Floyd Road* from a young opera singer who'd supported the team all her life, and was coming out onto the pitch to orchestrate the hymns of victory.

Tossing back her dark curls in acclamation, she sang from the heart, raising up the hearts of others as high as the afternoon air show.

As if from 7,000 feet above they looked down on the season that had gone, and the barren years before. She was sending them across the map of England, a division's worth of travels. Carlisle, Hartlepool, quarter of Lancashire, and half of Yorkshire, right down through Yeovil's December darkness, to the blue seas of Bournemouth.

Then, as she finished the song, with her voice melted seamlessly into the thousands around her, a tsunami of applause filled the stadium.

'And there's the Holy Grail we've chased for three years.'

The Championship trophy, shiny as a Torino, was ending its season's journey in the team captain's hands, as he stood high on a podium with his troops arrayed behind.

Then he handed the silver vase to Chrissie Powell, the manager, the man on the sideline who'd steered his team out of dark tunnels towards success. He'd changed this club's life. He'd changed the lives of these players, and their supporters. He'd changed the lives of Lance and Fergus, solidifying the name of Charlton Athletic into their flesh and bones.

And now he was a priest raising up a Eucharistic chalice of dreams, as songs of triumph engulfed the whole stadium, and his faithful congregation, '*We are the Champions.*'

As the players' wives and children came onto the pitch to celebrate, you couldn't help but feel the greatness in this moment. Chrissie Powell had built a team of men with good hearts led by Johnnie Jackson who'd played a captain's role in stabbing the Steel City's defences with classic free kicks. Yann Kermorgant, Ben Hamer, Chris Solly, Rhoys Wiggins, Danny Hollands, Dale Stephens, Bradley Wright-Phillips, Michael Morrison, and everybody else from the subs' bench to the ground staff.

This was Fergus's town, and his team now, not Liverpool FC.

'I've decided. I'm going to get a Charlton tattoo.'

Lance shook his hand. 'Welcome to addiction.'

Katy shook her dark head. 'Boys will be boys.'

Fergus laughed. 'And grow up as red men.'